SOFTLY SOFTLY
CATCHEE MONKEY!

SOFTLY SOFTLY
CATCHEE MONKEY!

by

Stephen Lister

LONDON: PETER DAVIES

FIRST PUBLISHED 1943
REPRINTED 1943
REPRINTED 1951

PRINTED AND BOUND IN GREAT BRITAIN FOR PETER DAVIES LIMITED
BY WILLIAM CLOWES AND SONS, LIMITED, LONDON AND BECCLES

Author's Note

I BELIEVE, and I state here with emphasis, that wrong-doing is wrong. Furthermore, I make the statement without ulterior motive or hope of profit. Bishops, archbishops and priests of all denominations frequently make the same statement, or paraphrases of it, with the difference that they are paid sums varying from a pittance to many thousands of pounds annually for making it. I wonder, therefore, whether my complete altruism in the matter does not make me a more trustworthy witness to this simple truth, for there is no disguising the fact that if a bishop or an archbishop were to declare publicly his belief in free love, for example, he would very quickly have his princely stipend cut off at source. I, on the other hand, can flit like a butterfly from flower to flower, committing adultery with the entire chorus of the Folies Bergère, with no more financial inconvenience than the incidental expenses of such a costly hobby. But, despite the insouciance of this relative freedom of action, I re-affirm that wrong-doing is wrong.

It is better to be clean than dirty. I believe this also to be true. I affirm my belief in all sincerity and am prepared to propound a logical argument in support of the belief. But I believe also that if upon the poster hoardings and in the advertising columns of every newspaper I read I were to see this simple statement conjoined with an appeal to buy Buggins' Perfection Soap, my faith in cleanliness would weaken.

The two decades 1919–39 were the Golden Age of the professional persuader, and if any of these professional persuaders—many of whom became very rich—were actuated solely by love for their fellow men, I can only say that I did not meet them. They persuaded from pulpit, in the press, from courts of law, on the floor of Parliament, over the radio, by posteresque art and every other known advertising medium. Some were just trying to sell soap. Some sought to whitewash swindling company promoters —if the reader will excuse the redundancy—while others just offered new lamps for old. But the most dangerous of all, and it is they who brought the world to its present sorry pass, were those who created new and tempting ideologies which were cloaks for fear, hatred, cruelty and oppression.

All the simple and straightforward issues have been fogged by the professional persuaders. Truth and justice still exist, despite all that has been done by lawyers to distort and pervert them. The Sermon on the Mount still offers the best way of life, despite all that has been done to obscure its simplicity and beauty by fat priests who, just as the lawyer has striven to deny us direct access to justice, have done their best to deny men direct access to their God.

We at times pride ourselves on our advanced civilisation, but I wonder what Christopher Wren would say if he returned to St Paul's Cathedral and looked around him as his epitaph enjoins others to do.

We have improved our plumbing, installed telephones which frequently work, but the greatest of all human ingenuity and industry has gone into weapons of destruction. For twenty years honest craftsmen by the millions were unable to find work. Half the world starved for goods of which the other half had a huge surplus. There was prosperity only among those privileged few who were born with the gift of the gab: the lawyers, the priests, the salesmen, the politicians (who never suffer in the crises they create), the advertising experts and the ordinary windy orators who hire themselves out to anyone. They dealt in words—all of them. They created nothing and destroyed much. The magic of their well-chosen words and silver tongues helped guilty men escape the gallows, invested shoddy goods with an aura of excellence and shoddy ideas with the trappings of profundity. The great mass of humanity, the wolf snapping and snarling close behind, were too busy with the serious business of obtaining food and shelter to be critical or analytical.

It is perhaps foolish to become too cynical and too suspicious of human motive, but it is hard not to be so in a world which is run for the benefit of the professional persuaders. If and when I am privileged to witness one of these gentry sacrifice £10,000 per annum because he cannot conscientiously lend his powers of persuasion any longer, I will recant. But until then I shall continue to believe that the professional persuaders of all kinds are actuated by self interest rather than a love for those to whom they address their persuasions.

Russia and Spain have afforded us two glaring instances of the diabolical harm done by these same professional persuaders. It is not long ago that we were told by these gentry—I wonder were they ex-shareholders in the Lena Goldfields—that Russia was our arch-enemy and that Joseph Stalin was the personification of the anti-Christ. Many of the same voices are telling us another story now but there must be many who listened to and believed the first story who are finding difficulty in swallowing the second, despite the evidence we have that Russia under the leadership of Joseph Stalin probably saved our bacon. The legitimate Republican Government of Spain a year or two ago was characterised by some of these professional persuaders—perhaps they were Rio Tinto shareholders— as something so bestial that no abuse was bad enough. But the fact remains to-day that Franco, who waved the

Christian banner so vigorously, hired Moslems to murder Christians and to-day professes open friendship with Hitler the self-confessed anti-Christ. These same professional persuaders tried to sell us not so long ago the tale that Hitler himself had no aggressive intentions.

Can anyone in his sober senses believe that the men who so misled us did so in all honesty? If they were honest, which I for one will never believe, they were fools and as such had no business to be in positions of authority and influence.

The great mass of people are nothing like so stupid as they sometimes appear to be. They would not even seem stupid unless they were denied access to unvarnished truth, which might have enabled them to form right judgments for themselves without the help of the professional persuaders.

Perhaps out of all the misery of the present time, which would never have occurred if these venal advocates had not occupied such a great number of high positions in this and other lands, there will come sanity. Then truth—plain, undoctored truth—uttered by men without an axe to grind, may rule our counsels.

Try a parlour game for the long winter evenings: get hold of back files of newspapers since 1933 and ask yourself how many prominent men in this and other lands would like to be confronted with their statements on international affairs. That will prove a good footrule by which to measure them.

S. L.

Chapter One

JEREMY DOWBIGGIN, aged ten, with the aid of an ingenious contrivance which enabled four pens to write simultaneously, was laboriously engaged in the task of copying out two hundred times the excellent old adage: 'Honesty is the best policy'. The bees were droning outside. Smells of freshly cut grass came through the window of the musty old classroom. From the distance came the tantalising click of a cricket bat striking the ball and occasional rounds of applause—very restrained applause—as some player distinguished himself. Wendleton Junior School was playing St Winifred's Preparatory School on that particular Saturday afternoon in June of the year 1904.

The Rev. James Muggridge, headmaster of Wendleton Junior School, took great pride in his strawberry garden. Jeremy Dowbiggin was fond of strawberries. Hence, instead of watching the cricket match, he was engaged with his quadruple pen in the prosaic task mentioned above. Even at the age of ten young Jeremy had a very inquiring mind. Honesty he defined as not stealing, but he found himself consumed with curiosity to know what a policy might be. From a tattered dictionary on the shelf behind the master's desk he learned that a policy was 'a prudent, expedient or advantageous procedure'.

The thoughts aroused by this ill-understood dictionary definition carried Jeremy through to the end of his imposition. Indeed, on counting the lines written, he found that he had written 204. Crossing out the last four hastily, he signed the sheet with a diagram which revealed a parrot sitting on ST as the best of its species visible.

Another trip to the dictionary revealed that 'expedient'

and 'advantageous' were synonymous. But the definitions seemed to lack clarity.

'What is an expedient procedure, sir?' Jeremy asked the Rev. James Muggridge a little later as he delivered the 200 lines to him.

'Why do you ask, Dowbiggin?'

'I read it somewhere, sir, and didn't understand what it meant. You told us, sir, that when we read words we didn't understand . . .'

'Quite! Quite! An expedient procedure, eh? Let me see. How shall I explain it?'

The worthy clergyman had to stop to think. He warmed to this handsome small boy, whose frank blue eyes looked up to him as the fount of knowledge. It was a full minute before a good hypothetical case occurred to him.

'Let us suppose, Dowbiggin,' said the headmaster smiling, 'that one of the boys here—I am only supposing you know—wished to eat some of my strawberries without my—er permission. Such a thing couldn't happen, of course, but let us suppose that it could. Very well. It would be an expedient procedure to make quite sure that at the time the strawberries were being—er picked I was not looking out of my study window. Now do you understand?'

'Yes, sir! Thank you, sir! Now may I go and watch the match?'

'Yes, run along, my boy, and remember that I shall be looking out of my study window as you pass the strawberry bed. Ha ha!'

In a little shiny black notebook which he used as a diary and for the committal to paper of his inmost thoughts, Jeremy that night wrote: 'Did an impot 200 lines. Honesty is the best policy. Must not pick strawberries when head is looking.'

This was followed by a painstaking reproduction

of a rather elongated parrot sitting upon the letters ST.

That night he dreamed he was stealing strawberries in a mist which crept conveniently between him and the headmaster's study window. Just as he was reaching out for an extra luscious berry the parrot—the one perched on ST—fluttered down beside him. Just then the mist began to clear and the parrot in a loud voice remarked: 'Stop stealing those strawberries. It isn't honest to steal them when the headmaster's looking. Wait until he goes to bed.'

* * * * *

Charles Dowbiggin, Jeremy's father, was fond of expounding to his only son the maxims which had governed his own life. Fathers often feel thus impelled. Jeremy, aged eighteen, put on the special face he used for listening to his father's homilies, keying his mind the while to more amusing things.

'There are no short cuts to success, Jeremy,' Charles Dowbiggin was saying. 'Success comes after years of hard work, pains-taking and integrity. Remember that. You have had a fine education and far more advantages than I ever had. It has not been easy giving you these things. Your mother and I have had to do without many things in order to make it possible. . . .'

All this was a somewhat oblique reference to his own success in life, his career having just been crowned, after over twenty years of punctuality, diligence and almost excessive honesty, by the post of chief clerk in the actuarial department of the London & Continental Assurance Company. The post carried with it £600 per annum, rising to £800 at some remote time in the future. Charles Dowbiggin was feeling justly proud that the directors had recognised at long last the loyal service they had received from him. Twenty years of catching the 8.14

train from Richmond to Waterloo; twenty years of cheap and indigestible lunches bolted in a City basement; twenty years of submission to petty tyranny such as only great financial institutions inflict upon those who serve them; twenty years without a debt unpaid; twenty years of cigar-smoking by proxy as the fragrant fumes of the actuary's after-lunch cigar eddied into the little cubbyhole which Charles Dowbiggin called his private office.

'And now, Jeremy,' Charles Dowbiggin continued, 'I have some news for you. I heard to-day that when you leave school—subject of course to a personal interview—a place will be found for *you* at head office. There is no finer company in existence than the London & Continental, my boy. Your future is assured.'

Jeremy looked at his father, taking in at a glance his flat chest, hunched shoulders, dim and watery eyes. He was genuinely fond of this prematurely aged man who had sired him. At forty-two Charles Dowbiggin looked sixty. Life for him had been fifty weeks of work each year and two weeks at mean Broadstairs lodgings. Jeremy gritted his teeth to thank his father, but could not repress a shudder.

'We have a premium income in excess of £6,000,000 now and we pride ourselves that our ratio of expenses to premium income—only 8.37 per cent—is the lowest of any company in the City, and therefore in the world, writing our class of insurance. Do you see what that means, Jeremy?'

'Yes, father!' was the dismal reply.

'By the way, Jeremy, your Uncle George is coming to lunch to-morrow. I want you to slip round to the wine merchants and ask them for a bottle of their sparkling Moselle. Your Uncle George likes a drop of good wine. And while you are about it bring me half a dozen Flor de Dindiguls. Try and get an empty box to put them in.

[4]

It looks better. I shouldn't like your Uncle George to think that I buy cigars specially for him. . . .'

Uncle George, Charles Dowbiggin's brother, was the living embodiment of the utter fallacy of all Charles's theories of life. George Dowbiggin carried gold sovereigns in his right-hand trouser pocket, all jumbled up with silver and copper. He paid two shillings each for his cigars at a time when most men thought sixpence a high price. His clothes were *built* for him, as distinct from made. He had begun life by entering the office of a firm of estate agents, valuers and surveyors, just about the time when Charles Dowbiggin had joined the staff of the London & Continental. He had lasted exactly one week as junior clerk, the senior partner of the firm taking the view that it damaged the firm's good name to receive a complaint from a lady client that she had found George *in flagrante delicto* with her niece upon an otherwise disused bed in a lumber room. With a sigh of relief George Dowbiggin accepted his dismissal and, rather than face an irate father, took up his abode in cheap lodgings near Camberwell Green. Being a young man, handsome and of pleasing personality, he had persuaded his landlady—a buxom young widow—to accept payment in kind rather than in cash. When the lady in question developed a single-track mind and coyly admitted that orange blossom was her favourite flower, George Dowbiggin decided that it was time to emigrate. In wanderings which took him to the Australian goldfields, Nevada copper mines and to a Mexican silver lode, always as a speculator rather than as one of those who toiled with pick and shovel, George Dowbiggin acquired much knowledge of the world and those who live in it, a cheerful cynicism regarding all human motive, a knife thrust an inch below his heart and a very considerable fortune. When he finally returned to England, where sundry lurid stories of his wanderings had preceded him, it was only the fortune which persuaded his horrorstruck blood relatives to have anything to do with him. For his brother Charles he had a good-natured contempt and was fond of telling him that on one spin of the roulette wheel in a mining boom town in Nevada he had once made more money in two minutes than Charles had ever made in five years of slavery.

The arrival of Uncle George for lunch on Sunday, a semi-annual event, was therefore a somewhat feverish occasion in the household of Charles Dowbiggin. It was always, contrary to the usual habit, a cold lunch, which enabled Ruth Dowbiggin to appear unruffled and be-satined. Although she had goggled more than once at some of his stories and the parts he had played in them, Ruth liked her husband's brother. He brought into her rather drab life glimpses of a larger and brighter world, where people did not peep furtively through machine-made lace curtains at the doings of the neighbours and where lusty hearty men handled their women as women were meant to be handled and where an insurance actuary was not God. It was all very ill-defined in Ruth's mind, but there were times when, amid the fumes of cooking and soapsuds, punctuated by the cry of the milkman and clatter of the butcher's boy at the back door, she found Number 7, Cornwallis Crescent, Kew Gardens, something of an anti-climax when set against her girlhood dreams. Charles had always been so considerate, so utterly reliable and so undemonstratively loyal and affectionate, that she could not bring herself to the disloyalty of comparing life with him to life with—say his brother. But lurking at the back of consciousness the thought was there. While she knew that George would have been unfaithful on a wholesale scale, showered jewels on her one minute and pawned them the next, and life with him would have been rather like life on the brink of an active volcano, Ruth

[6]

Dowbiggin sighed deeply when despite her best endeavours these disturbing thoughts would come to her.

Charles Dowbiggin at forty-two was the husk of a man. George at forty-six was in his prime, his zest for life unimpaired. He arrived just before lunch in a vast Minerva car, which parted every pair of lace curtains in Cornwallis Crescent.

George was a kind-hearted scoundrel. Although he loathed sparkling Moselle he drank it with apparent zest. Although his chauffeur smoked better cigars than those his brother offered to him, he smoked one and asked if he might pocket another to smoke that evening. He praised the lunch and said that Ruth's salad dressing reminded him of the famous French dressing at Delmonico's, adding that only at Fisherman's Wharf in San Francisco was it possible to get dressed crab comparable with that which was on the table.

'A friend of mine will take out a big policy with your company,' said George to Charles. 'I'll send him along to see you on Tuesday. You might as well pocket the commission on it.'

'I'm in the actuarial department, George,' replied Charles. 'I don't get any commission. But I'll be delighted to see your friend and you'll have the satisfaction of knowing that there's no finer company he could come to. Of course, I haven't told you the news, George. They've made me chief clerk. . . .'

'Sucker!' said George between his teeth. He wished he had not spoken, for he could have secured the commission rebated through a broker friend, but for the fact that he wanted to do Charles a good turn.

'Good for you, Charlie old boy!' he said aloud. 'About time they recognised a good man, too.'

'That isn't all, George,' continued Charles. 'Young Jeremy here joins the company next month, subject to the personal interview turning out all right. Isn't that so, Jeremy?'

'Yes, father!' was the weak reply.

'Like a drive in the car, Jeremy?' asked George.

'Rath-er!' said Jeremy, whose mind had all along been on the shining monster outside the door.

'You didn't sound very enthusiastic about joining your father's company,' said George as the car purred up Kingston Hill.

'I'm not,' said Jeremy, miserable at the very thought.

'What do you want to do, then? P'raps I can help you.'

'I don't know, Uncle George. I think I want to go abroad—like you did, and do things.'

'What things?'

'Everything!'

'Now look here, Jeremy my lad, it isn't for me to persuade you to go against your father's wishes. P'raps he knows best for you, but it does seem to me that you're not cut out for the insurance business. Talk it out with your father and drop me a line. If the worst comes to the worst I'll stand you a passage out to Mexico and get my partner out there to fix you up with a job. But have it out with your father first.'

Who should know better than Uncle George that you cannot open to a boy a vista of Mexican bandits, dark-eyed Señoritas, tinkling guitars and the loot of the Incas, and expect him tamely to submit to the horrors of life in a London assurance office.

'If you want to turn that into something worth while,' said George a little later, slipping a few uncounted sovereigns into Jeremy's hand, 'back Hasty Lad for the big race at Kempton next Saturday. But whether you do or don't, don't tell your father. He might not like it.'

The last remark was a monument of understatement.

Jeremy hid his golden hoard—five golden sovereigns—

under the linoleum in the bath-room and lived for the following Saturday. He escaped from the house immediately after Uncle George had left because he felt he could not endure his father and mother's usual *post mortem* after these visits. Uncle George had become his hero and he felt himself unable to listen to any disparaging remarks about him. He took with him a copy of *Whitaker's Almanack* and in the privacy of the shrubbery opposite Number 7 Cornwallis Crescent devoured every word about Mexico, resolving on the following morning to secure further information from the public library.

'What price Hasty Lad?' asked Jeremy nearly a week later, selecting the least revolting-looking bookmaker in the Ring at Kempton. He had secured admission on a borrowed newspaper pass.

'100 to 8 to you!' said Bob O'Brien, *né* Cohen, expecting to see two half-crowns at most. He swallowed hard when Jeremy thrust five sovereigns at him. The market price was nearer 10 to 1 and Bob O'Brien hated to lay over the odds. It was against his religion. 'Sixty-two-pun-ten to five Hasty Lad!' he added. 'Here's yer ticket and I'll lay ten to one Hasty Lad.'

Jeremy watched fascinated as the market for Hasty Lad hardened. The colt went to the post second favourite at five to one.

It is probable that the outcome of the race was one of the great turning-points in Jeremy's life, for when Hasty Lad won by a short head and Jeremy had collected £67 10s. from Bob O'Brien, the boy would not have been human if the thought had not come to him that in five minutes he had made more money than his father earned for five weeks of hard work.

Uncle George, who always felt naked without race-glasses slung across his shoulders, loomed large and prosperous through the throng.

'Back it?' he asked. 'Come and have a drink!' he added, seeing the answer to his question in Jeremy's face.

George Dowbiggin himself had his pockets full—literally full—of five- and ten-pound notes. Hasty Lad had won him a few thousands.

'Had that talk with your father yet?' asked George.

'Not yet,' replied Jeremy, 'but I'm going to talk to him to-night. It'll be easier somehow now.'

'It always is easier, my lad, when your pockets are full of these.' George pulled out a fistful of sovereigns. 'Remember what I'm telling you: never be broke. Being broke breaks your heart. Your father's been broke all his life, with the result that he lets that damned insurance company walk all over him. If they told him he'd have to crawl in the front door on his knees, he'd do it. Why? Because he's broke and they know it. I've been broke in one sense of the word—often. But I wasn't really broke, as nobody knew it. Your father's a good fellow, Jeremy. One of the best. A better brother no man ever had, but he's let them put chains on him and now he's so used to them he wouldn't feel happy without them. . . .'

The champagne was loosening George's tongue.

'But listen to me, Jeremy. Don't let the mean-souled tykes get their claws on you unless you want to spend your life in a rotten little suburban villa and wear yourself out for the benefit of a lot of bloodsucking financial bandits who'll throw you a little pension and retirement when you're too old and too worn-out to enjoy either. I don't care what you do or where you go, but don't go into that bloody insurance office or you're damned—eternally damned.'

'I'm going out to your mine in Mexico, Uncle George. That is, if you meant what you said.'

'I always mean what I say, boy. Tell your father and go. He'll never forgive me for this, but he's had his life, or the chance of it, and you have yours before you. Don't hurt him more than you've got to. He's a good fellow and he never hurt anyone except himself. Get into trouble if you have to. Trouble makes a man. Probably I'll get you out of it—once or twice. After that you'll have to find your own way out. Come and see me before you go. Now I've got to go out and back another horse. No! Not for you, my lad. You've multiplied your five by more than twelve. Leave it alone now.'

Jeremy stood in a daze while George, waving a fistful of Bank of England notes, rushed out of the bar and into the Ring. The champagne had not yet gone flat when Jeremy was sitting down to tea and crumpets at Number 7 Cornwallis Crescent, which suddenly seemed very shabby and unromantic.

'What's on your mind, dear?' asked his mother.

For reply Jeremy pulled out of his pockets the notes and gold which were burning a hole.

'What have you been doing? Where did you get this?'

Money, that is to say cash, in quantities greater than would suffice for the settlement of the weekly household bills, looked wrong to Ruth Dowbiggin. She assumed, although she had no reason to suspect Jeremy's integrity, that it had been acquired by immoral, reprehensible means. Charles, her husband, would have jumped to just such a conclusion. In point of fact, had the choice been open to him, it is probable that he would have preferred to learn that Jeremy had robbed a bank, rather than won it at Kempton Park.

'I won it, mother. I had a tip for a horse and it won. That's all.'

'What will your father say?'

'I'm not going to tell him.'

'But you must, dear. It would be deceitful not to tell him.'

'Mother dear,' said Jeremy, dismissing the subject, 'I have decided that I won't go into the London & Continental. I'm not made for that sort of life. I'm going abroad—now, at once. I shall tell father when he comes home.'

Ruth Dowbiggin shook with three huge convulsive sobs. Her world was dissolving around her. The enormity of what Jeremy had said in the last few moments was too much for her. She had an almost superstitious feeling that Jeremy would be blasted by his father's anger and so, because she was a mother, she hugged her boy to her. He was hers, she felt, until his father returned home and after that anything might happen. So she hugged Jeremy just that much more tightly.

Chapter Two

ALL THE WAY ACROSS from Liverpool to New York Jeremy was haunted by his father's horror-struck face. Charles Dowbiggin had said very little, had shown no anger. He had just looked unbelievably hurt, horrified and despairing. 'I can't think what the directors will say!' was the last coherent remark Jeremy remembered.

The London & Continental had closed its Mexican offices largely owing to the instability of the country's business fabric. Somehow Mexico, George Dowbiggin's irregular mode of life, bandits and immoral women were all inextricably muddled in Charles Dowbiggin's tight little mind. With the possible exception of Paris, he would rather have heard that Jeremy had gone anywhere else on earth. He could have restrained him forcibly, of course, but that would have done no good.

There was one bright spot for Charles after Jeremy had

sailed. The bursar of Wendleton posted him a receipt for one term's fees in lieu of notice. Charles was pleased that Jeremy had remembered this, though he wondered where he had got the money. Charles was not mean: it was the thought rather than the money which pleased him. Later he assumed, and rightly, that his brother George had found the money.

Jeremy travelled first class to New York in the *Baltic*, then one of the world's wonder ships.

'People who travel third class think third class,' George Dowbiggin had said. 'In the steerage you'd probably meet much nicer people, but they'd be no good to you. If they were they wouldn't be travelling steerage. It isn't what you know but the people you know that counts in this world.'

It cost Jeremy five pounds in tips to leave the *Baltic* at New York. Contemplation of this sum appalled him, but when he had disbursed it he found that it gave him a curious pleasure.

Uncle George's partner, who might have stepped out of a Wild West novel, was in New York when Jeremy arrived. He occupied a suite on the eleventh floor of a vast hotel overlooking Times Square, where night was if anything more noisy than day.

'Colonel Hunter's room, please!' said Jeremy to the lift attendant. Nor did it strike him as peculiar that among eight hundred or so other guests the name was familiar.

In visualising Colonel Hunter, Jeremy had created a picture of someone immaculate of dress who, after being parboiled and stuffed, was propped in the window-seat of a Pall Mall club. The fact was that Jim Hunter himself had forgotten when the label 'colonel' had been tied on him, by whom or why. But from the Sacramento Valley all the way down the Pacific Coast to the Mexican frontier and beyond, there were thousands of people who knew him as Colonel Hunter. The title was, therefore, fully as authentic as the Kentucky variety.

Jim Hunter's suite opened Jeremy's eyes. Scattered about it were upwards of a dozen people, the contents of one case of whisky and an unopened case in reserve, countless cigars and cigar ends, many of which had been trodden into the carpet.

'Hey there, Clara!' called Hunter in a voice that must have been heard in the hotel lobby. 'Put your pants on and act respectable. We got company.'

Through a blue haze of cigar smoke which nearly choked Jeremy, Hunter introduced him to the assembled company.

'How did you leave that gosh-danged old scoundrel of a partner of mine?' asked the Colonel, filling a tumbler with faintly diluted whisky and handing it to Jeremy. 'When's he coming out to do some work?'

Fortunately for Jeremy's blushes it was the sort of party where everyone talks and nobody listens. At the time of his arrival it had been going on continuously for three days and nights. His replies, therefore, were inaudible and quite unimportant.

Two days later Hunter, with Jeremy in tow, left for the mine. The last stage of the journey, almost perpendicular, was accomplished on muleback. For Jeremy it was two days of torture. In the rarefied air when they finally arrived—the mine was situated some 8,000 feet above sea level—Jeremy could not keep awake. He slept more or less continuously for forty-eight hours and finally awoke to the realisation, among others, that the Spanish grammar he had studied ever since he had left England did not help him to understand one single word of the language which was being spoken around him.

Jim Hunter in New York on holiday and Jim Hunter at *La Purificacion* mine were two entirely different men.

The mining itself was relatively simple. Great lumps of ore, some of them more than 70 per cent pure silver, were blasted and hacked out of the mountainside in incredible quantities. But the said ore was quite useless where it was. It had to be transported somehow to places where it was useful and, which is more to the point, protected at the mine itself and *en route* from the greater part of the population of the district, all of whom believed that they had a better claim than Jim Hunter to the shining wealth which was being mined.

There was no drink at *La Purificacion*, except in strictly medicinal quantities. The mine and buildings were surrounded by a high wire fence. After sundown it was the local rule that nobody but Jim Hunter and the mine manager, the latter a gigantic Cornishman named Pengelly, was permitted inside the enclosure. On Jeremy's arrival he was included. This considerably simplified the protection of the silver, for anyone else moving about the compound was shot on sight.

Hunter, Pengelly and Jeremy divided the night into three watches. The one on watch sat, a loaded shotgun on his knees, at one of several spots which commanded a view of the compound. The spot was changed frequently and without plan.

For Jeremy's first watch he chose the shadow of the mine mouth. Within a week he had from its security killed a man, narrowly escaping from blowing up the mine and everyone around. At four o'clock in the morning, just as the moon had sunk behind the serried mountain range behind the mine, Jeremy heard a faint ping. It was as though someone had plucked gently at the string of a 'cello. There followed a moment or so later a little cascade of stones and rubble from the same direction. The flash of his first barrel enabled Jeremy to see a man crouching beside the dynamite store. The second barrel, loaded with buckshot, found its mark. Several pellets tore through the flimsy woodwork of the dynamite shed and one actually penetrated a cardboard box in which was stored enough fulminate of mercury to have brought this story to a speedy close.

By the first morning light they found the night marauder some twenty yards outside the wire fence, on which were still trailing some of his intestines. The greater part of the buckshot had caught the poor wretch in the pit of the stomach.

'Good work, Jeremy boy!' said Jim Hunter, lifting the corpse and pitching it down a deep ravine, where it fell with a sickening crunch on to the rocks. All that day Jeremy was haunted by the sight of vultures swooping down to their ghastly feast.

The thought uppermost in Jeremy's mind, curiously enough, was what they would think of it all at Number 7, Cornwallis Crescent, which now seemed so remote as to belong to another world.

For the rest, life at *La Purificacion* was deadly dull, relieved only by the periodical guarding of a long train of mules which set out for the coast loaded with silver. On these occasions Pengelly, with half a dozen Mexican soldiers borrowed for the purpose, remained behind to protect the mine, while Jim Hunter and Jeremy, with a further escort of troops, set out with the mule train.

At Hunter's insistence Jeremy practised with rifle and revolver, until with the former he could hit a cigarette-tin three times out of four at two hundred yards and with the latter hardly ever miss a silver dollar on edge at twenty paces. Of mining itself Jeremy learned precisely nothing, and of mine book-keeping very little. Mexicans, who lived in a village over a mile distant, did all the mining under the occasional supervision of Pengelly. Jim Hunter's job was largely to placate with bribes the civil and military authorities, to keep the scale of bribes as low as skill and experience made possible, and to ensure that, having bribed the right people, they did what was required of them.

But if Jeremy learned nothing about mining during the two years he was at *La Purificacion*, he learned a good deal about life, human nature and frailty. He learned, too, the first part of the lesson that almost nothing in life is as it seems to be, which lies at the very roots of worldly wisdom; that the rich rewards of life do not go to the hewers of wood and the drawers of water, but rather to those with strong claws and teeth; and that the pattern of human conduct, as exemplified by his father, might carry its reward in a problematic hereafter but would never yield dividends in this world.

When in late August of 1914, a few days after Jeremy's twentieth birthday, news reached *La Purificacion* that the British and German Empires were at war, Jim Hunter announced his intention of going North to Canada to join the Canadian army. Jeremy accompanied him.

In New York, where Jim Hunter treated himself and Jeremy to a final splurge which lasted a week, the former dyed his greying hair black and, despite over forty tough rough years, would have passed—did pass—for a little over thirty.

In the summer of 1915 a magnificently handsome and stalwart young man, clear blue eyes shining out from a tanned face surmounted by almost blue-black hair, walked twice round Cornwallis Crescent, before he was able to summon the courage to knock at the door. It was Sunday. Charles and Ruth Dowbiggin were sitting down to a leathery piece of the Roast Beef of Old England, all the way from an Argentine *frigorifico*.

'Did you come by bus?' asked Ruth. She was so overcome that she did not know what she said.

She and Charles looked at each other and the unspoken thought between them was: 'Did we produce this bronzed, handsome young giant? And if so, how?'

Charles Dowbiggin forgave Jeremy when he learned that his son had no intention of returning to Mexico; and although Jeremy only gave his parents a heavily expurgated version of life at *La Purificacion*, it quite satisfied the father that Mexico was no country for a Dowbiggin.

His return home was enough to prove to Jeremy that he and his parents, even if they had done so in the past, would now never understand each other. Jeremy had outgrown them and their ways of life. Already, or so it seemed to him, he was older and more experienced than his father, at least as far as worldly wisdom goes. Charles made one feeble and unconvincing attempt to persuade Jeremy to join the London & Continental when the war was over, offering to abase himself before the directors to that end. There was a chance, he believed, that before long he would sit at the actuary's desk, which ranked in Charles Dowbiggin's imagination as on a par with the Throne of Heaven.

'I don't know what I shall do when it's over, father,' Jeremy replied as gently as he could, 'but I know I don't want to go into insurance. Something will turn up and, in the meantime, there's the war, which isn't over yet.'

Jeremy's battalion was cut to pieces at Vimy Ridge. He himself was slightly wounded and commissioned in the field. Amid the mud and blood he saw many things he hated. He saw incompetent senior officers wearing decorations earned by their juniors who had gone to a greater reward. He saw through the high pretensions mouthed by politicians, to the basic fact that the war was being waged for the benefit of two small groups of greedy and selfish men, who were prepared to shed rivers of blood—so long as it were not their own—to protect and bolster iniquitous financial and commercial empires, which were the very nullification of the democracy for which at least one side professed to be fighting.

When the bugles sounded on November 11th, 1918, Jeremy, who had already written himself off—for he had long since ceased to regard a future of any kind as a practical possibility—found himself faced with the problems of peace. He dwelled overmuch upon those who had been his comrades in war, most of whom were rotting under the sodden fields of Flanders. He dwelled, too, upon the causes which had sent them to their deaths. Nor did those causes seem adequate. There was much fine talk in those days of building a new world. If nothing else, it heartened people, for they felt that any change must be a change for the better.

By August of 1919 every penny of Jeremy's war gratuity was spent and he was no nearer solving the problems of peace. He wrote to Uncle George, who was in America, offering to return to *La Purificacion* if there happened to be a job there.

Jeremy had taken his discharge from the Canadian forces in London, feeling no desire to return to Canada with them. Pride, and a reluctance to allow his father to play any part in moulding his life, kept him away from Cornwallis Crescent. Here the wonderfully impossible had happened: Charles Dowbiggin was now Actuary of the London & Continental and, although these had become outmoded, he left for the City daily wearing a glossy silk hat. It would have been the crowning joy of Charles Dowbiggin's life if Jeremy had entered the service of the insurance company, but this was denied him.

Uncle George Dowbiggin replied to Jeremy's letter by cable, telling him to pick up £100 and a passage to New York at the Cunard office. Jeremy neither knew nor cared what his uncle had in store for him. He sailed as

[19]

soon as his passport formalities were completed.

As was almost inevitable, George Dowbiggin was making a huge fortune in Rum Row. Millions of thirsty American soldiers were being re-absorbed into the homeland; money was plentiful and prohibition was unpopular. He bought from a Great Lakes shipyard one of the fastest motor vessels afloat. When the Armistice was signed she had been nearly ready for delivery to the navy as a submarine chaser.

Jeremy enjoyed the life. Drink meant very little to him, but he felt strongly that prohibiton was a gross violation of individual liberty. Crouched behind a steel shield on the deck of the submarine chaser, with bullets from Customs craft and rival bootleggers pinging harmlessly, Jeremy found a certain cynical amusement. The end came when, dashing at high speed through a dense fog off Long Island, the little ship crumpled her bows against an anchored steamer, taking with her to the bottom 400 cases of genuine Scotch whisky. George Dowbiggin was not aboard. Jeremy and the two other members of the crew were picked up and landed at Havana. Back in New York a week or two later George Dowbiggin decided that he had made enough money and would turn respectable. Jeremy, with over £8,000 to his credit in the bank, returned to England.

*   *   *   *   *

Jeremy was still very sceptical about the new world which the politicians promised to build. He was sceptical about many things. In the early months of the war he and others had played a game, counting the totals of Austrian prisoners captured by the Russians, as published in the newspapers from official sources. When the Austrian prisoners totalled 14,000,000, or something like three times the entire strength of the Austrian army, Jeremy felt that there must be some slight exaggeration somewhere. Jeremy's was the inarticulacy of inexperience. He knew that few things were as they seemed and the knowledge disconcerted him. He had once seen an imposing general —a man with a great military reputation—clad in his underpants. Although the general in question had added to his laurels later, Jeremy always saw through the façade of the tightly-buttoned and beribboned tunic, the brass hat and scarlet tabs. He saw instead a funny little man with knobbly knees, thin legs and a pot belly, who was so helpless that he could not put his boots on without aid.

Jeremy remembered, too, the politicians, the policemen and the prohibition enforcement officers, who used to throng Uncle George's suite in New York—all of them sworn to do their duty without fear or favour.

All the real authors of Europe's blood bath had escaped scatheless. The worst fate to befall any of them had been luxurious exile. The politicians of Britain, the United States and France, to say nothing of the other allies, had at no time the smallest intention of implementing their promises to hang the war criminals. It would have been too dangerous a precedent and might have had repercussions on themselves.

Millions of other young men beside Jeremy entertained these thoughts and others more dangerous.

'I'm beginning to understand how it all works,' said Jeremy to George Dowbiggin on one occasion. 'So long as everything looks all right it is all right. The trouble is that there are some decent people in the world. Take poor old dad. He never hurt anyone. He's so darned honest that it hurts. He'd rather die than tell a lie, or steal, or make money the way we've been making it. But what good does it do him? What does he get out of life?'

'It looks like that, I know,' said George Dowbiggin soberly, 'but maybe old Charlie gets something out of his way of life that you and I can't understand. Mind you, I don't say that I disagree with your ideas of things, but I do say that you're too darned young to think that way. Half the fun in life lies in having illusions. Take the floor waiter here in the hotel. When I come back here he welcomes me like a long lost brother. I like it. He knows I like it. I dare say he hates my guts if the truth be told, but even if he does I don't want to know about it. Knowing wouldn't make my food or drink taste any better. No, Jeremy, hang on to a few illusions. It's better that way. I haven't got many, but the few I have keep me from cutting my throat. Don't you see that when you come to the point of realising how utterly rotten the world and most people in it are, the last reason for living has gone?'

Chapter Three

IT IS A CURIOUS reflection on our civilisation that so many men, without training of any kind, or any specialised knowledge, fly to three professions: advertising, journalism and teaching. Some of these men have never tried anything else; some have tried and failed. Both types seemingly deem themselves fitted for the task of moulding the habits and opinions of others. Bank clerks are chosen with infinitely more care than schoolmasters. The inevitable inference is, therefore, that the possibility of having money stolen is much more alarming than that the youth of the land should be corrupted. The chief requirements in a successful advertising man are personality rather than character, if these two things can be spoken of entirely separately.

For no better reason than that George Dowbiggin and George Hayward Fisher were old friends—it seemed a good reason to Jeremy—Jeremy joined the staff of the

Hayward Fisher Agency to learn advertising and, if he liked it, to make it his life's work.

'Ever sold anything?' asked Hayward Fisher.

'No!' replied Jeremy.

'Like to try?'

'I'll try anything.'

'Fine! That's what I like to hear. We'll soon find out if you can sell.'

Some years previously Hayward Fisher had acquired for a song one of those strange little trade journals of which there are so many scores published with varying degrees of success. It had once been called the *Lampmaker's Journal*. That was its name when founded in the 1850's. When electricity killed oil lamps it nearly killed the *Lampmaker's Journal*. But it managed to linger on until about 1910 when Hayward Fisher acquired it in payment of a bad debt. Its official title then became *Modern Illumination*, incorporating the *Lampmaker's Journal*. A dozen times Hayward Fisher had almost decided to let it die peacefully, but as many times had reprieved it. Many a salesman had broken his heart trying to sell advertising space in the journal, which had cost incredible sums in shoe leather alone. It was useful to Hayward Fisher as a proving ground for anyone who called himself a salesman and as a convenient way of getting rid of him when he reported failure.

When Jeremy set out from the office with a few specimen copies and order blanks in a shining new leather portfolio, Hayward Fisher smiled grimly. He had at least done what his old friend George Dowbiggin had asked him to do. It now remained for Jeremy to decide his own future. George Hayward Fisher almost forgot his existence from that moment.

As Jeremy was leaving the office a pretty girl intercepted him in the hall.

[23]

'Don't waste your time,' she whispered. 'He's only doing it to get rid of you. It's a shame, I think.'

'What's a shame?'

'Letting you waste your time on that rag. Nobody can sell space in it. Nobody reads it anyway.'

'What's your name?'

'Janet Seymour, why?'

'Will you have dinner with me to-night, Janet?'

'Mmm! All right. But I mustn't be late home.'

In a Fleet Street teashop Jeremy studied a melancholy list of all the prospective advertisers, each annotated with the even more melancholy remarks of salesmen who had vainly battered against their doors.

'Not interested.' 'Call again.' 'Thrown out.' 'Written applications only entertained.' 'Perhaps next year.' The entries went back over a period of more than a decade. It seemed as though these forgotten men had tried every firm in the country who could conceivably become advertisers.

Jeremy gritted his teeth. He would show that swine Hayward Fisher that he could sell space and when he had done so he would go somewhere else for a job. Why couldn't the man have said there was nothing doing in the agency? Hayward Fisher didn't know that Jeremy had money in the bank and was not desperately hard up, but he was willing to let him waste a week, a fortnight, being thrown out of strange offices, merely because the man lacked the moral courage to write and tell his old pal George Dowbiggin that there was nothing in the office for his nephew.

From Janet Seymour at dinner that night—Janet was a very junior stenographer—Jeremy learned that over a dozen ex-officers had been given their *congé* in the same way by Hayward Fisher.

'Prove to me that you can sell and I have a job for you,'

he had said to each of them, and when they had proved the contrary they had gone out to swell the embittered ranks of an army of men who were beginning to think that peace was worse than war. In war they had at least eaten regularly.

It was ten days before Jeremy saw Hayward Fisher again. He stalked into the office, through two doors marked 'Private', slamming down on Hayward Fisher's desk three signed contracts.

'Is that all you could do?' asked the latter when he had glanced through them. One was a series of twelve monthly quarter-pages from a concern which manufactured fireworks, another a trial half-page from a West End electrical wiring contractor, and the third from a novelty sign manufacturer. The grand total was a little over £80, of which 15 per cent belonged to Jeremy.

Hayward Fisher looked up at Jeremy and what he saw disconcerted him. The younger man's blue eyes had gone to tiny pin-points, his usually full lips to a fine line.

'It so happens,' said Jeremy in a voice vibrant with rage, 'that I don't need your filthy money, which is why I'm going to destroy those contracts. I wouldn't rest easily in my bed knowing that I had been the means of bringing you money—you fat, sly-faced, money-grabbing, cowardly crook.'

As he spoke, Jeremy threw the contracts into the fire.

Hayward Fisher sat back in his chair and laughed. He laughed until tears rolled down his cheeks. Hard words had been hurled at his head before this. He was quite impervious to abuse.

'You must come and have lunch with me,' he said, dabbing his eyes with a huge pocket handkerchief. 'Then we'll talk about a real job for you. I've found out what I wanted to know—you can sell all right. If you can sign up three firms for that'—he pointed with contempt to a copy of *Modern Illumination*—'you could sell Holy Water in an Orange Lodge.'

Hayward Fisher touched a bell.

'Miss Patterson,' he said to his faded secretary, 'how long is it since anyone sold any space in this?'

'I forget exactly, Mr. Fisher, but it was before the war. I know that. . . .'

'There you are,' said Hayward Fisher. 'You're a very lucky fellow, Dowbiggin. When you've cooled down I'll tell you why.'

Jeremy did not cool down until he was seated with a cocktail in his hand at a table in the Savoy Grill. He almost walked out of the office twice, but curiosity impelled him to accept this strangely-given invitation.

Jeremy had lunched in the Savoy Grill before, but never with anyone who was, so to speak, of it. To Hayward Fisher the famous eating place was more a club than anything else. He lunched there, frequently dined there, met his best clients there and most of the best deals over the years had been concluded there. If the shade of Hayward Fisher ever returns to this earth the most likely place to see it will be in the Savoy Grill.

'Now I'd like to know why I'm so lucky,' said Jeremy, trying hard to stifle the hostility which would not be stifled.

'Dowbiggin,' said the older man, looking at Jeremy over the top of his glass, 'there are two kinds of men to whom the world nearly always gives more than it receives from them. One is the salesman and the other is the orator. Neither kind produces anything—except hot air, but both of them flourish. In the complicated social and commercial structure we have created around us the greatest craftsmen, artificers, scientists, builders and other producers are helpless until they enlist the aid of the

[26]

smooth-tongued salesman to put the products of their industry and genius into circulation. Likewise, the most beneficent new laws and reforms are still-born until the harlot orator comes along to cast the spell of fine words and well-rounded phrases upon and about them. The orator, like the salesman, adds nothing to the excellence of the wares or ideas he propounds, but that excellence is not apparent to the masses unless it is presented to them behind a smoke-screen of verbiage. The hulking beetle-browed murderer, standing in the dock at the Old Bailey, becomes transformed by the oratory of his learned counsel into a gentle, ill-used victim of circumstances over which he had no control. The crooked politician worms his way into high office, with promises he has planned to break even before he makes them. Silver-tongued evangelists drag groans of piety and adoration from thousands by wrapping fantastic absurdities in the guise of divine truth.

'There are, Dowbiggin, no limits to the power and influence of the salesman—the orators are salesmen, too, just as much as the men who peddle vacuum-cleaners or hair restorers. Salesmanship and oratory, reduced to their one essential ingredient, are just hot air. Some men achieve this power by what we call personality, some by beautiful words, some by a glorious speaking voice. There are those who can sell by bullying the prospective buyer, and others who arouse pity. Some carry with them an aura of integrity, so strong that their least word has the force of an undisputed truth. But whatever the method, the essential thing is that these happy men, divorced from the need to toil and produce, have within them some vital spark which enables them to use their fellowmen and dominate them. . . .'

Hayward Fisher paused to examine the *Sole Colbert* which had been put before him.

'. . . There is probably a perfectly rational bio-chemical reason for this quality which is possessed by the few and withheld from the many. All I know is—and this is why we are lunching together—do eat your sole before it gets cold—that you, Dowbiggin, are a salesman. I thought it when I first met you. I know it now. You proved it by selling space in a moribund trade journal whose paid subscribers nearly all died at the turn of the century, and which now only exists at all through the courtesy of waiting-room tables in chambers of commerce and one or two public libraries which do not throw it unopened into the wastepaper basket.'

Jeremy glowered at the beginning of this harangue, but towards the end began to smile.

'You see, Dowbiggin,' Hayward Fisher continued with his mouth full, 'a glorious vista of the future is opened up for you. The world is your oyster. In filthy factories, in tunnels underground, in elegant show-rooms, at benches, lathes and on farms, there are men and women toiling for you. Some of them have hungry children, most of them are utterly miserable, all of them are grossly underpaid. But they await your pleasure, Dowbiggin. The major part of the profit from the useful and beautiful things they are toiling to make will go into your pockets. They will continue to wear harsh fabrics next to their skins, eat coarse and probably insufficient food, go to sleep, worn out, on hard and lumpy mattresses, and awake each morning to the sense of hopelessness and futility which goes with unrewarded industry. While for you, Dowbiggin—by the way, what'll you have after the sole—some grilled kidneys?'

'How much of what you're saying is serious, Mr. Fisher?' asked Jeremy.

'I'm perfectly serious, my dear fellow,' was the reply. 'You can sell, which means that you can sell yourself. It

[28]

remains for you to decide what you're going to sell—with yourself. You're too late for the law. There's politics, of course. On the other hand, and it's my advice that you do so, you can go into business, which will turn your talent into cash more quickly than other ways. Or there's religion. If you decide to go into business I hope you'll sell advertising with me. Of course, I shan't let you loose just yet among my clients. You'll have to spend a little time learning something about advertising first—say a few months, and then if I don't turn you into a first-class contact man my name isn't George Hayward Fisher. Think it over and let me know.'

*   *   *   *   *

It was three months before Hayward Fisher allowed Jeremy even to meet a client, or prospective client, and then only because he received a letter from the proprietors of Dr. Forsyth's Nectar saying that they were placing their business elsewhere at the end of the year. Fisher felt badly about this, for he had held the account for nearly ten years.

'Blundell's the man to see there,' said Fisher. 'He's a cross-grained swine, too. Try your teeth on him and see how you get on. Miss Patterson will give you their file.'

According to the claims made for it, Jeremy discovered that Dr. Forsyth's Nectar would tone up the nervous system, relieve constipation in adults, cure recurrent headaches, improve the circulation and give relief to sufferers from arterio-sclerosis, flatulence, acidosis and liver derangements. Grateful men and women in all walks of life had paid tribute to its efficacy in a host of other rare and complicated maladies, from peritonitis to hæmorrhoids.

'What's the stuff made of?' Jeremy asked a chemist of his acquaintance and buying a bottle out of curiosity.

'Chiefly the scourings of Algerian wine casks, fortified

with a certain amount of raw spirit and a microscopic quantity of God-help-us to take away the taste. Those who die of the stuff turn a nasty purple colour, while the survivors linger in alcoholic wards. I sell thousands of bottles of it every year.'

'Is it by any stretch of the imagination, do you think, good for anything or anybody?'

'There's a customer of mine who's been buying it for years,' said the chemist. 'He swears it cures his piles. They return after about six years and then he goes on another binge with it. I think it must cauterise them. Take a drink of it and see how you like it. To me it tastes like paregoric that's been filtered through the postman's socks.'

'Another time, thanks!'

*　　*　　*　　*　　*

'I almost hope you don't get the account, Mr. Dow-biggin,' said Janet Seymour when she had taken down a letter from Jeremy to the formidable Mr. Blundell, asking for an appointment. 'It's simply terrible stuff. When my Auntie Nellie died—that's my father's sister—they found hundreds and hundreds of the empty bottles under her bed. She'd been drinking it for years. I've never told my father that we do their advertising here or I'm sure he'd take me away. And now you've come here, Mr. Dowbiggin, I don't want to leave. All the others are a bit stuffy—dull somehow.'

'It can't be as bad as they make out,' replied Jeremy, 'or the law wouldn't allow it to be sold. There are public analysts and people like that who are paid to spot anything that harms the public. Anyway, that's none of our business, and I haven't got the account back for the firm yet.'

Jeremy went back to the chemist. He wanted more information.

'What sort of people buy that Dr. Forsyth's Nectar?' he asked. 'Are they mostly men or women, young or old, well or badly dressed?'

It was after closing time and the chemist was enjoying a large whisky and soda, a luxury he seldom permitted himself. He was resolved, furthermore, to get at least two more for the information Jeremy was extracting from him.

'It's hard to say, you know,' replied the chemist. 'I should say as far as the sexes are concerned that the people who buy it are about equally divided. But certainly they're not old people. You'd need a pretty young and strong constitution to stand a steady diet of it, I should imagine. But I have noticed more than once that it's the more respectable people who buy it—city clerks and so on who don't like being seen going into pubs. I think what really happens is that these people get a taste for drink through the stuff and then find that they get better and cheaper drink in the pubs. By that time they don't care a damn who sees them.'

The chemist looked at his watch.

'Yes, thanks! I will have another. But don't take my word for it. Go and have a chat with Dr. Williams round the corner. He'll tell you plenty. He tried to run the proprietors in once. . . .'

'I will,' replied Jeremy. 'Time for another?'

*   *   *   *   *

'Dr. Forsyth's Nectar, eh? You'd like my candid professional opinion of the stuff, eh? You want to know whether you ought to take some home to your mother? That depends, young man, on whether you want her to live or die. If you want to kill her relatively cheaply and still remain outside the clutches of the law, young man, by all means take her home a dozen or two. When you

[31]

observe that her memory is faulty, her eyes rheumy, her reflexes are no longer apparent and she tends to put her fork into her left ear rather than her mouth, you will know that she is on the last lap. I once wrote across a death certificate "Killed by Dr. Forsyth's Nectar." There were reporters present at the inquest. They told me later that their stories had been killed by their advertisement managers.'

'Then I gather that you have no high opinion of the stuff,' said Jeremy.

'Your assumption is correct, young man. If you are a newspaper reporter—as somehow I suspect you are—you may quote every word I have uttered. They are hanging a man next Monday at Pentonville. He killed his sweetheart and buried her in the garden. But I would rather be sitting in the condemned cell with his conscience than have mine burdened with Dr. Forsyth's Nectar. . . .'

Jeremy was about to tell the doctor the reason for his call, but he shrank from what the vehement little man might say. Jeremy was for a little while in doubt as to whether he wished to pursue the matter any further.

'If I don't, someone else will,' he murmured inwardly. 'Thank you, doctor,' he said aloud. 'And your fee?'

'Young man,' said the doctor earnestly, 'I don't know why you came here to see me. I do know that you were not contemplating giving this filth to your mother, or anyone else. But whatever your reason, I want no fee. You are at the beginning of your life and I am getting near the end of mine. You, therefore, will have more influence upon the future than I shall. Use that influence if you get the chance to put out of business the vendors of worthless and usually dangerous remedies. Good night, young man!'

As he left the doctor's house Jeremy lacked the moral courage to go back and hand him a fee, but he felt a little better when he had dropped a pound note through the letter-box. He felt that it released him from a promise by implication.

* * * * *

George Hayward Fisher leaned back in his chair, a broad grin on his face.

'My dear Dowbiggin,' he said, 'you're an advertising man now. You're not a reformer. Have you ever heard of the Pure Food & Drugs Act? It was passed to protect the public against just the sort of thing you've been talking about. This Dr. Forsyth's Nectar complies with the requirements of the Act, or it wouldn't be on the market. As to the claims made for it, if it can be established that they are fraudulent—and no such allegation has ever been made—there is the criminal law to deal with the vendors. I respect you for the attitude you are taking, but there is much good sense in the adage that the cobbler should stick to his last. Doubtless the law of the land could be improved, in this and other respects. If you think that you are the man so to improve it, then my dear fellow, your bounden duty is to go into politics. But I assure you that you can't muddle up advertising and medical jurisprudence. They don't mix. I have here indisputable proof that the vendors of this stuff have complied with the law as it now stands. Your job is not to question the wisdom or excellence of the law, but to devise a means of popularising this ab-so-lutely legitimate product and to convince the proprietors that you have in fact done so.'

'But, Mr. Fisher,' said Jeremy slowly, 'when a fully qualified medical man says things like that one can't forget them.'

'The man's probably hipped on the subject. Forget him. There'd be chaos if every fellow started turning reformer because of pet theories. Drink kills thousands every year. What are you going to do about that? Start a crusade? One of our best accounts, as you know, is *Flora McHaggis* whisky. Damned good whisky, too! It isn't the whisky that kills people; it's their own immoderate habits. If it wasn't whisky then it'd be something else. Are you going to ask me to turn down a good account like *Flora McHaggis* just because a few thousand drunken swine swill too much of it? But anyway, I'm glad we've had this chat. I respect you for your convictions, too. It's men like you we need in advertising. But don't lose your sense of proportion. Now, have you got any ideas on the subject of this Dr. Forsyth's Nectar?'

'Yes,' said Jeremy slowly. The stirrings of conscience were subsiding much as a pan full of boiling soup quietens on a dying fire. 'I've been through the old files of advertisements and it seems to me they cover every angle except one. I'd like the studio to do me a sketch of a fine, hale and hearty old couple sitting by a fire, sipping a glass of this—er—nectar. Then perhaps the copy department could work out something on these lines: "In the Autumn of life the blood runs thinly, the pulses beat more slowly. Dr. Forsyth's Nectar will rekindle the fires of Spring." Do you get the idea? Probably there are hundreds of thousands of old people who like a drink. They are too old or infirm to go out to the pubs. Probably the younger people won't go and buy booze for them. I've done a bit of investigation on the subject—talked to over a dozen chemists. They all say the same thing—that very few of the people who buy the stuff are old. Well, as I see it, this opens an entirely new field. . . .'

'Yes, you've got something there, Dowbiggin. I like the idea of the old fogies sitting boozing by the fire with the chemist's errand boy delivering relays of the stuff.

Why shouldn't the old ones have their bit of fun? Yes, I think you've hit it, Dowbiggin. I'll get the studio and the copy department working. With one or two nice lay-outs and a bit of persuasion you may land the contract. I suppose you've often been told that you're a damned good-looking fellow, Dowbiggin? You wear your clothes well, too. You talk convincingly, as though you really meant what you said from the bottom of your heart. You almost had me fooled with all that stuff the doctor put into your head. Good lad! That's salesmanship. You'll show 'em. Even if that swine Blundell turns you down, don't let it dishearten you. There'll be the satisfaction of knowing that you've been kicked out by one of the toughest men in business to-day. Now I'm busy.'

Chapter Four

'YOU CAN TELL Fisher from me,' said Blundell, 'that I'm not renewing the contract because I like him, or because I am reluctant to break an old association. I'm renewing it because you, Dunvegan, or whatever your name is, are the first intelligent man he's ever sent to see me. You've brought me an idea that will create new business. Hitherto I've provided all the ideas and Fisher has merely fiddled about with them. It's about time he had some new blood in the agency. Tell him so from me. He's slipping. He's getting old and fat and careless. You'll get the renewal by the first post in the morning. . . .'

So Blundell is what they call a tough nut to crack, is he? Jeremy soliloquised as he strolled back to the office. That must make me a nut-cracker. How much is one and three-quarters per cent of £55,000? That's the same as thirty-five bob per hundred quid, three hundred and fifty bob per thousand quid, seventeen hundred and fifty bob per five thousand quid. So it's eleven times seventeen hundred and fifty bob. Twenty thousand shillings is near enough— a thousand quid. Hope that swine Blundell doesn't change his mind!

Jeremy was walking along the eastern end of the Strand. In one of the side turnings he caught sight of a lawyer's brass plate. One can't be too sure, he reflected.

'Which of the partners do you wish to see?' asked a clerk who might have stepped out of the pages of a Charles Dickens novel.

'Any one of them,' replied Jeremy, 'but preferably one who deals with commercial contracts.'

'If you'll take a seat in there I'll see if Mr. Merryweather is disengaged.'

Mr. Merryweather turned out to be a chubby little man, just such as his name suggested. He looked rather too pink and innocent to be an astute lawyer, but Jeremy comforted himself with the thought that the matter was a very elementary one.

'I just want to know whether this letter constitutes a binding contract between me and the man who wrote it,' said Jeremy, handing over the desk the letter which Hayward Fisher had written confirming the terms of Jeremy's employment, with particular reference to a commission of one and three-quarters per cent on business secured.

'You are, I take it, Mr. Jeremy Dowbiggin?'

'Yes!'

'This Mr. Fisher who signs the letter, he is, I take it, what he is purported to be on the letter—the Chairman of the Hayward Fisher Agency?'

'Yes!'

'A contract to be valid, Mr. Dowbiggin, must be for a specified length of time. This letter specifies no time.

[36]

Nevertheless, its purport is quite clear and unless you have reason to suppose that the writer of the letter wishes to repudiate the contract—or shall we say the arrangement—I would say that this letter, duly stamped, places you in a very strong position.'

'But it is not, as you know the word, a properly drawn-up legal document?'

'No, emphatically it is not!'

'Then I wonder, Mr. Merryweather, if you would be kind enough to write to the writer of the letter and send him in draft the contract or exchange of letters which you consider adequate to protect me, pointing out the omissions in this?'

'I would prefer in such a matter to deal with your firm's legal advisers, Mr. Dowbiggin.'

'May I use your phone?'

'My clerk will get any number you require. . . .'

'Is that you, Janet? Listen! It's me. Be a good girl and find out from Miss Patterson, or someone, who the firm's lawyers are. Yes, I'll hold on. . . . Spurgeon, Micklethwaite and Crabbe . . . and the address . . . thanks, Janet. Good-bye!'

'An excellent firm, Mr. Dowbiggin,' said Mr. Merryweather, beaming. 'But I think as a matter of courtesy to this Mr.—er Fisher you should inform him that we shall be communicating with his solicitors on the subject. Let me congratulate you also on your extremely sensible action. Few young men, if I may say so, act with such entirely commendable prudence. . . .'

'Well, as I see it, Mr. Merryweather, a contract has no value while both the parties are on good terms. It's only when one side or the other turns nasty that anyone refers to the contract. I'd like to know then that I've got a good one.'

'If everyone thought like that, Mr. Dowbiggin, our

judges would be on perennial vacations and we poor lawyers would starve.'

* * * * *

Most of Fisher's harangue regarding the power of the salesman went over Jeremy's head at the time it was delivered. Jeremy was not introspective. He had never wasted time analysing himself and his motives. But much of what Fisher had said stuck in his mind. He began to notice things he had never noticed before. There was, for example, the little pub in Fleet Street where he drank a pint of beer every day about noon. No matter how crowded the bar might be, one or other of the barmaids always thrust his pint to him over the heads of men who had been waiting longer. It was the same thing in the office. When Miss Patterson mentioned to the staff that Mr. Dowbiggin was to have a stenographer to himself —she carefully avoided saying private secretary—three of the girls came to him and asked if he would choose them. He chose Janet Seymour, but even then the others seemed to go out of their way to do things for him. He could always get hold of a file more quickly even than Fisher himself.

People really do seem to like me, Jeremy reflected. He found that with angry and disgruntled clients, although he knew nothing at all about their accounts, he could smooth them down and make them forget their troubles. At the Bayswater boarding-house where he lived, Mrs. Bromley-Bellenger, the proprietress, relict of Colonel Bromley-Bellenger, popularly known in her establishment as The Dragon, was all over him. When he returned too late for dinner there was always a pile of sandwiches and some fruit by his bed. It transpired in conversation with the other guests that he had been singled out for this attention.

Complete strangers smiled at Jeremy in a friendly way. Some even told him what a delightful speaking voice he had. Slowly he came to realise that, whatever it might be called, he had the power within him to exert a subtle mastery over most of his fellow creatures. Since his schooldays he had always been able to hear, without listening, while people talked nonsense. His grave and deferential manner while clients aired their views would have brought him a fortune in Harley Street, without the formality of studying medicine. What made it so effective was that he was never sycophantic. He could express disagreement without giving offence, leaving the other party to the conversation feeling he wanted to revise his own judgment. Clients who had dealt direct with Fisher for years showed a desire to deal with Jeremy, who avoided them where he could, as the basis of his remuneration gave him a commission only on accounts which he himself introduced.

'I think you'd better remember, Dowbiggin,' said Fisher irritably one day, 'that the Chandos & Perkins account is mine. I happened to hear you speaking to Perkins on the phone as I passed your office. Perkins is an old friend of mine and I do not want the relationship disturbed in any way.'

'Very well, Mr. Fisher, I'll give instructions for the future that I'm out when Perkins phones. It will suit me excellently well. He pesters the life out of me and—since we are talking on the subject—Perkins and other of your own clients are taking up a great deal of my time, for which I get paid nothing. I had intended speaking to you about it. If it continues I shall have to ask you to revise our arrangement.'

'But my dear chap,' protested Fisher, 'the contract which the firm's solicitors agreed with yours has only run a year. Surely it's a little soon to talk of revising it. Let me remind you, Dowbiggin, that there aren't many men —inexperienced men—earning anything like your income. . . .'

'I don't want to revise the arrangement, Mr. Fisher,' said Jeremy pleasantly. 'I'm perfectly content with it. But I'm not paid a salary and I am entitled under the agreement to devote my entire time to my own clients. If you would be kind enough to instruct the staff outside— particularly the girl on the phone—that your clients have nothing whatever to do with me and that they are to deal with you exclusively, I shall be very grateful.'

As Jeremy and Fisher both knew, it was not practicable to expect clients to concern themselves with the purely domestic matters of the firm. Clients liked to feel free to consult whom they pleased in the firm. Fisher said this to Jeremy with some emphasis.

'Then it is not I, Mr. Fisher, who have varied the original agreement. . . .'

'I'm sure I haven't,' protested Fisher.

'No, but circumstances have,' said Jeremy quietly. 'The only fair suggestion I can make, therefore, is that in addition to my commission for the introduction of new business, I receive an over-riding commission on all the firm's business. Then I don't mind what accounts I spend my time on.'

Realising that he had created this situation, Fisher made his tongue bleed before he retired to his own office.

When Fisher finally submitted, Jeremy enjoyed a tremendous sense of power. He exulted in the knowledge that much of what Fisher had told him at their first lunch together was true. He was a salesman! The mysterious force within him, whatever it might be, that Fisher called salesmanship, could if it were handled properly and diverted into the correct channels, raise him high among his fellows.

'For a young man, if you do not mind me saying so, Mr. Dowbiggin,' said Merryweather during the drafting of the second contract with the firm, 'you have enjoyed a remarkable success. You have ambitions, I think.'

'I have ambitions,' replied Jeremy in a monotone, his eyes wearing a far-away look.

'And I wouldn't care to be the one to stand in the way of them either,' said Merryweather to himself, looking up at Jeremy's set face.

Ambitions, mused Jeremy, wondering as he did so just what his ambitions were. Money first, and the things money would bring. But beyond this he wanted power. In the few years he had been loose in it Jeremy had come to regard the world through dark spectacles. As he saw it, for every one who enjoyed the sweets of life there were a thousand who did not. People preached equality but did not practise it. If there were any, he did not understand the rules, but there was plenty of time to learn them. Meanwhile, wise men looked after themselves and the devil took the hindmost. That much Jeremy understood. When and if he ever achieved power, Jeremy mused, there would be things he would try to change. But how could a reformer work from obscurity? What was he going to reform anyway?

Jeremy seldom went to see his parents these days. They irritated him in some vague way. His father's patent adoration of the London & Continental Assurance Company irked him, so did his mother's placid acceptance of everything. These two seemed to Jeremy to live in a dream world. They believed in things and institutions which Jeremy knew were hollow shams. Although they knew that Jeremy was, by their standards at least, making a great deal of money, they would have been happier if he were catching the same train as his father in the morning to earn the miserable pittance which the company paid its junior clerks.

'I can't believe that Dr. Forsyth's Nectar is as bad as you say it is, Jeremy,' Charles Dowbiggin said on the only occasion when Jeremy discussed his work with him. 'You're just making a good story of it to amuse me. If you really thought what you say you think, I know you wouldn't play any part in putting it on the market.'

His father said this with an air of finality that left Jeremy with nothing to say.

To Jeremy his father represented just one of the millions of 'suckers' who, working hard, living honourably, exercising no imagination whatever, were the victims of those few predatory individuals who ran society to suit themselves. In later life Jeremy divided society into two classes: 'the boys' and the rest. The boys had plenty of everything, and the rest had just enough left to them to provide the strength of body to go on working so as to maintain the boys in the style to which they had become accustomed. The noble dukes who lived fatly on coal royalties would have to pull their belts in if the workers refused to mine the coal. They didn't refuse because they had to eat. So, treated like dogs, herded underground like moles, they slaved for a pittance to maintain lavish ducal establishments.

The system was indefensible. It was rotten, corrupt, selfish, brutal, and the very antithesis of the promises made by mealy-mouthed politicians when they were herding the masses into uniform to save democracy. The heroes were selling matches in the gutters, while others—a few—for no better reason than that some remote ancestor was alleged to have come across with William the Conqueror, were wringing wealth from the misfortunes of the underprivileged and spending it on riotous living in the world's playgrounds. The few continued to exploit the many and, appalling as he believed the system to be, since he lacked the power to change it, Jeremy was determined to be one of the few.

What Jeremy did not know, or knowing did not concern himself about, was that he was a throwback to a remote ancestor of Elizabethan times.

The Dowbiggins were a Devonshire family. Jeremy's grandfather had been the last of his line to farm the land, not far from Plymouth, which had been in the possession of his forbears since the days when Elizabethan sea-dogs put into Plymouth with their ships deep-laden with Spanish treasure.

It is recorded by one Sir William Brimstage, lord of the manor of Yellumpton, and Justice of the Peace, that on a cold December night in the year 1580 his servants found in a snowdrift near the gates of the house a tall, handsome, swarthy stranger, almost dead of exposure and exhaustion. The stranger was brought into the house, given brandy and warm clothing and, after hovering between life and death for some days, was gradually restored to health. Concealed about the stranger's waist were rolls of Spanish gold coins and certain valuable but unspecified jewels. The stranger spoke a tongue which later turned out to be French. Such slender account as he gave of himself is recorded in Sir William Brimstage's diary. He had been set ashore near Plymouth by the crew of an English ship which had picked him up as a castaway on some remote island of the Spanish Main. The stranger gave his name as Jules d'Aubigné.

The parish records of Yellumpton reveal that three years later Jules d'Aubigné married Lucy, only daughter of Sir William Brimstage, whose death took place shortly afterwards, and the next reference to the stranger or his family is the birth of a succession of sons and daughters, eleven in all. The headstone which marks Jules

[43]

d'Aubigné's grave refers to him as Julius Daubigny. One of his sons went to live near Exeter, dying under the name of Daubeny. In the middle seventeenth century the manorial rights of Yellumpton were owned by a William Dowbiggin, who also owned an area of land far greater than the Brimstage holdings, which were acquired through the marriage with Lucy Brimstage.

The decline of the Dowbiggins began with the repeal of the Corn Laws, and Jeremy's grandfather, William Dowbiggin, unable to set his sons up on the land, sent them to London to fend for themselves. With his death the Dowbiggins were landless.

Although some years were to pass before Jeremy acquired it, there was in existence a portrait of this Jules d'Aubigné, painted when he was about forty years of age. Jeremy had his somewhat voluptuous lips, his blue-black hair of rather coarse texture, his well-chiselled features, broad intellectual forehead and ruthless jaw. From this remote ancestor, it is reasonable to believe, Jeremy inherited the mystic quality which we, for the limitations of our language, have come to call salesmanship.

A stranger, a Frenchman—at a time when Frenchmen and Papists were detested in England—arrives in a remote village and is found half dead in a snowdrift. The account he gave of himself was sketchy and inconclusive in the extreme. He must have been an object of suspicion. He could not even speak the language of his hosts. But within a short space of time, despite all these handicaps, we see him married to the most considerable heiress in the locality. He must have had personality, assurance—unbounded assurance. One can only fill in the blanks of this incomplete human story by conjecture, and the train of thought this sets up sheds much light upon his latter-day descendant, Jeremy Dowbiggin. If it were not for

[44]

those bright blue eyes of his it would have been easy to look at Jeremy through half-closed lids and to see him with massive gold ear-rings in his ears, leather breeches, a bright scarlet sash round his waist, a turban of some bright colour on his head, standing beside a cask of rum on the after-deck of a pirate ship while his captives walked the plank.

All this may be doing an injustice to the memory of Jules d'Aubigné, but any man who dropped into a village of Elizabethan England, speaking no English and carrying a small fortune in Spanish gold and jewels, must have known, with his highly intelligent face, that then and afterwards tongues would wag and eyebrows be lifted. He will forgive us if we assume that he had the very best of reasons for being so vague as to his origins.

This Jules d'Aubigné sired a mixed bag of descendants. One of them, Henry Dowbiggin, ordered a maidservant to be whipped for laughing on the Sabbath. It was he who helped Cromwell kill the joy-of-living in England for a few decades. His son, Charles, for a wager of ten guineas, ate a whole goose and drank four gallons of ale at a sitting. It was said of this Charles that he had illegitimate children in nine parishes, and this be it remembered, before bicycles and Henry Ford between them made this a commonplace feat. Several Dowbiggins took holy orders, one entered a monastery in Spain. Two Dowbiggins, brothers, fought on opposite sides in the Revolutionary War in America.

But these things touched Jeremy not at all. His father, Charles, was, as Jeremy saw matters, a failure, as his father had been before him. Jeremy had very little patience with failures in or out of his family.

Chapter Five

IT IS EASY to be wise after the event and to look back on the uneasiness of the 1920's. But thinking men and women had already observed that in the patching-up of one war the seeds of another had been sown. Thoughtless people just knew that something was wrong and hoped that someone would come along and put it right. The social strata resembled a Neapolitan ice-cream that someone had trodden on. Britain was just beginning to realise that it had not been so clever to take all Germany's obsolete ships and thus force her to build completely up-to-date ones. It wasn't so clever of the United States, Britain and France to collar most of the world's gold, making it just that much harder to sell American machines, British textiles and French luxury goods to countries whose national exchequers rattled like drums. Then there was the general strike and the crime wave in Britain, gang warfare in the United States, wholesale unemployment because industry could not absorb men. Rich men said that high taxes were at the root of it. Poor men said that the rich had been allowed to make too much out of the carnage and that better—therefore more expensive—social services were needed.

It was an anxious, troubled world, that of the 1920's, a world in which false prophets flourished. Astrologers began to addle heads that were already addled almost beyond comprehension. At cocktail parties decorative halfwits overworked Freudian jargon that was quite beyond their capacity to understand, and while hospitable Americans offered to introduce a friend to their bootlegger, British people of amazingly varied social status whispered the name of the pet psycho-analyst. It is still a debatable point whether synthetic whisky, distilled from embalming fluid and coffin handles, killed more people than were frightened to death by the professional searchers-into-dark-places-of-the-soul. Certain it is that the latter and the bootleggers flourished mightily.

People who looked below the surface of things were frightened at what they saw and they came, understandably but without logic, to the conclusion that any change, any new thing or idea, must be for the betterment of humanity

People who had never troubled to read Darwin damned him for things he never said. People whose mathematical educations had taken them no further than simple equations deemed themselves fitted to expound Einstein's theories to others less fortunate, while at cocktail parties lugubrious alcoholics proved conclusively that in a given set of circumstances next Thursday preceded last Sunday in the calendar.

Then there were the diet cranks. One of them, a pest who told his patients that two rusks, three lettuce leaves, a nut and some tomato-juice daily were the secret of longevity, happily pre-deceased most of his patients. He died of ptomaine from an infected pork pie.

There were always plenty of people who would listen to any nonsense, however fantastic, provided that it was dressed up with a lot of long and preferably new words.

It was, for other reasons as well as these, the advertising man's Golden Age.

The world had learned all the tricks of production. Cheap tractors made it possible to cultivate vast new areas of land. Machines were turning out manufactured goods of all kinds at a rate far beyond the capacity of the world to assimilate them. The word bandied about at cocktail parties for a while was 'saturation point'. Its aptness was frequently lost.

Jeremy went to America for a short trip. He had become an advertising man. From all he had been able to learn, the Americans had progressed further along this road than any other people. Jeremy went to see, stayed for a while to marvel and returned to England anxious to put into practice some of the things he had learned.

Hayward Fisher was beginning to feel his years. He allowed Jeremy a free hand because he was obsessed by a fear that Jeremy would leave the firm. He had already planned to retire just as soon as he was convinced that Jeremy could carry on without him. Hayward Fisher wanted to breed pigs in the country, leaving Jeremy to do the hard work.

It was at this time that Jeremy met Sybilla Davenport.

Jeremy met her at one of the cocktail parties which were the rage. It was one of those Anglo-American parties where the principal topic of conversation was who-sleeps-with-whom? and where businessmen, their wives, stage and literary celebrities and would-be celebrities, nobodies, anybodies and a smattering of gentle people, met without rhyme or reason, drank inordinately, probably didn't know their hosts, and left cigarette-ends burning on furniture, while the more considerate trod them into the carpets. Sybilla was talking in animated fashion with London's most eminent abortionist, a young surgeon of high attainments, who found cocktail parties a prolific source of new business. Sybilla's conversational *forte* for some while had been Freud, but at the time Jeremy met her she was in the throes of becoming a convert to Christian Science.

Jeremy knew very little about women. At school he was innocent of them. In Mexico he saw none. In New York George Dowbiggin and his associates were somewhat too hearty for the sort of women Jeremy might have liked if he had met them. There was a little too much sudden death in bootlegging circles. Then in London Jeremy had been too busy. Women—most women—

looking at Jeremy, saw in him a most experienced erotic. His lips were sensual, with a hint of cruelty in them. He had a way of looking at women which made them feel that they had no secrets from him. It disconcerted some and attracted others.

Jeremy stood a few feet from Sybilla, watching her and deciding that she was the most attractive woman he had ever seen at close quarters. She was tall and dark. Her body was at once athletic and voluptuous. Massive jaw-bones just missed giving her ugliness, but gave her something striking instead. High cheekbones and faintly slanting eyes, together with a husky contralto voice, suggested Russian or West Indian negro blood, or both. Jeremy believed in physiognomy, so her wide-set eyes and big generous mouth completed an almost perfect picture for him. When he barged into the conversation she was having with the fashionable abortionist, Jeremy found they were talking shop. That is to say that Sybilla was endeavouring to prove to the surgeon's satisfaction that it was possible to be a Christian Scientist and have a baby.

'But be reasonable, my dear Sybilla,' he was saying. 'You can't have it both ways. The body is, or is not mortal. Which is it?'

'The body is mortal, of course.'

'The same applies to two bodies?'

'Of course!'

'The body, being mortal, is a manifestation of error. Error, being in its turn a manifestation of the mortal mind, is non-existent. The so-called lusts of the flesh—of the body must, therefore, be erroneous and non-existent. Euclid would tell you conclusively that the union of two nothings, whether by addition, multiplication, or sexual intercourse can only result in nothing. Now I happen to have delivered several Christian Scientist mothers in my time, and I can assure you that the births were in every way normal, even to the pains, which I understand are erroneous and non-existent. I don't mind admitting that, in view of the fact there is no sensation in matter, it struck me as highly peculiar that the ladies in question made such a fuss of them. But the most curious feature of the whole business to my mind was that the ladies found themselves in that condition at all. I came to the conclusion that they must have forgotten to put a copy of *Science & Health* beside the bed one night.'

'You're hopeless, Paul,' said Sybilla. 'You're just reducing something very fine to absurdity.'

'Because I believe that truth—any basic truth—can be reduced to absurdity without suffering in the process. Mrs. Eddy graced her theories by the name of "science". Very well then, she cannot grumble if it is criticised by scientific methods. That diamond on your hand, if it's a real diamond, will stand up to any of the tests which proclaim the genuine stone. . . .'

'Won't someone introduce me to this handsome man?' asked Sybilla, to the world at large, indicating Jeremy and bringing him into the magic circle. She was getting the worst of it and was glad of his arrival.

'Never argue with a professional man, Miss Davenport,' said Jeremy a little later. 'You are bound to get the worst of it.'

A more experienced man, Sybilla noted, even though when introduced the 'Mrs.' had been slurred, would have seen the wedding ring she still wore.

'Funny!' she reflected. 'And he looks as though women were his hobby.'

The young surgeon, whose eyes were as quick as his fingers, caught the look Sybilla and Jeremy exchanged.

'Who and what,' he asked his hostess a little later, 'is that handsome brute talking to Sybilla over there. My

God!' he added. 'He's looking at her as though he wants to eat her.'

'Well, he seems to have a fine enough set of teeth,' was the reply. 'Don't you know him? That's Jeremy Dowbiggin. He's supposed to be a very brilliant young advertising man. From what I know of him, anything he tried to do he'd do well.'

'Lucky Sybilla!' he said, leaving his hostess with a laugh which proved, if proof were needed, that men also are cats.

Jeremy had never been in love. He did not know, therefore, what the precise symptoms were. But Sybilla attracted him so much that for several days he neglected his work. They lunched together two days running, dined and went to a show on the same evenings. While walking home along the embankment, after dropping Sybilla at her little house in Chelsea and dismissing the taxi, Jeremy decided that Sybilla was his woman. He never had to explain things to her. They seemed to like the same things, even the same food and drinks, laughed at the same kind of humour and were both frankly selfish. Marriage? Jeremy was not quite so sure. He had a dream-wife already staked out in his imagination and it was hard to reconcile Sybilla with her. Jeremy could not visualise Sybilla at breakfast, nor wearing a gingham apron which she held up to drop flowers into as she cut them. Although she was in fact the mother of a little girl, whom Jeremy had not met, he could not imagine her as a mother. There did not seem anything maternal about her.

Sybilla just at that moment was thinking about Jeremy. He's quite nice, she mused, but I can't make up my mind whether he's damned clever or just very simple and innocent.

Sybilla was twenty-seven. She had married Davenport in a fit of pique when she was twenty-three. Before she had really had time to regret it he had solved all his problems and some of hers by drowning himself on the Belgian coast where they were spending a holiday. Claire, aged three, had never seen her father. Sybilla, and she was acute enough to know it, had drifted dangerously into that class of smart young women who hover on the fringe of things. She was deemed good value at a party. Men liked her. Few women did. When they compared notes, other women agreed that Sybilla had a conversational knack which irritated them. She always talked to men—even husbands with their wives present—in a way that implied that she and they shared some understanding, or little secret, to the exclusion of others. It was done very lightly and harmlessly, but it had been enough to win for her the nickname among women of 'The Man Eater'. Sybilla, sensing the mistrust of most other women, had always been very circumspect. She had listened in her time to many scandalous confidences, but had given none. That had not endeared her to other women.

Sybilla's few 'affairs' since the death of her husband had been with married men who had had the best of reasons for maintaining a discreet silence. Of Sybilla, therefore, her little world suspected much but knew nothing.

*　　　*　　　*　　　*　　　*

Jeremy had returned from the United States in the firm belief that people—the people who read advertisements— were more concerned with personalities than facts, and that when facts had to be used they carried more force when linked with personalities. There was not the remotest ground for believing, for example, that Mary Pickford and Douglas Fairbanks had the smallest knowledge of internal combustion engines, the health-giving properties of cocoa or the efficacy of a rat poison. But it did not alter the remarkable fact that a motor car, a brand of cocoa or a rat poison would sell more quickly if it became generally known that these two distinguished people had given them the seal of their approval.

It was this knowledge which prompted Jeremy to cultivate the eminent dietician, Dr. Juniper Berry, whose theories had been so widely publicised that he had achieved the status almost of a national institution. Jeremy had also taken the trouble to do a little quiet investigation of the said Dr. Juniper Berry in the matter of the remarkable hair-restoring properties the doctor had attributed to a rare drug which had been named 'gyomin'.

Two Danish explorers had returned from Central Asia with tales of a tribe living in a remote valley whose old men and women retained fine heads of hair and perfect teeth to the age of over one hundred. The secret appeared to be a drug prepared from a tree which grew exclusively in that valley. Newspapers and magazines carried well illustrated articles regarding this new wonder, and in due course Dr. Juniper Berry wrote a learned article on the subject, following which the two Danes floated a small company to market the drug, which now acquired a capital 'g' and became Gyomin.

A clerk in the employ of Mr. Merryweather, a man named Vosper, who looked and behaved rather like a ferret, was lent to Jeremy for purposes of investigation. He ran to earth the two Danes who in a moment of alcoholic exuberance admitted that the story of this hirsute Central Asian tribe was unvarnished fiction. They themselves had never been nearer to Central Asia than the Chinese Maritime Customs station in Szechuan from which they had been dismissed for accepting bribes.

From all of which Jeremy deduced that Dr. Juniper Berry, provided the proper kind of inducement were offered, might be persuaded to assist in securing a very large new account which Jeremy was eyeing hopefully.

Professor Sigismund Pulitzer, proprietor of the Sigismund Pulitzer Correspondence School—'I-will-spring-clean-your-Brain' Pulitzer—had let it be known around those circles most likely to be interested that he was not satisfied with his advertising agents.

'I want ideas!' he remarked loudly at an advertising luncheon. The ears of several contact-men within earshot had flapped visibly for, said in such company, his words were tantamount to an invitation.

Sigismund Pulitzer was an American citizen of Polish-Hibernian extraction. Before coming to England he had owned a flourishing business in Birmingham, Alabama, de-kinking Afro-American hair. The Ku Klux Klan ran him out of Birmingham when it was reported that he attended personally to the de-kinking of the hair of his lighter-complexioned lady customers. It was when meditating in a Northern New York State sanatorium for some weeks, while doctors endeavoured to remove an elegant coat of tar and feathers without removing too much of his epidermis, that the idea of the correspondence school originated in his fertile brain. A few months later he began to advertise his course from an accommodation address in Oxford Street. He addressed himself to the British public through the medium of several religious news-papers, East Anglian agricultural weeklies and other publications whose readers were staunch rather than numerous.

At the time Jeremy called on Sigismund Pulitzer the latter was buying substantial spaces in the national dailies, spending a very large sum of money annually. He had installed himself in a delightful country house near Guildford where, in a converted barn, an office staff numbering over one hundred persons dealt with a huge mass of letters from all over the world. Sigismund Pulitzer had arrived.

Jeremy's opening remark in his first conversation with Pulitzer almost made certain of the account.

'I'm afraid I haven't a single idea in my head, Mr.

Pulitzer,' he began. 'I have purposely tried to keep an open mind until I know a little more about the course itself and your methods of approach.'

'Some of the bright boys have been to see me lately,' observed Pulitzer scornfully. 'They knew as much as you do about it all, but they came here spilling bum ideas all over the place. I got plenty of bum ideas myself. . . .'

Jeremy spent the day with Pulitzer while the latter showed him the 'works', and when he left for London was fully convinced that ideas and only ideas would secure the account. He took away with him, too, several of the courses, one of which he intended to read himself, while the others were for distribution among selected members of the staff of the Hayward Fisher Agency.

On the way into London—Jeremy, by the way, now lived in a Knightsbridge service flat—a black and gilt sign caught his eye: 'The St Martin Hospital for Diseases of the Mind'.

Pulling up the car hastily, Jeremy rang at the heavily-barred front door and asked to see the doctor in charge. Noting that the hospital was maintained by voluntary contributions, Jeremy attached a five-pound note to the slip of paper which the attendant gave him to state his business. On it he wrote: 'I shall be happy to make this contribution to your funds in return for fifteen minutes of your time.'

'What can I do for you, Mr. Dowbiggin?' asked the doctor, a tired and prematurely aged man, who looked harassed.

'Assume that I have come to you, doctor, with a view to having my brain and its working improved. I am not a lunatic, or I hope not. Just a normal person who wishes to improve a quite ordinary brain, with particular reference to the memory. Would you be able to do anything for me? If so, what?'

The doctor thought for a moment before replying.

'I dislike replying to hypothetical questions on principle,' said the doctor. 'I know nothing whatever of your brain, your habits and so forth. But in replying to you—we need your five pounds—I am going to think of a man I know personally and of whose life and habits I know a great deal. I am also going to rule out the possibility of mental defects through congenital disease. The man of whom I am thinking has a good brain—or had one. I shall tell you what I have told him. Try to reach finality over worrying matters. Worry causes the brain to deteriorate, in my judgment, more quickly than any other cause. Eat light, easily digested foods. It stands to reason that the more blood which goes to the stomach to digest heavy meals, the less there is available for the brain. There are other reasons as well. Tobacco is a drug. It should be used sparingly. But against this, a heavy smoker might suffer more from a sudden cessation of smoking than from continuation. Pay a great deal of attention to comfortable, restful sleep. A healthy body, needless to say, is an aid to a healthy mind. Observe, therefore, all the elementary rules of health. Plenty of fresh air, exercise, no excesses of any kind. You speak of memory in particular. Take one of the recognised mind and memory training courses. The concentration required to master the course cannot fail to assist you. Most people have, I find, butterfly brains. Concentration—on anything almost—will help. I hope that is worth five pounds, Mr. Dowbiggin.'

'There are five minutes still to go,' said Jeremy, looking at his watch. 'You mentioned diet. Do you think a skilled dietician could work out a special diet for improving the memory and mental powers generally? One that would be really helpful?'

'I do,' replied the doctor, 'in conjunction with the other matters I have mentioned. I almost go so far as to say that a sensible balanced diet is one of the most urgent human needs. The more one learns of biological processes the more one realises that diet is what may be termed the controlling factor in plant, animal and human life. Considerations of diet have been at the root of every great human and animal migration. Diet has . . .'

'Thank you, doctor. You have answered my question.'

'Now perhaps, Mr. Dowbiggin, you will answer one. Why do you want this information and why did you come to me?'

'I require the information for advertising purposes, doctor, and I came to you because, while I was driving past here, turning the matter over in my mind, I saw your notice board. I argued that in an institution which tried to heal diseased minds there was bound to be someone who had some ideas about improving normal minds. That's all doctor and thank you.'

There was an angry light in the doctor's eyes.

'And I suppose now, on the scanty information I have given to you, and without any scientific attainments yourself, you feel justified in bursting into print with a specious argument on behalf of some crank brain food? If I had known why you wanted to talk to me I would not have given you a particle of information for your vile purposes. . . .'

The doctor fairly spluttered with indignation.

' . . . We scientists and medical men labour for years to secure one small grain of truth on behalf of suffering humanity. We take nothing for granted and say nothing of our discoveries until we are sure. But ghouls like you are prepared to broadcast undigested theories, which you do not even understand, using them to batten on human misery. The people are fuddled enough as it is with half-understood knowledge of a dozen kinds. I don't know what purpose you intend putting this conversation to, but if you have any sense of responsibility, any sense of what you owe to your fellow men and women, I beg you not to use me, however unwillingly, as your accomplice. I see too much sorrow and suffering here every day to wish to be the means of sowing the seeds of more. Here is your money, sir. I will not touch it. I am not a carrion crow. . . .'

'Hold hard, doctor!' said Jeremy, who had listened without interrupting. 'Aren't you rather jumping to conclusions? I don't think you have the smallest right on the facts I have mentioned to suggest that I intend making any improper use of the information you have been kind enough to give me. If what you have told me is the truth —and I do not doubt it—surely the more people who know that a sane diet, worked out scientifically by an eminent physician, can in fact improve their mental power, the better for everyone concerned. Do you condemn John Wesley out of hand for saying that cleanliness is next to godliness? Would you condemn me for using the statement in an advertisement for soap or some disinfectant? You and I are aware that soap and disinfectants, properly used, could save the people of this world an infinity of suffering and disease, a huge proportion of which is caused by dirt and insanitary conditions. Do you doubt the accuracy of your own statements, that you are so reluctant to have them widely known?'

'I do not doubt the truth of anything I have told you, but I do not credit you with the sincerity, the honesty of purpose, to use what I have said for the benefit of humanity in general rather than for your own base commercial purposes. You have made out a pretty argument, just as doubtless you will when the time comes to foist some quack remedy, or food or whatever it is, on to people who lack the discrimination and the scepticism to distinguish between scientific truths and prostituted science. It is your intentions that I doubt, Mr. Dowbiggin. I have no doubt whatever that you will protect yourself and those for whom you work with great cleverness. But underneath it all you will know—you know at this minute—that your arguments are fundamentally dishonest and selfish. You do not care what misery you spread. You do not care about the poor people who will be ill able to afford the shillings they scrape up for your catchpenny schemes. Your conscience will be satisfied if you have kept within the law. Yes, Mr. Dowbiggin, it is your intentions that I doubt, and before you leave here let me remind you that morally and legally the only difference between murder and manslaughter is one of intent. Yours is a dirty trade, Mr. Dowbiggin. Good afternoon!'

* * * * *

'I won't keep you more than five minutes, Janet, but I've just had a marvellous idea. I got it from the doctor in charge of a booby hatch in Kensington or Fulham, or somewhere like that. Try and get hold of Dr. Juniper Berry, or his secretary. Ask him if he will lunch with me to-morrow.'

There were two or three letters to do, and it was nearly seven o'clock before Janet Seymour put on her hat and coat.

'Buy yourself a nice dinner in town, Janet!' said Jeremy, handing her a pound note.

'Jeremy Dowbiggin! It's after six o'clock. I'm a woman now and not a secretary. You can keep your pound. I don't want it. I've never presumed on the fact that we were terribly friendly before you became a big shot here and I'm not going to. But when you would like to take me out to dinner yourself I should love to come, and I wish . . .'

'I didn't mean to be rude or nasty, Janet. I'm sorry. We'll go out to dinner one night this week and we'll make an evening of it. Unfortunately, to-night I just have time to change and keep a dinner appointment. . . .'

'With the husky contralto who's always ringing you up these days, I suppose!' said Janet, slamming the office door as she swept out.

'I wonder what's got into *her* hair!'

* * * * *

'What a marvellously interesting life you do lead, Jeremy dear!' said Sybilla over her fourth gin-and-French. 'You meet interesting people, do interesting things. I've often wanted to be a man. . . .'

'From someone as gloriously feminine as you are, Sybilla, that's just sacrilege.'

'What I mean is that I envy you the chance you have to do so much for other people. This mind-training business, for instance. You stand as an interpreter, so to speak, between great scientists—men who have made a life study of the mind—and the millions of poor people like me, who wouldn't know what the scientists were saying until you come along and tell them in simple language how they can better themselves. . . .'

'I haven't got the account yet, you know!'

'But you will, Jeremy. You're one of those strong people who always get what they want.'

Sybilla glanced upwards into Jeremy's steady, cold blue eyes to find with a shock that they and he were far away. For a few seconds he was shut away with his inner self, wondering just what he did want. Sybilla was used to men who in moments like these made burning fatuous replies. It would not have flattered her to know that Jeremy was also wondering whether marriage would prove the only key to possession of her. Without knowing that she was doing so, Sybilla answered the question that evening by spending the night with him at his flat.

'If I get the account let's go to Paris for the weekend!' Jeremy suggested at the breakfast-table.

'I'd love to, darling! I suppose instead of being so very, very happy, I ought to be feeling terribly ashamed of myself as a brazen woman. But I'm not. Christian Science has taught me that bodies are not very important, really. It is our minds that are *us*, Jeremy. . . .'

Jeremy, who had once been persuaded to read Mrs. Eddy's best-seller, *Science & Health*, remembered putting it down with the impression that bodies were unimportant, but wondered whether Sybilla had the context quite right. He decided to read it again. There might be pointers in it which would help him with the Sigismund Pulitzer account.

Chapter Six

THE SIGISMUND PULITZER 'Walk-with-the-gods' series of triple column by ten inch advertisements in the national press aroused tremendous interest in the British Isles and overseas. To Jeremy they represented the culminating point of three months of intensive work. Sigismund Pulitzer, as Jeremy had anticipated, jumped at the idea, especially when assured that the illustrious name of Dr. Juniper Berry would be associated with the campaign. There were, of course, captious souls who asked why the B.M.A. permitted such flagrant abuse of medical privilege, but for every one of such there were a thousand who felt that the lucidly expressed arguments were their own justification.

Dr. Juniper Berry, in a series of lectures which supported the advertising campaign, showed lesser people how diet was the determining factor in moulding racial characteristics of mind and body. Aesthetic people were light-feeding, often vegetarians. The placid cow ate grass, while the snarling fury of the tiger came from a diet of raw meat. It stood to reason that the diet which suited a dock labourer would not suit a musician.

'Let any man or woman tell me,' said Dr. Juniper Berry, 'the peculiar mental qualities he or she needs to develop —always pre-supposing a certain natural aptitude and inclination—and I will prescribe a diet to feed the proper cells of the brain. . . . The first requisite is bodily health and the contentment which springs from it. The body is to the brain what the peel of an orange is to the orange itself. A damaged, diseased peel cannot house a perfect orange. A diseased body seldom if ever houses a finely balanced brain. As the body is to the brain, the brain is to the Mind. If I may be allowed another analogy, the brain may be likened to a gramophone and the shellac disque we know as a record. Like these, the brain is mechanical, physical. It consists of a few simple chemicals which can be bought for a few pence at your chemists. It is an organ of the body, like the heart and the lungs. The Mind in its turn may be likened to the sounds which come from the shellac disque of a gramophone record when the machinery functions. But those sounds, im-printed on the disque, have no weight nor substance. They are impressions, as thought is an impression on the brain.

'Mind, likewise, has no weight or substance. Through-out the ages it has defied definition. It *is*. More than that we cannot say. But we do know that the perfect function-ing of Mind can only be achieved through the physical well-being of the thing we call the brain, just as we know that the perfect reproduction of music from a record depends upon the accurate timing of the gramophone turntable, the sharpness of the needle and the unblemished surface of the record itself. . . .

[62]

'The body, the brain and the Mind must function smoothly. The Mind cannot, for example, function smoothly in the brain if the brain itself is disorganised by constantly receiving pain messages from an aching tooth. Bodily fitness, therefore, comes first. With bodily fitness it is no longer necessary for the smooth working of the brain to be disturbed by the impulses which come from bodily irregularities and dis-ease. The brain becomes a perfect housing for the Mind—a temporary housing, but still as near perfect as we can hope to attain. . . .

'The Mind knows no limitations of any kind. It can soar at will out into the cold abyss of infinity, beyond the confines of mortal conceptions, bringing back to the brain which has been fitted to receive them thought impressions which transcend in their majesty, immensity, beauty and accuracy anything which mere words of mine can hope to describe.

'Let diet mend your ailing body. Let diet attune your brain to the infinite. Mind, over which no mortal can exercise control or influence, will do the rest. You, any one of you, have the power within you to walk with the gods.'

Dr. Juniper Berry delivered the first lecture of the series in London to an audience of some 3,000 persons on the evening before the Sigismund Pulitzer campaign was launched in the press. The press advertisements invited people, as a preliminary to taking the Pulitzer New-Minds-for-Old course, to prepare themselves for it by going on the 'individually prepared, Dr. Juniper Berry Mental Perfection Diet'.

'LET DR. JUNIPER BERRY HELP YOU TO WALK WITH THE GODS!'

Jeremy felt that he could afford some of the witticisms in which his friends and rivals indulged at his expense, but it was more than a little embarrassing when, entering

[63]

the Savoy Grill with Professor Sigismund Pulitzer and Dr. Juniper Berry, a loud and penetrating voice was heard to remark: 'Hullo! there, Dowbiggin. Walking with the gods, I see!'

It was, perhaps, needlessly hurtful on Jeremy's part when, on the day before leaving for Paris with Sybilla, to celebrate the Sigismund Pulitzer victory, he sent Janet Seymour to book two tickets.

It was Janet Seymour who had given up three weekends to work during the hectic weeks while the campaign was being prepared, and the nearest to the promised dinner in town she had had was some sandwiches snatched hastily at her typewriter about 10 p.m. Curiosity, or something, impelled Janet to be at Victoria Station when Jeremy and Sybilla joined the Golden Arrow. She wanted to see for herself the owner of the husky contralto voice which talked so impersonally to her and so very personally to Jeremy, as Janet had learned from a judicious manipulation of the two-way switchboard between her and Jeremy's private office.

Men can give loyal service to institutions, but women cannot. A woman's loyalty is personal. A good secretary frequently knows more about a man as he really is than his wife knows. It would be a gross over-statement of the case to say that a good secretary is always in love with the man she serves, but automaton-like as some appear to be, and however impersonal the relationship may be in the eyes of the man concerned, there goes with the personal loyalty a sense of possessiveness which can very easily be confused with what is generally known as love.

Janet rejoiced when things went well for Jeremy, was unhappy when he met reverses or was moody and depressed himself. When she believed that one—man or woman—was taking advantage of him she became as jealous and watchful as a cat.

'I wonder am I in love with him?' Janet asked herself as she watched Jeremy, Sybilla and four shiny new suitcases decanted from a taxi into the Golden Arrow.

'I don't know,' she replied to herself through clenched teeth, 'but I do know that I'd like to scratch the eyes out of *her*. I bet Jeremy bought her that silver fox cape, and I'll bet it'll cost him plenty to get out of this mess. . . .'

Janet had to go into the ladies' cloak room to hide the ravages of her tears when the train pulled out. They were hot, blinding tears of rage, which play havoc with make-up.

Jeremy had left Janet the number of the Hotel Scribe in case of emergency. The emergency arose on the Monday morning.

Sybilla's voice answered the telephone and Janet heard her say, sleepily as though just aroused from deep slumber: 'Jeremy, beloved, your tiresome office wants you. It's that girl with the impertinent manner who usually answers me. . . . I suppose you'd better speak to her.'

When Jeremy reached the telephone Janet was off the line, a fact which Jeremy interpreted as being due to the vagaries of the French telephone system, but which Sybilla interpreted correctly, resolving to pay a surprise visit to Jeremy's office one day. Sybilla had few illusions as to what would happen if she spent four or five hours daily in intimate association with a man, sharing his ambitions and most of his private affairs. Sybilla was not really anxious—she was too vain for that, but she was also too intelligent to overlook the possibilities of the situation. Thirty seconds face-to-face with the woman would suffice, and then Jeremy's pleasure, embarrassment or annoyance at this unexpected invasion of his office would tell the story.

Sybilla intended that this weekend in Paris was to be a good d   nore than a pleasure jaunt: it was to become the turning-point in their relations. She intended that before they returned to London Jeremy should have

3*

[65]

committed himself to a great deal more than a clandestine love affair. There were circumstances in Sybilla's private life which made the securing of a husband an imperative necessity. Her late and not very much lamented husband's estate had been a bitter disappointment, nor was there anything more to be expected from any of his relations. The little house in Chelsea, her own pretty clothes, occasional parties and the incidental expenses of leading the pseudo-smart cocktail existence in London, had caused Sybilla to dip deeply into the nest-egg left to her by her father.

It might be thought that a clever woman like Sybilla played her cards badly by allowing Jeremy an apparently easy conquest without benefit of orange blossom. But she relied on her own charms to make Jeremy toe the line, and she believed that Jeremy as a lover was easier to control than Jeremy as an acquaintance. Sybilla was one of those women who contrive to smother men with chains, to make them feel obligated in all kinds of ways.

In Paris they kicked the high spots. Sybilla spoke fluent French, but she concealed the fact from Jeremy, allowing him the privilege of airing his schoolboy French, which he did with surprising fluency helped by champagne. Champagne is a curious drink. It elates and then depresses its devotees with amazing speed. There is a stage in champagne-drinking which, taken at the flood, so to speak, gives the illusion of greatnesss. The tongue is loose, the brain quick—but not of perception. The guard is down. At this stage strong silent men babble, women laugh and weep by turns, difficulties melt away as though they had never existed and the human Ego asserts that its judgment is infallible, its prescience godlike. Jeremy reached just that stage in the 'Alcazar' night club.

'This has been a wonderful, glorious weekend, Jeremy darling,' said Sybilla as, hand in hand, they returned from the tiny dance floor to their table. 'Nothing and nobody can take it away from me. I shall remember it when the memory of all sorts of other things has gone. . . .'

'Don't sound so melancholy, sweetest,' said Jeremy. 'There'll be plenty more. Pulitzer wants me to superintend the launching of the Continental campaigns. He's opening offices in Paris, Brussels, Amsterdam, Berlin, Madrid and Milan. We'll do it all by car and . . .'

'Jeremy darling, even if you take me on top of a high mountain and tempt me with all the cities of the world, you won't make me feel differently. I don't regret this one tiny little bit, so don't think it, but you must see that it can't go on. Sooner or later women who make a habit of going away to Paris and Berlin and Madrid for the weekend with men acquire reputations—bad ones. I don't care a great deal for myself, but I'm not going to forget that I have a small daughter. I've not inflicted her on you, Jeremy. You saw her that night when she was asleep. But she's mine. I brought her into the world. She didn't ask me to. I'm not going to bring her up in a beastly, irregular atmosphere. Claire's going to have every chance in the world and I'm not going to have her discover in a few years' time that her mother is an immoral woman.

'Shush! I am one, I know. Although I never think that anything you and I have done can be immoral. No, Jeremy. No more champagne. I want you to listen to me. I've nearly finished and then you can drink as much as you like. So, when we get back to London we must just behave as though we've never met. It'll hurt—both of us, I expect, but women who have babies have responsibilities, and they must live up to them. I'm going to, that's all. This has all been mad and wonderful. Let's drink and dance and forget our troubles and pretend that we're children and there are no nasty wagging tongues in the world. All right. Now you may have that drink. . . .'

The thought of returning to London the next day and not seeing Sybilla any more hit Jeremy like a pole-axe. He felt that he simply could not face it. The lilting Hungarian music seemed to mock him. A world that a few moments before had seemed quite perfect had gone flat and stale. Across the table was Sybilla, a forced cheerfulness on her face, while her great lustrous eyes were filled with unshed tears.

'Sybilla!' he exclaimed, stretching out his hand. 'Don't. . . .'

'Sorry to make an exhibition of myself,' said Sybilla brightly. 'I'll be all right in a moment. Let's dance.'

Perhaps it was the sensuous music; perhaps it was the feel of Sybilla's lithe warm body, clinging a little helplessly to him; perhaps it was the champagne, or the combination of all three. Who cares? Jeremy knew as they swung round the dance floor together that he had been a callous brute. This little woman, alone in the world, deeply conscious of her duty as a mother, had given herself to him, trustingly and completely. Her surrender had been spontaneous and unconditional. There had been a time when he had wronged her—thought her a clever, calculating female. A woman, or man, he mused, would have to rise very early in the morning to get the better of Jeremy Dowbiggin. The very idea was laughable. Then came a horrible thought: would she, after the way he had lightly planned a series of immoral weekends all over the continent, as though she were a tart, want to marry him now? Life with Sybilla would be gay, scintillating, glorious, beautiful, and he like a fool had perhaps dashed away from his lips the cup of happiness which had been offered to him.

Contritely, brokenly, Jeremy asked Sybilla to marry him.

'Are you just being gallant, Jeremy? You don't have

to, you know. I'm not the little girl who's been done wrong. . . .'

'I'm asking you to marry me because I want you to, and for no other reason,' said Jeremy masterfully.

'In that case, Jeremy darling, I'd love to.'

The night staff of the hotel, accustomed as they were to British peculiarities, found it impossible to understand why this handsome couple, obviously on the most affectionate terms, demanded a second bedroom and separated for the night.

'I'd rather, Sybilla darling,' said Jeremy, kissing her on slightly fluttering eyelids and closing her door from the outside.

'I understand, dearest!'

*　　*　　*　　*　　*

George Hayward Fisher met Sybilla at lunch a few days later. It took him fifteen minutes to decide that the marriage, when it took place, would be the cue for his own retirement from active participation in the business.

'She'll make him toe the line, by God!' he said to himself.

'You're a very lucky man, Jeremy,' he said aloud, 'and I'm going off in a few minutes to my lawyers to see if we can't work out a very nice wedding present for you two young people. I'm getting old. . . .'

'That means,' said Jeremy, when Hayward Fisher had left the table, 'that the lazy old so-and-so thinks he's going to spend the rest of his life breeding pigs in luxury and idleness while I slave my guts out for him. I *am* the Hayward Fisher Agency, and he knows it. I could take ninety per cent of the business with me, wherever I went. . . .'

'I like him, darling!'

'So do I, my sweet, but business is business.'

With which dictum Sybilla was forced to agree.

*　　*　　*　　*　　*

Since this story is concerned more with the business than the domestic side of Jeremy's life, let it suffice to say that the honeymoon was a busman's holiday, during which Jeremy made contact with various men of affairs in daytime, while in the evenings the happy pair danced and amused themselves in the gay haunts of most of Europe's capitals.

On returning to London they rented an expensive flat overlooking the Park, furnished it in ultra-modern style, though be it said with excellent taste, settling down to a life which seemed to both of them rather too good to be true.

George Hayward Fisher, as predicted, dropped out of any kind of active control of the agency he had founded, though on very much harder terms than those he had planned.

'You're an ungrateful young dog, Dowbiggin,' he said on the one occasion during the negotiations when tempers ran high.

'I'm nothing of the kind,' said Jeremy, 'for I've nothing to be grateful to you for. I've given you sixteen ounces in the pound and you know it, and to be fair about it, I can say the same of you. Gratitude doesn't enter into it. This is business.'

Hayward Fisher was glad afterwards that he settled when he did, for within a few months of the settlement being reached the Wall Street crash shook the world's business structure to its foundations, and to Jeremy was left the task of piloting the agency through a very dangerous and difficult period.

As very little of the Hayward Fisher Agency's business came from the other side of the Atlantic it was able, better than most, to maintain its position.

Jeremy, happily, had the wit to realise that, first and foremost, he was a salesman. His knowledge of advertising, as such, was more limited than he had allowed others to know. He had relied to a great degree upon Hayward Fisher's mature judgment and knowledge, his complete grasp of the internal mechanism of a modern advertising agency and, fully as important, his shrewdness in finance. Details bored Jeremy, but knowing how important they were, he set to work to find someone who would handle them for him. To this end he laid siege to Robert Scrymgeour, accountant and secretary to the Wideawake & Universal Agency, who had been notoriously meanly treated by his directors. He was a mean little man himself, so was able to recognise meanness on sight.

When Robert Scrymgeour was installed in the Hayward Fisher Agency's new offices in the West End—London's centre of gravity had already begun to move westwards from the City—at a salary nearly twice that he had been earning, Jeremy was able to throw off the shackles of business detail and devote himself to the selling at which he excelled. During the months which followed Scrymgeour's installation, and at the suggestion of the latter, Jeremy secured a young man named Hartnell from the Wideawake & Universal Agency who, with more freedom for his talent, became an outstanding copywriter.

Most people at this time regarded Jeremy as a very successful man. He alone knew that he had hardly begun.

Chapter Seven

'WHAT DO YOU believe?'

Entering Hyde Park at Marble Arch for a stroll before dinner, Jeremy encountered an elderly man who was just folding up a banner bearing this inscription:

'What do *you* believe?' asked Jeremy.

'I believe that it is folly to bandy words with the idle rich who come to mock me,' said the old man, hurrying out to the bus stop.

'What do I believe?' said Jeremy aloud, so that a passer-by glanced anxiously at him.

There wasn't very much when Jeremy came to sort it out, nor on reflection did he regret the fact. Beliefs—that is to say the beliefs founded on faith rather than reason—were in his judgment the leaning-posts of the ineffective. Curious for a man whose life was spent inculcating beliefs in others! When he came to think of the matter he had very little belief in the things he advertised, or in the integrity of those who paid him. Pulitzer sold hot air to the credulous—hot air wrapped up in fine phrases. The less said about Dr. Forsyth's Nectar the better. Gosling & Murphy's Popular Pickles, which was one of Jeremy's most profitable accounts, were able to undersell their competitors because, instead of using good malt vinegar at several shillings per gallon, they used acetic acid at about one-twelfth the price. Gloria Winsome Beauty Soap was another fake. The owners spent over £100,000 per annum on advertising, but Jeremy knew that it contained enough caustic soda to take the hide off a rhinoceros. The tooth powder put out by the same firm, relied for its remarkable cleansing and whitening properties on the abrasive action of volcanic dust, guaranteed to remove the enamel from the healthiest teeth inside a year.

McCracken & Boldrewood's, proprietors of 'Glorious Devon' jams and preserves, advertised widely their beautiful orchards where the fruit was picked and packed into jam jars the same day. The truth was, as Jeremy knew, that their orchards were capable of supplying about five per cent of the firm's fruit requirements. The rest was imported in casks from various parts of Europe, preserved heaven alone knew how.

Jeremy laughed as he turned over these and other of the Hayward Fisher Agency's accounts. How could he have many beliefs? What was there left to believe in? His father still believed in the London & Continental Assurance Company. George Dowbiggin believed in prohibition, which had enabled him to make a large fortune bootlegging. Jeremy decided that he believed in Jeremy Dowbiggin.

This was one of the evenings when their flat was filled with Sybilla's guests. They came to see Sybilla, for long ago Jeremy had made it very plain that while he had no objection to her giving cocktail parties, he felt no obligation to attend them himself. Sybilla rather fancied herself as queen of a salon. It would not have flattered her vanity to know that four-fifths of those who came were attracted chiefly by free drinks.

Jeremy was allowing the crush to depart before he put in an appearance. There were three or four of the guests staying to dinner, among them a man he wanted to meet. Jeremy had heard much of Paul Lefroy, first from Sybilla and then from others. Paul Lefroy had been responsible for interesting Sybilla in Christian Science before she had known Jeremy.

Jeremy had pricked up his ears when he heard Paul Lefroy described as 'the slickest publicity man in the United States'. The man who said this was one whose judgment Jeremy respected.

On arrival at the flat Jeremy filtered through the departing guests, being mistaken by them for a late arrival, which made him laugh. Sybilla caught his eye as he entered the hall and steered him towards a small room they called the library, where Paul Lefroy and those who were remaining to dinner had been segregated.

Sybilla was rather proud of knowing Lefroy. Among the crowd of second-rate people who came to drink her cocktails he stood out as a personality, and she was conscious that Jeremy's abstention from these gatherings was due to his contempt for them.

'It's a pity you didn't come home earlier,' Sybilla had said on one of these occasions, 'as there've been some very interesting people here to-night.'

'For instance?'

'Well, there was Molly Alderswick, the daughter of the R.A., John Alderswick. Then there was Joe Wilsher—his brother Jack won at Wimbledon last year. . . .' Sybilla rattled off a few more names of the near-great who had honoured their home.

It was on the tip of Jeremy's tongue to say what a pity it was that Alderswick himself hadn't put in an appearance and that the wrong brother Wilsher had come along. But, he reflected, if useless nonentities amused Sybilla, why should he interfere with her pleasure?

'Another time, darling, I probably shan't be so busy.'

Paul Lefroy, seen through the half open library door, impressed Jeremy. He was standing talking to the other guests, giving Jeremy the opportunity to look him over in a way which would be insulting if the looker were visible.

'A beautifully finished job!' was Jeremy's dictum

A few years later someone was bound to have applied the adjective 'stream-lined' to Paul Lefroy. He wore good clothes as though he had never worn any other. His linen, like his clean-shaven, smiling face, was immaculate. His voice was beautifully modulated and his accent noncommittal. Many Americans would have said that he was an Englishman, while most Englishmen took him for a highly educated American, which he was. Even to Jeremy, who was an acute observer of men, it was not apparent that Lefroy's every word and movement was studied, like that of a finished actor, but this was a fact. Although his manner was that of a well-bred man of leisure, behind

Paul Lefroy's suave mask there worked at lightning speed a mind which had the precision and accuracy of a card index.

Jeremy was interested because for the first time in his life he was confronted by a highly intelligent man who was also a Christian Scientist, and he was curious to know how the two became reconciled to each other.

Paul Lefroy described himself as a 'Public Relations Counsel'. It is hard to improve upon his own definition: 'My task is to stand between my principals and the Great American Public and to interpret each to the other. My function is largely that of an attorney pleading a case at law, except that I plead to a larger and often biased court —the court of public opinion.'

Among Lefroy's principals—perhaps clients is a better word—were numbered some of the world's most brutally monopolistic corporations and the personalities which were their driving force—the robber barons of the late nineteenth and early twentieth centuries—who had swept into their greedy maw an unbelievable proportion of America's natural wealth. Because of the pressure of public opinion the *tempo* of this wholesale pillage had slackened. A more respectable age had dawned. John Citizen no longer stood by in inarticulate apathy while his country was looted. Besides, the robber barons had grown old. The fires of avarice no longer burned so fiercely in them. They had founded dynasties, and if those dynasties were to be perpetuated, public opinion must be courted, for ultimately public opinion became law.

There had begun in America, therefore, the greatest whitewashing campaign in history.

Lefroy's first client had been James McBride Cargill, who had risen to fame—or infamy—when he and his associates at the turn of the century had cornered lard. When Cargill and his fellow pirates made a bear raid on the prosperous New York, Philadelphia & West Virginia Railroad, over a hundred suicides were attributed to the panic which followed. Cargill came out of the deal with $20,000,000, but the taste of it was ruined by the constant fear of assassination.

At Lefroy's suggestion Cargill grew a beard, to hide his ruthless mouth. Without any publicity of any kind a fine new athletic club for New York's poor children was built on the lower East Side. When some eighteen months later the name of the anonymous donor was disclosed by a carefully calculated indiscretion on the part of one of the committee of management, it transpired that he was none other than James McBride Cargill, who still made no admission of the fact.

Lefroy had an aunt—none other than the famous hostess, Mrs. Charles Sumner Vanderstraaten. It required two years of diligent persuasion before she would consent to entertain Cargill among her guests at Southampton, Long Island. A discreet reference to this amazing occurrence was sent to a society weekly and other great hostesses took their cue, deciding that the Cargill peculations had been so large and so long ago that they might be forgotten.

Since reference to the whitewashing of Cargill is relevant only in so far as it illustrates that Paul Lefroy was an artist with the whitewash brush, it suffices to add that when the latter had finished his task Cargill was known to the Great American Public as a benevolent old gentleman who was happiest when among his flowers, patting the heads of small children and doing all manner of good deeds by stealth, to blush and complain bitterly when the press made them famous.

In a locked drawer Cargill kept for his private amusement several albums of press-cuttings, dating back three decades. Various cartoonists had portrayed him as a wolf, a devil—complete with tail and horns—a snouted hog

[76]

and so forth. He had been compared in print with Nero, Caligula and Judas Iscariot.

We may agree, therefore, that in his chosen profession of 'Public Relations Counsel' Paul Lefroy was an adept.

All these things Jeremy knew as he appraised the man preparatory to meeting him. A sixth sense also told Jeremy that the meeting would prove important to him. He also found himself wondering whether, in bringing Lefroy to the flat, Sybilla were not re-kindling the ashes of some old fire.

Jeremy had to introduce himself to everyone in the library, although they all seemed to know Sybilla well. Lefroy's greeting was so frank and friendly that Jeremy's faint hostility died within him.

It was Sybilla who later brought the conversation round to Christian Science.

'I am a student of Christian Science,' Lefroy declared himself. 'Perhaps one day I shall be able to call myself a Christian Scientist, but not yet.'

'Jeremy thinks it's a great joke,' said Sybilla, who seemed anxious for these two men to test each other's metal. 'I suppose I ought to call myself a student too.'

'I don't think it's true to say that I laugh at it,' said Jeremy, 'at least not out loud, but I confess I regard it through the same sceptical eyes with which I regard other pseudo-sciences. I'm afraid I'm a very practical man. I spend so much of my life wrestling with real and tangible problems that I haven't much patience with the intangibles of life.'

'Yours is a very common attitude, Mr. Dowbiggin,' said Lefroy, 'and, if I may say so, you declare yourself very lucidly.'

It soon became obvious that as fast as Sybilla steered the talk to Christian Science, Lefroy steered it back to more mundane subjects. Jeremy deduced from this that Christian Science with Lefroy was, as it was with Sybilla, a conversation piece. Jeremy had found long ago that Sybilla's knowledge of the cult consisted of a few phrases, heavily charged with jargon, chiefly used out of their context. She used Freud and Einstein in much the same way as she used Mrs. Eddy. She talked freely about complexes; 'relatively' was one of her favourite adverbs. Sybilla was not a fool. On the contrary, she was highly intelligent. But associating mostly with mediocrities, she seldom found the need to use her intelligence. Jeremy would have been astounded to know that Sybilla spoke French, German and Italian so well that she could unerringly tell by ear a Hanoverian from a Bavarian, a Neapolitan from a Piedmontese, or the accents of Paris and Dijon, which are nothing like so easy to distinguish. It suited Sybilla to let Jeremy believe her to be rather superficial. It so happened that she knew very little about business, the one subject which interested Jeremy, so he had fallen into the error of rating her intelligence on a much lower plane than it really was.

Jeremy lived chiefly by deception—by over-statement, under-emphasis, by withholding essential facts, by glossing over uncomfortable facts. He was, perhaps with some justice, deceived in his turn. Eminent judges, who spend their lives trying to unravel the tangles caused by wealthy men dying intestate, frequently do the same thing themselves. Burglars are careless of the latches in their own homes. Doctors forget that they, too, are mortal, and more than one lawyer has found himself the defendant in a breach-of-promise action.

But Jeremy's mind on this particular evening was fixed upon Paul Lefroy. He knew that Paul Lefroy's presence was not just social. He sensed that Paul Lefroy, like himself, never set himself out to be charming without some

[78]

definite purpose in mind. Paul Lefroy was being charming. Why?

Not very many people had been charming to Jeremy, and those who had—or so he believed—had been actuated by self-interest.

When the other guests were leaving Jeremy signed to Lefroy to remain behind. Sybilla made her excuses and went to bed.

'I took the liberty of telling Sybilla that I wanted a quiet hour's chat with you, Mr. Dowbiggin—may I call you Jeremy? I'm only over here for a short while and I have to arrange certain matters at once. I shall come to the point straight away, therefore . . .'

Jeremy, without interrupting, pushed the whisky decanter towards Lefroy.

' . . . and the point is that I want a European associate. You'll excuse me being so abrupt, but if you're definitely not interested I'd like to know it to-night, whereas if you think you may be interested—and I hope you will be— we can continue our discussions to-morrow.'

'You may take it that I am interested,' said Jeremy, 'but I'd naturally want to know a great deal more about what's in your mind before being in any sense committed. I'll be as blunt as you are being and tell you that, when I knew you were coming here—Sybilla has often spoken of you —I informed myself a little regarding you and your methods. . . .'

'Fine! That's going to save us a lot of time, because I don't mind admitting that I have done the same where you are concerned. May we take it then that what we have discovered about each other is—shall we say— satisfactory?'

Jeremy nodded assent. This was swift work, with a vengeance! But there was something about Lefroy's utter frankness which appealed to him. So much of his time was spent with boards of directors who hum'd and haw'd, with advertising committees which raised futile points to cause delays, that there was a refreshing touch about a man who said what he had to say quickly and concisely.

'See here, Jeremy,' Lefroy continued, 'I've come to you because you and I see eye-to-eye about one important matter. We both believe that the job of an advertising or publicity man is not to advertise or publicise himself. You have some smart advertising men here in London—I'll not deny it—but to my way of thinking they'd be a lot smarter if they didn't advertise themselves so much as they do. The advertising man and the hunter are just that much more effective and deadly when they approach game from cover. When the circus "barker" gets up on his platform, wearing a checkerboard suit, and begins to shout through a trumpet, the public knows without being told that he isn't going to tell them it's a lousy show.

'I'm over here, Jeremy, representing a small group of men with an idea. It's a good idea and it's as old as civilisation itself. It is best expressed by the old saying "Thy duty towards thy neighbour is to love him as thyself." My principals in this matter have no corporate existence. As a group they have no name. They do not, as you might suppose, represent any religious body. They are drawn from a wide group of interests in the United States and they share only this one idea: that unless something is done and done quickly to improve the social and economic structure of the world, the thing we call civilisation is headed for the toboggan slide. . . .'

'Pacifists?'

'No, pacifists are people who say peace at any price. Call them just men of good will. They command, I may tell you, sums of money which we may call unlimited. . . .'

'Just who are these people?' asked Jeremy.

'That I am not at liberty to disclose. These men desire

[80]

no personal *kudos* for themselves. They are actuated by a desire to prevent a catastrophe to civilisation. They believe that by opening men's eyes to the dangers which exist, men of good will in all countries will play their parts. Lastly, they believe that, as has always been the case, the English-speaking peoples must make the first move. Look, my friend! To-day hundreds of millions of people in the world are short of the bare necessities of life, but in Brazil they are talking of burning the surplus coffee that has accumulated. In our Southern States cotton is being grown and stored at a rate beyond the present capacity of the world to buy and consume it. The grain elevators in Western Canada are bursting. Factory workers in all countries are being laid off because production has gone so far ahead of consumption that industrialists despair of ever being able to restore the balance.'

'Well, there's one very simple remedy: you Americans have hogged most of the world's gold. Devise a means of putting it back into world circulation and you will soon thaw frozen credits.'

'I am not trying to shift from American shoulders the onus of blame which belongs there. We, like other nations, have been selfish, short-sighted and narrow in the way we have tackled the problem. We, like other peoples, are actuated by fear, and that the fear is vague and formless makes it just that much more real. Fear is at the back of all economic nationalism. It is fear which is keeping tariff walls so high at home and elsewhere. It is fear which causes the French to complete their Maginot Line. Fear was the root cause of your Wembley Exhibition, just as fear lies behind all the propaganda of the Empire Marketing Board. It is all this fear that the men who sent me here want killed, and it will not be killed until men of good will in this and other lands demonstrate that the world's fears are groundless.'

'That's why the League of Nations was created, and the reason that it has been a joke from its very creation is not hard to find.'

'I know,' said Lefroy sadly. 'Wilson was an idealist and a not very practical one.'

'In principle, of course,' said Jeremy, 'I'm in full agreement with you. Things are in a rotten state everywhere and, like you, I'm quite convinced that unless we pull up short we're heading for chaos. But you haven't made it clear to me how I can do anything in the matter. I'm not a politician and I haven't even got any political affiliations. . . .'

'Which is one of the chief reasons why I'm talking to you at this minute. See here, Jeremy,' said Lefroy earnestly, 'I've never spoken to you until to-night, but I have the advantage of you in one respect: two years ago I was in the room when you argued your case before the board of directors of the International Tourist Agency and got the contract. I am, as you may know, a member of that board. I tell you, Dowbiggin, I never heard a case better argued in my life. When you entered the room they had almost made up their minds in favour of another agency . . . then when I heard that you had married Sybilla . . . well you can guess the rest. Dowbiggin— Jeremy! I'm offering you a grand job because I know you can do it. I sail Friday. . . .'

Sleep stayed away from Jeremy a long while that night. It seemed as he turned the conversation of the evening over in his mind that at long last he had something to put his teeth into. He had made money and would make more, but it had all been done within the small orbit of an advertising man. He had influenced a few million people to spend their shillings and pence upon this or that triviality, but it had never made him feel that he was a propagandist, or that he had been able to bring to bear influence in any worth-while matter.

From the hour that Jeremy found that he was a salesman—that he had the gift of imposing his personality on
others, he knew that he had within him the seeds of power.
He did not want the power that comes from public
acclaim. As Lefroy had said, Jeremy liked working in
the background. It had given him enormous satisfaction
in a small way to see a well-planned advertising campaign
from the viewpoint of a spectator and to know that he
was the anonymous power behind it. He remembered the
thrill it had given him once, when passing in the early
morning one of the suburban depots of the London
General Omnibus Company, to see rows of shining omni-
buses displaying on their side boards his messages, and
knowing that because of them and of other co-related
messages the buying habits of millions would be influenced.
The novelty had worn off, and latterly he had the uncomfortable feeling that he was successful because he had never
pitted his wits against a worth-while problem.

Now this smooth, suave Lefroy, almost as though he
had read Jeremy's thoughts, was holding out the tempting
prospect of a seat at the table where big men made big
decisions in the biggest game ever played—and he would
take a hand.

Jeremy for once in his life was not thinking of money.
He knew, of course, that there *was* plenty of money in it,
for men of Lefroy's type lived always close to money.
Jeremy was in the grip of the craving for power, the craving that is greater than greed for money, that transcends
the desire for a beautiful woman or the hankering of an
opium addict for the poppy. In that after-dinner conversation there had been opened up to Jeremy the vista
of a new future. All the smothered vanity of his life came
to the surface and he was able to recapture some of the
thrill and excitement there had been in the mad dash
through winter fog, the evasion of coast-guard cutters and

the successful landing of his first cargo of bootleg whisky in New York. It had not crossed his mind then that the evening's work was worth $1,000 to him, nor did it cross his mind now that large sums of money were being dangled before him. It was power he wanted.

It had more than once been suggested to Jeremy that he enter politics, but the men who suggested it did not realise that even the prospect of cabinet rank one day did not attract him. Cabinet ministers were, in Jeremy's conception, merely puppets. The men who had the power were those who stood in the background and pulled the strings.

Jeremy had no illusions about the motives of this mysterious group of philanthropists behind Lefroy. In his own good time and in his own way he would find out all there was to know about them. As Lefroy had said, the world was in a sorry mess. Wealthy men—the men with the biggest stake in the *status quo*—naturally did not want to see chaos or violent change. They were probably big shipowners, whose ships were sailing empty; big industrialists, whose mills and factories were running at less than half capacity; speculators who were overloaded with unsaleable cotton, wheat, metals, chemicals and other commodities. Naturally, they wanted to see the wheels of international commerce turn smoothly once more. It would be worth millions to such men—tens of millions— if the barriers erected in the name of economic nationalism were torn down.

'Philanthropists, my left foot!' Jeremy ejaculated, and to that degree his summing-up of the talk with Lefroy was correct. More important still was the fact that Jeremy had reached the precise conclusion which Paul Lefroy had expected him to reach. The astute Lefroy had judged his man well.

Jeremy, believing that he was on the threshold of a

future in which he would be able to leave the tiresome trivia of advertising to paid servants, was very well content. Let someone else blandish housewives into buying fifth-rate jams. It would no longer be necessary to bribe and cajole Dr. Juniper Berry into lending his name and dwindling prestige to thinly-veiled commercial advertising. Since man had to sham, pretend, dissemble and shift in order to live—for that was the nature of things—Jeremy wanted to be privy to large-scale sham and pretence, an associate of the princes of the craft. Was it not true that the world condoned theft, pretence, common swindling and even killing, always provided that these things were done on the grand scale?

Sybilla, lying awake in the next room to Jeremy, guessed something of what was passing in his mind, and when at last there came through the communicating door the sound of his regular breathing she knew that, one way or the other, he had made up his mind. But there was a lot Sybilla did not know about Jeremy. Each of these two had a big part of the mind locked and shut away from the other. Sybilla did not know what it was that Paul Lefroy had proposed to Jeremy, but knowing the proposer, had a fair idea that it would not be what it appeared to be.

Paul Lefroy had telephoned Sybilla shortly after arriving in London.

'I want to meet your husband, Sybilla,' he had said. 'I've something that will interest him, I think.'

'Then come to dinner to-night, Paul.'

'No, I'd like a chat with you first,' Lefroy had replied.

'Now look here, Paul, it isn't any good trying to bring to life something that's so dead it might never have existed. I was very young and rather foolish that summer in Italy, but I'm neither now. Just try to remember, will you, that

I'm a very respectable, happily married woman, who doesn't want to be reminded of—a lot of things.'

'Sybilla, my dear,' Paul replied, 'hurtful as it may sound, I do assure you that, beautiful and charming and utterly delightful as you are—and I would call out anyone who said the contrary—I had, until you reminded me, forgotten these things. If you will honour me by lunching with me to-morrow I promise not even to refer to them. I have reason to believe that your husband is a remarkable man. I wish to meet him. I would like, also, to hear from your own beautiful lips a few things about him which will help me to make a decision. I am asking nothing disloyal, I assure you. Is it a date?' . . . .

'Are you comfortably fixed?' Lefroy asked at lunch. 'Financially, I mean?'

'Very, thank you, Paul!'

'Does your—does Jeremy like money?'

'Who doesn't?'

'But does he like it more than most people?'

'Ye-e-s! he does. I don't mean by that that he's mean. He isn't. He's always been generous with me—surprisingly generous.'

'Why do you say *surprisingly*?'

'Surprisingly, for a man who is so fond of money, that's all.'

'Is he ambitious?'

'Do you know, Paul, and it's a funny thing to say, I can't answer that question. I just don't know. There are times when I suspect Jeremy of the most colossal ambition, and then I begin to doubt it because he becomes so very pleased over some small triumph. . . .'

'I take it, of course, that Jeremy knows nothing whatever about—well, about any romantic interlude, shall we call it, between us?'

'Nothing at all, Paul. I don't intend that he shall know.

It all happened years ago, long before I knew him, and I can't believe that he wants to know. . . .'

'I think you're quite right, Sybilla.'

That had been that. Sybilla had asked Lefroy to dine.

But when Sybilla at last heard Jeremy's restlessness end in sleep, she too composed herself for sleep.

'You're a clever swine, Paul,' she murmured, 'but Jeremy isn't a fool. There's bound to be a lot of money in whatever it is, and Jeremy has an instinct for money. I'd rather be his friend than his enemy, so watch out, Paul, and don't try to be too clever.'

Chapter Eight

JANET SEYMOUR was engaged in the pleasing task of arranging sumptuous furniture and carpets in a four-room office suite on the fifth floor of a new block of offices which had invaded the centuries-old calm of St Charles's Square. Although brand new, the furniture and fittings did not look new. They did not smell new. There was about everything an air of dim, restrained opulence. In Jeremy's private office there had been installed the latest thing in safes, built into solid concrete and fitted with a combination device, which if it did not, as the makers claimed, defy thieves, should have done so at the price paid.

The leather upholstery had almost the texture of velvet. Telephones rose up mysteriously and silently from recesses in the desks, the drawers of which ran smoothly on ball-bearings. To walk on the pale green cork-lino was to think of the ecstasy of walking through a pine forest on hard earth cushioned by pine needles. The soft-coloured oriental rugs seemed superfluous.

Janet Seymour loved luxury. There had been little enough of it in the offices of the Hayward Fisher Agency. Here, being the only woman in the office, she had a small tiled washroom and lavatory to herself, plenty of clean towels and hot water. Although Jeremy was going to spend less and less of his time at the old offices, he still went there for an hour or so in the mornings. Shortly after Paul Lefroy had returned to the United States, Jeremy had rented temporary furnished offices for his new venture, making it clear to Janet that he wanted no overlapping between the old and the new.

Janet would have been much happier about things if she could have understood what it all meant. Jeremy had not been very communicative. He had raised her salary to six pounds a week, impressed upon her the need for discretion and silence, but there had been little chance of any indiscretion, even had she been disposed to be indiscreet. There had been a few letters to type to important people, a few rough drafts of newspaper articles, very few telephone calls and fewer callers. Janet Seymour was a very competent, sensible young woman. She was also an extremely attractive one, a fact which, as she noted with some bitterness, had escaped her employer, who treated her like part of the office equipment—which she was.

In a room next to the waiting-room, looking out into the well of the building, was a young man named Roderick Gillespie Macdonald, who struck the only wrong note in the offices during the hours when he was in attendance. He is worth more than passing mention, this young Macdonald, if only for the fact that he was the living embodiment of the truth that a good brain cannot overcome the handicaps of an unpleasing personality. Macdonald had a good brain—a really first-class brain. He knew it, too, just as he knew that the vast majority of the

people he met either actively disliked him or ignored him
—which was worse.

One must suppose that nine-tenths of the men given the
baptismal name of Roderick in youth would be known to
their intimates as Rod, Roddie, or some such abbreviation.
But even Macdonald's father, mother, brother and sisters
called him just plain Roderick, while the rest of the world,
with the exception of Jeremy Dowbiggin, called him
Macdonald. To Jeremy he was always Roddie.

So far as it lay within the power of Macdonald's warped
little soul to be loyal to anyone, he was loyal to Jeremy,
who stood for all the things Macdonald would have liked
to have been and was not—good clothes worn properly,
popularity, physical stature, a good speaking voice.
Macdonald had a pimply face, which made him appear
even more youthful than he really was. He looked as
though he slept in his clothes, which might have been
made for a larger man. His hair defied the best efforts of
a hairdresser on the widely spaced occasions when he
visited one. His watery eyes peered out through ugly
steel-rimmed spectacles.

Macdonald had been brought up in a pawky little
Scottish town where they believed that it was 'what you've
got in you, not what you've got on' that counted. It may
have—there; but from the hour of Macdonald's arrival in
London—even in sartorially careless Fleet Street—the
little man was doomed to spend much of his life, unconsidered and unnoticed, in outer offices.

He had then become a 'free lance journalist' and in this
precarious manner had picked up a few guineas here and
there, mostly from kindly Scots. Out of all London's
millions only one man—Jeremy Dowbiggin—had shown
him kindness, courtesy. Jeremy had done more: he had
seen that behind the little man's intellectual if pimple-
ravaged forehead was a good brain. They had arrived in

London within two weeks of each other. Macdonald had watched Jeremy climb, while Jeremy—from the days when they frequented the same little teashop—had always held out a helping hand.

Macdonald had given Jeremy more than one idea—useless to its unprepossessing owner—but which Jeremy's salesmanship had been able to turn to good account. During his years of furtive comings and goings there was little which happened in Fleet Street which somehow did not come to the ears and notice of Macdonald. Possibly it was that, having only the bare bones of life himself, he took an untoward interest in the lives of others.

Now, in the amazing luxury of the new offices in St. Charles's Square, 'Roddie' was earning the stupendous sum of ten pounds weekly, plus out-of-pocket expenses.

'But I don't need new clothes,' he had protested when Jeremy sent him to his own tailor, with instructions to have himself turned out decently at Jeremy's expense.

'I don't care whether *you* need them or not, Roddie,' Jeremy had said heatedly. '*I* need you to wear them. From now onwards you've got to get rid of those damned pimples, wear good clothes as if they belonged to you, get your hair cut at least once every two weeks and acquire some expensive vice. It doesn't matter what it is so long as it's expensive. I'll pay for it all. You've allowed your niggling parsimony to mess up your own affairs, but you're not going to mess up mine. Which reminds me that Janet told me yesterday that in the last month you've drawn from the petty cash 4s. 1od. for bus fares and two shillings for telephone calls outside the office. It's got to stop, Roddie. . . .'

'It saves time to take a bus sometimes,' said Roddie, looking hurt and uncomprehending. 'I walk always for short distances. . . .'

'Exactly! From now onwards don't walk—or ride in

buses. Take a taxi. Leave taxis outside places where you call, ticking up the shillings. It'll do you good. Find yourself a fast expensive woman. She'll show you how to spend money.'

But it was no good. Macdonald looked like a tramp even in Savile Row clothes, which merely looked like somebody else's Savile Row clothes. His hair was the despair of every hairdresser to whom Jeremy sent him. Taxi-drivers took one look at him and drove on. Men looking as seedy as Macdonald simply didn't ride in taxis.

Jeremy called in the aid of one of the dance hostesses at the 'Eighty-one' club, where he occasionally entertained clients.

'Now look, Norma,' Jeremy said, 'I want this fellow made human. You can do it if anyone can. I'll give him some champagne and start the good work, but the rest's up to you. Take him back to your flat for the night. Keep him there a week if you like. I'll pay the bill. . . .'

'But Jeremy darling!' Norma protested innocently. 'You know I don't do things like that.'

'I know you don't, my little angel, but do it just for me —and for the twenty quid.'

With the help of Jeremy and the commissionaire Norma got Macdonald into the taxi. Jeremy followed in another taxi and watched while, protesting, the little man was dragged into the hall of the flats.

'This is Norma speaking,' came a voice over the telephone at noon the next day when Macdonald had not yet put in an appearance.

'Everything all right?' asked Jeremy. 'Is he still there?'

'Yes, he's still here,' came a weary voice. 'At two o'clock this morning he made me send my maid out to an all-night chemist . . .'

"You mustn't mind that, Norma. He probably didn't intend it that way.'

' . . . to buy some bicarbonate of soda for his indigestion. While the maid was out he bolted himself in her bedroom and he's still there.'

After that Jeremy gave up trying to change Macdonald, contenting himself with the virtues which went with the little man's failings.

*　　*　　*　　*　　*

There are two ways of securing publicity for this and that in the daily press: one way is to buy it. Advertising space in the national dailies costs up to £9 or so per column-inch, which automatically restricts the number and class of the potential buyers. The other way is to get it for nothing.

Newspaper editors, like most other people, give nothing for nothing. Aside from all other considerations, they don't have to. Editorial space is tremendously valuable. It is upon the palatability, or otherwise, of what fills this editorial space that the newspaper lives or dies. A well-edited newspaper attracts readers. Readers mean circulation. Circulation draws advertisers—paid advertisers, and it is upon the advertising that the newspaper ultimately lives.

In every newspaper under the sun a perennial war is waged between the editorial and business sides. The former wants news. The latter wants revenue. The advertisement manager is delighted when the editor gives a little free publicity to one of his star advertisers: it makes the task of selling more advertising space to that particular advertiser just that much easier. The advertisement manager, likewise, is fiercely indignant when the editorial department gives free publicity to some person or company who are not advertisers.

'How the hell,' asks the advertisement manager, 'can you expect me to sell advertising to John Smith when he knows damned well he can get all the publicity he wants out of you for nothing? Is this newspaper a philanthropic institution? Don't you know that your salaries depend on whether we downstairs here get in enough advertising revenue?'

'That's your lookout,' replies the editor in effect. 'My job is the collection and printing of news. Wherever it may come from, my meat is news. If I have to be governed by financial considerations the tone and quality of the editorial columns of this newspaper will suffer. We shall lose readers and circulation and you won't be able to get such a high advertising rate as you do now.'

The perfect newspaper, therefore, from the standpoint of its proprietors, steers roughly a middle course between these two views.

It is upon these elementary facts that a not inconsiderable industry has been founded in all lands where there are newspapers: industrious persons, working for various interests which pay them handsomely, use every art and guile in the box to prevail upon newspaper editors to publish innocent little paragraphs—and some not quite so innocent—calculated to grind the axes of all manner of persons, products and institutions. Until a few years ago these industrious axe-grinders were usually called publicity men. In America, where undertakers are called morticians and mud-pack-slingers are beauticians, publicity men were promoted to 'public relations counsel.'

Let us suppose that Miss Greta Garbo's publicity man walked into the editorial sanctum of the *Los Angeles Daily Sun*, if there is such a newspaper. His arrival coincides with the *première*—only he would call it *premeer*—of Miss Greta Garbo's just finished picture.

'I've got a story here that will interest you,' says the publicity man.

'Oh yeah! I've heard that one before,' replies the editor courteously.

'But this is good.'

'I've heard that one, too. What is it?'

'I have here a signed affidavit to the effect that Miss Garbo hasn't got a home. How's that for you?'

'Well, why didn't you say so before?' asks the editor. 'I'll print it—it's news.'

Everyone, thus, is happy. Miss Garbo gets the publicity for her new picture. The publicity man gets his salary. The newspaper gets a story. A perfectly fair arrangement all round.

When the vicar sends in an announcement of the forthcoming bazaar to the local newspaper he is a publicity man. Religion always being good for a little free publicity, he will get a paragraph or two. If the bazaar is being opened by the wife of the paper's leading advertiser, the vicar will secure a paragraph or four, while if he were to announce that during the bazaar the town harlot would do a strip-tease act, he would ensure the success of the bazaar.

The basic ingredient of the story is the bazaar itself, which even to the editor, who hasn't the least intention of being there, and will send his least efficient reporter to cover it, is a pretty dull affair. The skill of the publicity man, therefore, lies in wrapping the basic ingredient—which is usually pretty dull reading—in such an attractive manner that an editor, who lives on the news value of what he publishes, will use it in print.

Paul Lefroy was an adept in this fine art. Jeremy Dowbiggin, as Paul Lefroy's European colleague, had a tremendous advantage in the fact that, as head of the Hayward Fisher Agency, he spent some £600,000 annually with all sorts and conditions of newspapers and magazines. Jeremy may have lacked—did lack Paul Lefroy's fine handwriting in such delicate matters, but he would learn. Indeed, he learned very fast. Roderick Gillespie Macdonald also lacked experience in the larger aspects of publicity work, but he wrote consummately well and he knew from long and bitter experience what editors wanted and did not want. Because he had no personality with which to thrust his point of view upon others, nature had endowed him with other qualities. Macdonald was patient—infinitely patient. He had learned that while waiting in outer offices. Because it was not in him to be forthright, he understood the subtle aspects of innuendo. Because men and life had never treated him very kindly, little Macdonald had learned how to be sly and malicious, how to dip his pen in acid and let its corrosion work slowly for him. He was well read, too, regarding ancient and contemporary history. Unlike more attractive men, he had never wasted his evenings with drink and cards and wild women. These hobbies cost money, while a ticket for the public library cost nothing.

Macdonald was, therefore, well equipped to sit in the dimly lit room which looked out on to the well of the building in St Charles's Square and to do his work in secret like the mole and the ferret. He loved his work because it meant the daily toying with names, some of them great, which but for this would always have remained just names. Now he was able to clothe these names with well chosen words, to weave stories round them to order. Sometimes these stories were in praise of men and women, but Macdonald loved his work best when orders came from Jeremy to vilify this person or that, this cause or that. It was then that Macdonald shone—even scintillated. It seemed too good to be true that for all these delightful hours Jeremy—good friend Jeremy—was paying him ten pounds weekly.

There was a glorious mirror in the washroom, too, with a bright light above it. Here Macdonald was able to gaze lovingly upon the pimples which others—jealous, they were—professed to dislike.

Macdonald was very happy in St Charles's Square, probably for the first time in his life. He was there early and late, except when seeing Fleet Street acquaintances. The office accentuated the squalor of the attic bedroom in Battersea, where he slept and kept his other shirt, and experimented with razor blades, sharpening them on the curved surface of his tumbler, to make them last longer.

'Remember, Roddie,' Jeremy had said, 'nothing must go out from this office direct to any newspaper or agency. Everything we have to say must be put into the mouth of someone else. It then becomes the responsibility of someone else. Perhaps a newspaper will refer to us for something. We will get them the information they want, but it will go to them via some third party. John Smith, for whom we may be acting, may say to an editor "Better ask Dowbiggin about that". Dowbiggin has nothing to say, but he will tell John Smith what to say. That's a rule that must never be broken.'

Chapter Nine

IT WAS SIX months before Jeremy's office in St Charles's Square was what might be called a going concern. Paul Lefroy had made it a part of their arrangement that, aside from the work he wanted Jeremy to do, Jeremy must work up a publicity connection on his own. Most of his new clients were old clients, which is to say that they were clients of the Hayward Fisher Agency, to whom Jeremy now gave what was termed an 'editorial service'.

In St Charles's Square originated, for example, remarkable stories regarding ex-students of Pulitzer's, one of whom had by means of the mind-training course, plus the Juniper Berry diet, memorised twenty-four pages of *Bradshaw's Railway Guide*. The student in question had left a secondary school three years previously. His last school report read: 'Very forgetful. Will not concentrate.'

When a Birmingham-Simplex car—another Hayward Fisher account—under carefully supervised test conditions, demonstrated—the twelve h.p. model—that it could pull a trailer containing one ton of lead ingots up Porlock Hill, to say nothing of five passengers, it transpired that the test was the result of a wager between the manufacturer and the motoring correspondent of the *Daily Sun*, who acknowledged his error in a column of undiluted praise for the Birmingham-Simplex car. The makers of the tyres used, who paid Jeremy a retaining fee for editorial service, came in modestly for their share of the glory.

When a cat burglar was arrested on the sixth floor of a block of luxury flats, having climbed up the outside of the building, it was the observant Macdonald who discovered that the man had been wearing a set of special climbing shoes made by Alpine Requisites, Ltd., stolen on a previous burglarious raid on the house of Lord Excelsior, who had bought them for his attempt on Everest. Alpine Requisites, Ltd. were, of course, clients of the Hayward Fisher Agency.

But these things were very elementary. They were little more than the preliminary canter. Paul Lefroy, who never wrote letters, arrived in person to give his instructions and to explain the wishes of his clients.

'The men behind me—I hope before very long you will meet them,' said Lefroy, 'want the searchlight of truth put

4*

into dark places. One of the world's great cankers to-day is corruption in high places. Corruption and communism are the two great enemies of society. You know it and I know it, but our job is to make the world know it. I want results, and to get them the sky is the limit as far as money is concerned. Our job will be done and our utility ended, Jeremy, when the common people of the world have faith once again in their institutions and their elected representatives. Use what methods you like. You understand people and conditions here. Don't write to me about your work —I don't trust the mails. Arrange a safe cable address, which doesn't appear to be connected with you, so that I can communicate with you at short notice. When you want me cable to this address—cables sent to it aren't traceable to me. I'll be over here three or four times a year. . . .'

Jeremy whistled when he saw the sum which had been credited to his private banking account.

'Whatever these fellows want,' he murmured, 'they must want it damned badly!'

Communism, Jeremy reflected, was an easy target to shoot at. All respectable and influential people abhorred communism. The trouble was, as Jeremy saw it, that all respectable and influential people did not abhor corruption. To stir up mud in certain quarters was to make vastly influential enemies. Then Jeremy looked at his bank pass book and saw there a comforting shield against enemies, however powerful.

*   *   *   *   *

Before Lefroy left London what has come to be known as the Hanworthy scandal burst upon the world. George Hanworthy was an inventor. After years of patient research he perfected an electric storage battery which in storage capacity per lb of its weight transcended anything previously made. Nobody had ever heard of George Hanworthy until an article appeared in an electrical magazine of a highly technical nature disclosing that 'a foreign power' had acquired the patent rights. The article concluded with a vicious attack on George Hanworthy:

> While we are the first to agree that the inventor is entitled to reap the pecuniary rewards of his toil and ingenuity, we also believe that, even in time of peace, an invention of this nature belongs primarily to the country of which the inventor is a citizen or subject. It requires very little technical knowledge to guess at the uses to which this far-reaching invention might in certain circumstances be put by a foreign power inimical to ourselves. Careful enquiry reveals that Mr. George Hanworthy, a British subject, attracted by the magnitude of the sum offered, sold the rights of his invention outright to a certain foreign power, without giving his own country the opportunity of refusal. In so doing—and we weigh our words carefully—Mr. George Hanworthy has committed an act which morally, though unhappily not legally, is an act of treason.

This article, appearing as it did in a technical journal, circulating entirely among electrical engineers and the like, did not attract any general attention, and probably nothing more would have been heard of the matter if the said George Hanworthy, fiercely indignant at the allegation of treason, had not consulted his solicitors and brought suit for libel against the publishers.

At this point the daily press took notice of the affair, though it was still far from being a *cause célèbre*.

'There's a fine case for you to handle,' said Paul Lefroy, handing Jeremy a newspaper report with its very scanty details. 'Dig into that and you'll find what you'll find.'

It did not occur to Jeremy to ask Lefroy what he knew nor how he knew it, until the latter had sailed.

'I've a job for you, Roddie,' said Jeremy. 'Go and find this man Hanworthy and get his story from him—not for publication yet. I want to know everything there is to be known.'

Macdonald found Hanworthy only too anxious to talk. He was a very angry man indeed.

'No man is going to call me a traitor and get away with it. Before selling my patent abroad I spent six months hawking it in England. Three government departments in turn considered it, and then, after a lot of talk which ended in nothing, refused it.'

'Have you got the correspondence?' asked Macdonald.

'Not here, but I've got it safely and when it's read in court it'll be a sensation. Come and see me to-morrow.'

Macdonald was in time to catch the late editions of the afternoon papers. With Jeremy looking over his shoulders he typed his story.

'Hurry now,' said Jeremy when it was finished, 'and take a taxi, and don't forget that you're a free-lance. See that they pay you well for the story, too.'

Macdonald had an appointment with George Hanworthy for the following day at eleven a.m. in the latter's office in Victoria Street.

'I'm afraid I can't show you the correspondence to-day,' said Hanworthy in somewhat chastened tones. 'My lawyer tells me that at this stage I oughtn't to do anything. He says the matter is *sub judice* and I might land myself for contempt of court.'

Macdonald phoned Jeremy.

'I wouldn't ask you to do anything that might get you into trouble, Mr. Hanworthy,' said Jeremy, 'but I think you owe a duty to the public in this matter, apart from your duty to yourself.'

It was apparent that for some reason Hanworthy was a very frightened man, whereas less than twenty-four hours previously he had been full of fight. Why? With much persuasion he consented to come out to lunch. After two glasses of sherry he recovered some of his fight.

'Look here, Mr. Dowbiggin,' he began, 'I'm in a terrible position. Just before Mr. Macdonald called this morning I had a telephone call. A very important person was speaking. I can't mention his name. He told me that I was doing something very unpatriotic by letting the newspapers get hold of all this. He advised me to withdraw the libel action, too. Said that the consequences might be very serious—for me. . . .'

'In other words, he threatened you,' said Jeremy.

'He didn't exactly threaten me,' said Hanworthy. 'But he said that the paper would publish a handsome apology and if no more was heard of the matter, pay me £2,000.'

'Good God, man, they haven't got £2,000, that crowd. . . .'

'Then there was another phone call,' said Hanworthy as though he had not heard Jeremy. 'It was my bank manager. All the money I got for the sale of the patent has been put into a manufacturing business in connection with another patent of mine. The bank was going to lend me a further £15,000. Now they tell me that, as I've embarked on expensive litigation, they must reconsider their decision. That isn't all. My house was burgled last night and all my papers stolen.'

'Look here, Mr. Hanworthy,' said Jeremy, 'when you've won your case you'll have no trouble getting extra finance. People will tumble over themselves to give it to you. It's your duty to go through with this thing. . . .'

'But how can I in my present circumstances brief expensive counsel? I'm told that it will run into hundreds and hundreds.'

'I'll stand your costs, Mr. Hanworthy. Don't let that worry you. I'll phone my solicitor and we'll try to make an appointment with counsel this afternoon. . . .'

Jeremy knew that if he lost sight of Hanworthy the man's courage would evaporate. Someone had frightened him badly. Who was that someone? Jeremy intended to find out.

Merryweather hesitated for a little.

'I think Congleton-Jones is the man for this sort of case,' he said at length, 'but whether he'll see us at such short notice is another matter. I hardly like to ask him. . . .'

'We're going to try to get Congleton-Jones,' Jeremy told Hanworthy, who was drawing comfort from a glass of liqueur brandy. 'He's scared of nothing and nobody. Your troubles are over if he'll take the case.'

Congleton-Jones did take the case, although it took him some hours of questioning before he could extract the whole truth from Hanworthy.

Men in very high places were involved in what followed. The public stood aghast when Congleton-Jones established in court that the intermediary commission agent who had negotiated the sale of the storage battery patent to the unnamed foreign power was the brother-in-law of the high official to whom the patent had been offered. The latter, it transpired had resigned hurriedly, while the brother-in-law took up permanent residence in South America. Certain smaller fry had sudden and unaccountable lapses of memory, drawing down upon themselves a rebuke from the Bench. A great newspaper commented after Hanworthy had won his case:

> There cannot fail to be great public uneasiness at the disclosures made in this case. There seems not the smallest doubt that right up to the eve of its going to trial a variety of attempts were made to dissuade—a

mild word in this context—the plaintiff from vindicating his character in open court. Even then, last minute efforts appear to have been made to have certain evidence given *in camera*. The judge's own words on this point cannot have failed to make a deep impression upon the public consciousness: 'Representations made to me that certain parts of the evidence in this trial should not, in the public interest, be given in open court with press and public present, failed to convince me that such was the case. I formed the opinion that these representations were made without thought of any public interest which might be involved, but rather with the underlying purpose of shielding the guilty.'

'Nice work,' cabled Paul Lefroy from New York.

'I don't understand all this, Jeremy,' said Janet Seymour. 'There doesn't seem to be any sense in it.'

'There are lots of things you don't understand, my child,' replied Jeremy, and he might with equal truth have added that there was much he, too, didn't understand. 'But I can understand *this*,' he reflected, looking at his bank pass book.

Nevertheless, a few months later Jeremy, too, was telling himself that none of the things he was doing made sense and even the large sums of money passing into his possession did not still the queries which were constantly arising in his active mind. During those months Jeremy had, prompted by Paul Lefroy, uncovered dirty work on the part of two City financiers. There had been a celebrated divorce case in which a guinea-pig co-respondent had been found to substitute for the exalted person who was really guilty. Despite great pressure from unexpected places, Jeremy had been instrumental in turning the spotlight upon the guilty man and from being a hush-hush undefended cause, as had been hoped by all concerned, it became the joy of the sensational press. Real tit-bits of the evidence, which the British press could not publish, were printed in Paris and distribution effected among all English-speaking visitors.

Through Macdonald, Jeremy established contact with two Englishmen deported from Russia, arranging syndication of an article by one of them which alleged that the prime purpose behind Russian policy was the destruction of the British Empire. Accompanying the article was a diagrammatic map of the British Empire which purported to reveal a complicated system of communist cells at all key points. British opinion, already hostile to Soviet Russia, became inflamed, and the few who dared to defend the Red *régime* were howled down as traitors.

People still recall the wedding of Sir James Kinnell-Forbes (who inherited the fortune and baronetcy from his father, who had made the fortune as an army contractor between 1914 and 1918) to Mademoiselle Renée Justin, daughter of the French brandy king. According to contemporary newspaper accounts, which were reasonably accurate, the wedding guests consumed champagnes and other wines to the tune of £6,000. A special aeroplane was flown from the Caspian with caviar. The bride's parents presented the happy pair with a palatial villa on the Riviera, while the groom's present to the bride was an emerald necklace for which he had paid £40,000.

On the evening before the wedding Macdonald, with a newspaper cameraman to whom he promised a 'scoop', took a taxi from Fleet Street to the mouth of a foul alley not far from Surrey Commercial Docks. Here, in a basement whose walls sweated great drops of water, was living a family, father, mother, seven children and an aged grandparent. The father of the family worked as night watchman at the Kinnell-Forbes warehouse near the docks, for which he was paid thirty-three shillings weekly and had to rebate two shillings of this to a grasping foreman. The rent of the basement was eight shillings per week and the house was owned by Kinnell-Forbes himself, together with three rows of similar properties.

The story, complete with photographs, which showed the emaciated family in their basement, appeared in a morning newspaper alongside all the fantastic details of the wedding. The police were compelled to provide the bridal couple—together with their guests, who numbered some three thousand persons—with special protection. A French left-wing newspaper went further, and when Kinnell-Forbes and his bride arrived at their Riviera villa for the honeymoon they were pelted with filth before the police arrived to disperse an angry crowd.

The story was so horrifying that there was no voice raised in defence of Kinnell-Forbes. The Midland constituency which had adopted him dropped him like a hot brick, and newspapers which had hailed this Anglo-French marriage as having a significance it did not have, deplored the whole business in guarded terms.

'Now look here, Paul,' said Jeremy when the scandal had died down and the former was in London on one of his periodic and unheralded visits, 'I just can't work in the dark any longer. I've got to know more about everything. I want to know who I'm working for and why. What can you, or anyone, hope to accomplish in this way? First you tell me that communism must be discredited. All right! There's been plenty of dirt slung at Communist Russia. Then you tip me off about this Kinnell-Forbes business, though how you knew some of the details is more than I can see. I agree that the whole business stinks, but there can't be the smallest doubt that the disclosures made must have given a lot of fuel to communist arguments. I know what I'm talking about, for I've heard sober, decent British working-men say what they think about it.'

[105]

'I expected you to say this, or something like it, Jeremy, and I don't blame you for saying it. My principals in this make the mistake that a lot of rich men make—they think they understand how the public mind works. I've told them that what has been done is merely destructive and I think I've persuaded them that if they want value for the money they spend they've got to be constructive. Set your mind at rest, Jeremy. There won't be any more of this sort of thing. . . .'

'When do I meet these people you keep calling "the principals"? You've been very square with me, Paul, but constitutionally I'm not able to go on like I've been going without knowing more. So far it's just been what you might call isolated incidents, and even they don't hang together. I've got to be able to see a picture of it all— a pattern. Otherwise, I'm afraid you'll have to count me out.'

'You're going to meet the boss to-night, Jeremy, so put your mind at rest. I've booked one of the private dining-rooms at the Piedmont for the evening. We shan't be disturbed there and then you can ask questions until all's blue. Let's leave it till then, eh? How's Sybilla?'

'Fine, thanks!'

Jeremy tried to inject a note of heartiness into his voice and hoped that he had succeeded. The truth was that things were far from fine where he and Sybilla were concerned. There had been no actual breach, but they were fast drifting into separate ways of life. Trying to be fair about it all, Jeremy was not quite sure which of them was to blame. He himself worked early and late, but against that he provided Sybilla with plenty of money. When he was able to spend an evening at home there was usually such a crush that they hardly saw each other.

'Let me think, now,' Sybilla had said to him in the drawing-room the previous evening, 'I know I've seen you before somewhere. No, don't tell me. Let me guess.'

She was balancing a cocktail in one hand and a plate of stuffed olives in the other.

'Have one while I think,' she said.

She was easily the best-looking woman in the room, Jeremy reflected, while Sybilla played out her little comedy. There was something so arresting about her pose and voice that conversation in the immediate vicinity ceased for a few moments.

'I know,' she said when the tenseness could be felt all round. 'You're my husband!'

There was a roar of laughter and Sybilla sailed gaily on her way. More than a dozen of those who had heard all this learned for the first time who Jeremy was.

'Sybilla's quite irrepressible,' said one woman. 'She's the life and soul of any party. If she'd been born fifty or sixty years sooner she would have been one of those grand Victorian hostesses you read about. . . .'

'And you'd have been able to go to her parties, darling,' said a vapid young woman who looked as though she doped. 'Wouldn't that have been nice?'

Just then Jeremy spied Claire, now a self-possessed little girl of eleven, who was occasionally allowed to spend a few minutes at these parties. Claire, Jeremy reflected with some bitterness, was the innocent cause of much of the estrangement between him and Sybilla. The role of stepfather had never been to his liking. He resented this constant reminder of a predecessor in Sybilla's affections. There had been times when he found himself hating the very memory of this unknown man whose waterlogged body had been washed up on a Belgian beach. Every time he tried to pay some little attention to Claire, the picture of her father, framed in the distorted colours of jealousy, would rise up between them and some kind phrase on Jeremy's lips would be strangled.

He took Claire once to a matinée, but never repeated it. The play was for children. Without knowing what she was doing, Claire piped up, apropos of some incident: 'I suppose they've all got daddies of their very own. Aren't they lucky?'

Chapter Ten

THE PIEDMONT WAS, if one could forget its reputation, an extremely good restaurant. Its speciality was private dining-rooms, some of which were equipped with couches and other unusual features. Couples dining *tête-à-tête* in the restaurant downstairs sometimes had their coffee upstairs. They would part ostentatiously in the restaurant vestibule. *He* would take his hat and leave, while *she* would depart upstairs, ostensibly to the cloakroom. *He* would re-enter the premises by a door fifteen yards down the street to join her in the *cabinet particulier*, where the coffee and liqueurs were set out in readiness. The Piedmont was famed for its coffee.

'Odd sort of a place for Paul to have chosen,' Jeremy remarked to himself. 'He probably doesn't know its reputation.'

He instinctively looked around him before entering the place, being unwilling to be recognised.

'Mr. Lefroy's room, please.'

'Come this way please, sare!'

From force of habit the waiter delayed entering the room until a full twenty seconds had elapsed after knocking and being told to enter. Paul Lefroy and his companion were by this time looking expectantly towards the door. With some ceremony Lefroy introduced Jeremy to Mr. Ignatius Turner.

Jeremy had been expecting to meet some iron-jawed, beetle-browed, domineering captain of industry. Mr. Turner in the flesh was by way of being an anti-climax. He appeared pink, round, fifty-ish, benign, innocent and so utterly unlike Jeremy's mind picture that his surprise must have shown itself.

'You will never know, Mr. Dowbiggin, how much pleasure this meeting gives me and I hope you will forgive me and acquit me of any intentional discourtesy for having postponed it so long. I will be frank with you, Mr. Dowbiggin, and I hope now there will always be frankness between us—man to man, soul to soul, in perfect understanding. I wanted to be sure, Mr. Dowbiggin, that my dear friend Paul here had made no error in choosing you for the great work we have in hand. I *am* sure now and it distresses me that I ever harboured doubts.'

'Jeremy understands, I know,' interposed Paul Lefroy. 'He is the soul of discretion himself.'

Jeremy murmured something about understanding perfectly, but he had been rather knocked off his balance by the meeting. All his carefully prepared remarks seemed now rather banal and stupid. This pink little man, Turner, would require an entirely different way of handling and Jeremy didn't for the moment know what that way would be. He confined himself, therefore, to listening.

'I am first of all going to tell you all about myself, Mr. Dowbiggin,' Turner began. 'Courtesy demands that you know as much about me as I know about you. I shall begin, therefore, with the reasons which impelled me to leave the ministry. . . .'

Jeremy glanced at Paul Lefroy, believing he saw a faint flutter in the other's right eyelid.

'I believed, you see,' Turner went on, 'that God's Kingdom would not make itself apparent on earth while the Christian faith was rent with schisms. If Christianity is to redeem mankind, all Christians must pull in the same direction. But they don't, Mr. Dowbiggin, they don't. We have seen the awful spectacle of Christian nations fighting each other, introducing God's Holy Name into their godless struggles. After ten weary years I gave up the struggle. The Christian sects clung more tenaciously to their sectarian teachings than they did to the ungarbled word of Christ. The churches had forgotten Him who overturned the tables of the moneychangers in the Temple: they had become vast business institutions. The redemption of mankind, I knew then, would have to come from without the churches.

'I am an American, Mr. Dowbiggin, although I feel this to be my home also. Whatever culture I may have absorbed in my short journey originated in these islands. But my active life has been spent in my native America. Do you know America, Mr. Dowbiggin?'

'Slightly, Mr. Turner. I spent a few months in New York and a couple of years in Mexico.'

'New York! New York! A godless city that, Mr. Dowbiggin! But as I was saying—let me see. Yes! I had many heart-searching talks with an old friend. The newspapers used to call him a multi-millionaire. He is an immensely wealthy man, Mr. Dowbiggin. Much of his wealth, it grieves me to say, was made in an unworthy manner. But he has atoned—at least in part. He and I—his name will never cross my lips—he has not long to live and it is his most earnest wish that he be allowed to end his days in peace. The newspapers, you know! He and I, as I was saying, reached the conclusion—one which any thinking man must have reached—that the world is in a parlous state, Mr. Dowbiggin. Yes, a parlous state. Men have taken the broad highway which leads to destruction. Gambling, drink, the craze for speed and pleasure, extravagance, corruption, cruelty—these have taken the place of the Sermon on the Mount in the hearts of men. Blessed are the meek, Mr. Dowbiggin, for they shall inherit the earth. The very words ring strangely, do they not? It is long since you heard them.

'This old friend and I resolved to do what we could to redeem the world from its evil ways. To that end he placed at my disposal all his great wealth. Since then there have been others. I have at my command very great wealth, Mr. Dowbiggin, and at my waking and before I put my head on my pillow I pray to God for the grace to use it with wisdom and understanding.'

'He's a bit cracked!' was Jeremy's inward comment.

'After due thought and, I believe, divine guidance,' Turner continued, 'I founded a Movement. I called it the Christian Movement. Those who have made themselves part of the movement, and they number some fifty thousand, men and women, call themselves just Christians. We have no churches, no corporate property, no written constitution, no formality. As Christians we believe that the whole world is one great temple, erected to the greater glory of God. We meet on the beaches, in the privacy of our homes, on ships and in forest glades, by the banks of rivers and wherever the fancy pleases us to meet. We have no service as the word is known. We talk, we exchange ideas, try to imbue each other with beautiful thoughts, and when our meetings are over we go away refreshed and thankful. To those who are in trouble we try to lend a helping hand. It does not sound much, Mr. Dowbiggin, but out of such an association of men and women of good will there may come the redemption of mankind. We believe that as this movement spreads, as spread it surely will, the barriers of race will break down, man will be less inhuman towards man. Greed and oppression will vanish, industrial strife will cease, for there will be a new basis of understanding. Privilege will go, for men will believe that no greater privilege can exist than to be a citizen in good standing of God's Kingdom.'

Turner paused and drank a little soda water from a syphon at his hand.

'Will you do your part to help us, Mr. Dowbiggin?'

There was a great deal more in the same strain. Jeremy resolved, as a mere matter of business precaution, to have Mr. Ignatius Turner 'looked up'. Evidently, this pink and innocent man had persuaded someone to back him. That someone was probably some ferocious financial bandit who, as the grave loomed in sight, had undergone a change of heart. By making restitution in some good cause, the man probably thought he would stand a better chance in the hereafter. There were such people, Jeremy believed, but he marvelled that such a simple type as Turner had been able to talk a hard-boiled American out of his millions. Since all this money was being spent, Jeremy mused, he might as well have his share. If Pliny were still alive he would have said: Out of America always something new.

Jeremy realised that in dealing with people like Turner the ordinary standards didn't work. So far as he could see Turner was prepared to spend huge sums of money, wanting nothing in return except the problematical redemption of mankind. Jeremy most emphatically did not want to be mixed up in any kind of scheme for extorting money from gullible converts. He would have to inform himself on this point.

'Tell me, Mr. Turner,' Jeremy asked, 'is it your intention to raise funds here in England?'

'By no means, Mr. Dowbiggin. That has been a great problem in America. All manner of well-disposed persons have sent me offerings, large and small, but we have no need of them. I have been unable to use them because, as I told you, we have no corporate existence. In cases where money has been sent to me anonymously—and in the aggregate these have amounted to a large sum—I have passed them on to worthy charitable objects, among them a home for incurables. You see, it is my firm belief and the belief of those behind me financially that the churches have become business institutions. We Christians will not fall into that error. . . .'

'One more question, Mr. Turner. Am I, as a condition of the continuation of our arrangement, obligated to become a member of your movement?'

'Why no, Mr. Dowbiggin. One cannot have a change of heart made a condition of a purely commercial arrangement. You will have every opportunity of seeing us as we are. It will be a real joy to me if you decide to join us. Paul here has told me that you are not an active member of any Christian sect, so nothing you are called upon to do for us can possibly conflict with your conscientious beliefs. The only condition I feel I should make—if condition is the right word—is that should you now, or at any other time, feel yourself actively out of sympathy with us, you will as an honest man tell us—tell me.' . . .

'I do believe in fairies. I've had dinner with one to-night,' said Jeremy.

'Beg pardon, sir?' said the taxi-driver.

My trouble, Jeremy mused, is that I've become so hard-boiled myself and so damned sceptical, that I don't recognise unselfishness when I meet it. God knows there isn't much about. Turner really thinks he can reform the world. All right! Let him. It wants reforming badly enough.

The taxi was crossing Piccadilly Circus. He might as well start right here, mused Jeremy. Within a one-mile radius of here there's enough vice, corruption and all the other deadly sins, to keep Turner and ten like him busy for a few years. But I expect he gets his slice of cake all right. Well, I don't begrudge him that. He probably had

[113]

years of hard work bringing the repentant millionaire up to scratch.

*   *   *   *   *

'He's not likely to come back, is he?' asked Mr. Ignatius Turner, indicating the seat which Jeremy had recently vacated.

'Not he!' replied Paul Lefroy.

'Then ring for a pot of strong black coffee and some liqueur brandy, Paul. We've work to do and I'd like to get the taste of that soda water out of my mouth.'

'What do you think of Dowbiggin, Iggy?'

'Don't call me Iggy! I don't like it.' The mild, benign look left Turner's face for a few seconds. His eyes flashed angrily. He continued: 'What do I think of Dowbiggin? I think there is very little he would not do for money, but it would have to be a great deal of money. I compliment you on your choice, Paul, for I believe with you that he is precisely the man we need. But—and mark this well—don't ever make the mistake of under-rating Dowbiggin's intelligence. I knew a man once with just that shape of jaw and forehead. He was the most formidable human being I have ever encountered. Like this Dowbiggin, he was greedy for money. For a while greed blunted his intelligence. He saw only those things which he wished to see. But I made the mistake of under-rating him and I paid dearly for my folly. . . .'

*   *   *   *   *

'How long have you known Paul Lefroy, Sybilla?'

'Years and years and years. Why?'

'I wondered, that's all,' replied Jeremy.

'Don't you like him, then?'

'Yes, I like him well enough. I was dining with him this evening. I suppose you know I'm doing a fair amount of business with him these days?'

'I guessed you were, Jeremy my pet. You don't spend your time with people who aren't useful, so I put two and two together and made four.'

'Well, I have to live, don't I? This place doesn't run itself on cigarette cards.' Jeremy restrained his temper. 'I was thinking this evening how funny it is to be doing so much business with the man when I know positively nothing of his antecedents. I like to know something of the background of men I am associated with. It helps in all sorts of ways.'

'I suppose so,' said Sybilla languidly. 'I first met Paul at Myra Kennedy's place on Long Island. . . .'

'Who's Myra Kennedy?'

'I was forgetting. I thought you knew her. I was at school with her in Switzerland. She returned to New York and married Justin Kennedy. . . .'

'Do you mean old Justin Kennedy, owner of the *New York Clarion*?'

'Not the old man, silly. His son.'

'If Paul was friendly with the Kennedy family,' said Jeremy, 'he must have been someone.'

'Yes, I think Paul is very well connected over there. He's Harvard and all that sort of thing.'

'I'm glad you told me, Sybilla. It sets my mind at rest.'

'There's been no trouble with Paul, has there, Jeremy?'

'Good Lord, no! We're on the best of terms. I was just curious.'

*   *   *   *   *

Mr. Merryweather was dictating a letter to the New York correspondent of his firm:

We write on behalf of a valued client, who wishes, under conditions of the utmost secrecy, to ascertain something of the early life and antecedents of a certain Mr. Paul Lefroy, whose present office address in New York is No. —— Park Avenue. We understand from our client that Mr. Lefroy was educated at Harvard University and was some ten or more years ago a friend of a Mr. and Mrs. Justin Kennedy, who at that time maintained a large establishment at Southampton, Long Island. . . .

*   *   *   *   *

It consoled the dying days of Charles Dowbiggin to know that all his pessimistic forecasts regarding his brother George's profligate—the word was Charles's—mode of life had been justified by events. George Dowbiggin returned to England almost penniless. A large fortune evaporated when his New York brokers began to call for more and more margins.

Charles Dowbiggin survived Ruth, his wife, by only a few months. With her death he gave up the struggle to live. Sitting with his father in the living-room of No. 7, Cornwallis Crescent (Charles had been gravely doubtful in his later years whether the little house was consonant with the dignity of an Actuary), after Ruth's funeral, Jeremy could see in Charles's face the hopelessness in the old man's heart as he faced the prospect of living on alone.

Jeremy could not and did not pretend to any great grief. His father and mother had lived in another world. His refusal to enter the service of the London & Continental Assurance Company had proved a landmark in their relations. Charles to the day of his death was unable to understand how any man, privileged to have such a chance, could reject it. The fact that Jeremy was a rich and successful man in other fields did not mitigate this feeling. To the very last day of his service with the company Charles felt uncomfortable in the presence of the Directors at the thought that a son of his had not seized avidly the opportunity to shelter himself under their beneficent wing.

Then towards the end, when Ruth had been in her grave two months, George Dowbiggin returned home. George, despite his penniless condition, looked well, prosperous, slightly amused by it all and entirely unrepentant. This last was to Charles the most difficult to swallow. It was, as he conceived these things, almost the duty of a man without money in the bank and his debts paid to look humble and to talk humbly. George was nearly seventy years of age—sixty-seven to be precise. He had brought home with him a handsome woman of barely forty, whom he described airily to his brother as 'my secretary'.

'But what on earth do you want a secretary for?' asked Charles, aghast. 'You have no business and she can only be an expense.'

'Liabilities take a good deal more looking after than assets, Charlie old boy,' George replied, 'and I've a hell of a lot, haven't I, Flora?' he asked, turning to her for corroboration. 'Anyway, Jeremy's been a good lad. He's offered to start me up in something. I'll look around, I think. I heard yesterday of a half interest in a starting-price book that could be picked up for a couple of thousand. I'll cut you in on a share, Charlie, if it comes to anything.'

'You'll do nothing of the kind, George,' replied Charles, who was not quite sure what a starting-price book was.

Then in a few weeks Charles, in the little house which contained all his small store of memories, lay down and died. He ate his lunch and walked over to the couch in the dining-room where on Sunday afternoons for over forty years he had been in the habit of reading the Sunday papers. Charles had an inner knowledge that it was the end. In the brief moments before lethargy overcame him there passed before his eyes the uneventful kaleidoscope of the years.

There was a moment, almost at the end, when Charles was near to deciding to make a struggle to go on living. The Assistant Actuary, who would almost certainly be appointed in his place, was a careless man. He had once omitted an 'o' from a report and Charles knew for a fact that he spent four shillings on his lunch every day. It was the thought that by dying he might feel Ruth's comforting presence again which decided him. So he died.

If Ruth at that moment could have returned from that bourne from which it is said no traveller ever returns, the little house in Cornwallis Crescent would have heard her deep sigh of contentment. From Ruth's sewing basket, which still occupied its accustomed place at the end of the couch, came the creak it had always given—from the very day they had brought it back together from the Army & Navy Stores, using George's membership number—a few minutes after Ruth set it down.

When the maid-of-all-work found Charles lying there she saw, before she went sobbing for help, a large piece of plaster fall from the ceiling which for fifteen years had been threatening to drop. It was as though Number 7, Cornwallis Crescent, seeing that its work was done, had begun to disintegrate.

Sybilla did not come to the funeral. Jeremy's parents had disliked her. They thought her fast. George Dowbiggin and Jeremy went, of course, while Ignatius Turner and Paul Lefroy decided at the last moment to go, too. Three or four of Charles's colleagues came from the office.

There was a ghastly, uncomfortable hour in the drawing-room at Cornwallis Crescent after it was over. There was a lump in Jeremy's throat so big that it nearly choked him. The red-eyed maid served tea and from the recesses

[118]

of a cupboard under the stairs brought forth a bottle of sparkling Moselle and a bottle of port.

Jeremy, who had not been upstairs for twenty years, went into the room where he was born. His mother's clothes were still there and her few pieces of jewellery. A few strands of her grey hair still clung to her brushes. He picked up a silver-framed photograph of his father and mother and himself at the age of three. He would keep that. In his father's dressing-room was Charles's most prized possession, a seven-day case of German razors. In the attic he found the wooden playbox he had taken to and from school, still filled with forgotten treasures. There was room in it for the razors and the photograph and a bundle of papers from the desk downstairs.

The others were waiting in the car. Jeremy let them go back to London alone, all except George Dowbiggin, to whom Jeremy clung for a moment as the last link with his parents.

Jeremy handed to his uncle Charles Dowbiggin's will, amended a few weeks before his death.

He left his entire fortune, some £8,000 in all, together with the freehold of the house, to Jeremy. But there was a request that 'if I pre-decease my brother, George, and if the latter's extravagant mode of living should leave him in straitened circumstances, my son Jeremy will make such provision for him as will keep him from actual want.'

'May he rest in peace,' said George Dowbiggin, draining the bottle of sparkling Moselle and grimacing as he did so. 'Dear old Charlie wouldn't have liked to see it wasted. Now let's get out of here, boy. The place is full of ghosts.'

There was silence in the car until they were crossing over Kew Bridge and making for the Chiswick High Road.

'Who is that guy Turner, Jeremy?' asked George. 'I've seen him before and he's seen me, too!'

'I WANT TO meet people, Mr. Dowbiggin,' said Ignatius Turner. 'A lot of people. Before I begin my work over here I want to know how British people think and talk.'

'What sort of people?' asked Jeremy.

'I would like to meet people of all classes and all shades of opinion—the best and the worst. Before I declare myself I would like to mingle with them as an ordinary visitor to England . . .'

'Then I think as a start you'd better come to one of my wife's cocktail parties,' said Jeremy. 'I'll guarantee you'll meet there some very ordinary people—very ordinary indeed, some of them.'

Sybilla gave Jeremy an idea. 'Why not,' she suggested, 'let me have a chat with old Lady Penmanby? She's very hard up, I happen to know. . . .'

'How do you happen to know?' asked Jeremy.

'She's owed me a bridge debt now for three months and she shies whenever I go near her. She knows everyone and goes everywhere. I'm perfectly sure she'd be glad to tow Mr. Turner round and introduce him.'

'Good idea!' said Jeremy. 'In his time her husband was one of The Boys and The Boys always stick together. He made a hash of every job he attempted, but they always found him colonial governorships, a seat on some Royal Commission, and when he was too old to do anything but sit and wheeze in a bath chair, The Boys got together and gave him some directorships which brought him in a few thousand a year—at someone else's expense, of course.'

'I shall see her this afternoon, I expect. I'll see what she thinks about it. If she agrees I'll take good care to get what she owes me out of the first cheque.'

During the ensuing weeks Jeremy found little enough to occupy him at the office in St Charles's Square and devoted himself to the Hayward Fisher Agency, wondering that, in return for the handsome remuneration paid, Turner made such small demands on him. Paul Lefroy had returned to New York.

Before he moved his office temporarily back to the Hayward Fisher Agency, Jeremy instructed Macdonald in one or two matters, leaving him in sole charge of St Charles's Square. Macdonald was one of those men who had to be active, or he went to pieces.

'I want you to do something for me, Roddie,' said Jeremy, 'and it's a bit out of the ordinary run of things. I hope you won't mind.'

'I'd do anything for you, Jeremy,' said Macdonald. 'You know that.'

It comforted Jeremy to believe that this was literally true. There were not many people in the world who were so devoted to the interests of anyone else.

'You know Turner by sight, don't you? Good! I want him trailed for a few weeks. When he's going around with old Lady Penmanby it isn't important, but I'd like to know where he goes and what he does when he's alone. Get hold of someone else, two if necessary, and make it a twenty-four-hours a day job, and for God's sake don't lose him for fear of spending a few bob on taxis.'

'What sort of thing do you want me to look for, Jeremy?' asked Macdonald, his eyes lighting up. This was, as Jeremy had said, a bit out of the ordinary, but it delighted the little man. Having had no life himself, he liked to live vicariously. He would have made a wonderful private detective. When he was not at the movies—his only extravagance—he derived much pleasure from shadowing people he disliked. He loved Lombroso and obscure books on medical jurisprudence, and prized greatly a piece of the rope which had hanged a celebrated murderer of the nineteenth century.

'Anything at all,' replied Jeremy. 'I know what Turner is like when I'm face-to-face with him, but I don't know what he's like when he thinks he is unobserved. That's what I want to know. Take your time, but do the job thoroughly. I don't think he could know you by sight, but be careful.'

In many ways Jeremy had a very prosaic mind. As he knew the world and the people in it, people did things with a reason. More particularly was this true when people parted with large sums of money. Jeremy had made money, for money-making came more easily to him than it does to most. Those from whom he had obtained money had always demanded a *quid pro quo*. In Jeremy's philosophy they were entitled to it. But here was Ignatius Turner handing him on a silver platter every month a sum fully ten times as great as the trifling services given in return would warrant.

The true philosopher would have shrugged his shoulders, endorsed the cheques and hoped that the golden sun of providence would continue to shine. While it was undoubtedly true that Jeremy loved money, it was equally true that he loved the chase. Furthermore, elementary logic demonstrated to him that, since this man Turner paid him a great deal more than his services were *apparently*—that was the key word—worth, it followed with the relentless certainty of night following day that either Turner was half-witted, or he was in fact securing, or intended to secure in the future, some entirely adequate return for his very considerable expenditure. Now Jeremy had reached certainty in his mind on one point: that Turner's actual and declared motives were as the poles apart.

It is in such situations as these that the prosaic mind, as

distinct from the mind of genius, is most helpful. The prosaic mind looks for a prosaic explanation of the unknown, for the prosaic mind knows that in 999 cases per 1000 the apparently inexplicable is capable of a prosaic explanation.

Although there is much in these pages to suggest that Jeremy Dowbiggin was not over fastidious in the manner of making money, he played the game according to rules laid down a thousand or more years before he saw light. But he was not a criminal: he was merely a predatory businessman, conducting his affairs in the world's most predatory city, which sucked sustenance from every land on earth. Because Turner did not conduct his affairs according to any known standard of procedure, Jeremy concluded that Ignatius Turner was a crook, and invited his bank manager to lunch.

'Money used to be liquid, Mr. Dowbiggin,' said the bank manager. 'I won't go so far as to say that it isn't possible —just possible—to-day to cover up the movements of large sums of money, but you may take my word for it that it's a very difficult thing to do. I've noticed these large payments to your credit myself, I don't mind admitting, and I've wondered about them, because there didn't seem to be a corresponding series of payments out made against them, if you know what I mean.'

'They are sent to me by a Mr. Paul Lefroy of New York. I want to know where he gets the money from. . . .'

'They do not come to you from Mr. Paul Lefroy of New York,' said the bank manager with emphasis. 'That much I can tell you. The payments may, of course, be made on his instructions originally, but they are made on the direct instructions of a firm of lawyers. I can't remember their name, but I have a record of it.'

'Is that unusual?' asked Jeremy.

'No, not necessarily. Payments from a trust fund are

frequently made like that and also payments of which the payer for some reason or other desires to conceal his identity.'

'I'd like the name of the firm of lawyers, if you have no objection, and I'll come back to the bank with you.'

'If there's any other way I can be of assistance,' said the bank manager, who was by this time consumed with curiosity, 'I shall be only too pleased.'

'Would you care for a bite of dinner with me to-night, Uncle George?' asked Jeremy over the telephone when he returned to the office.

'If it's a good dinner,' was the cautious reply.

George Dowbiggin had often reproached Jeremy with being a careless feeder—careless, that is to say, in the choice of food rather than in the manner of eating it. Food to Jeremy had become merely the means of life. George Dowbiggin regarded it as one of life's great pleasures.

'You choose the place, Uncle George, and you can also choose the food and wine.'

'In that case, my boy, I'll see to the ordering immediately. The Regency at seven, shall we say. We can eat at eight and get the talk over by then. Never spoil a good meal by talking too seriously over it. When you reach my age . . .'

'Okay! The Regency at seven!'

*   *   *   *   *

Jeremy found Uncle George in a quiet corner of The Regency, secure from being overheard. The latter knew his nephew and argued that there would be an hour of highly confidential talk.

'You remember telling me that you'd seen Ignatius Turner before?' began Jeremy, sipping a glorious dry sherry—as dry as a sherry can be without being doctored. 'Have you remembered where?'

[124]

'No. I'll be shot if I can remember. Funny you should ask me. I felt that you wanted to talk about him.'

Jeremy knew that George Dowbiggin was the very soul of discretion. He told him all he knew of Turner, and his dealings with him and Paul Lefroy.

'Depend on it, Jeremy, my boy, they're a pair of crooks! You may be sure this Turner was in some racket or other over there, or the chances are that I shouldn't have met him, and meet him I did somewhere.'

'I've told you all this, Uncle George, because I know you know your way about New York. You've got ways and means of finding things out over there, haven't you?'

'Give me a lead of some kind and I've got friends over there who'll find anything out. What particularly do you want to know?'

'I'd like to know all about a legal firm there—Mercutier, Flashman & Gulbrandsen. Here's their address. They're the people through whom the monthly remittance is sent to me. I want to know all about them and—if such a thing is possible—I'd like a list of their principal clients.'

'Nothing's impossible in New York,' said Uncle George. 'If you're prepared to pay enough I'll have their grand-mothers dug up. But I wonder are you doing the sensible thing, my boy? Granted that Turner and his pal are crooks. What then? They haven't asked you to do any-thing illegal. They have no strings on you. If you start stirring things up over there, a pair of fly crooks like that will soon tumble to who's at the back of it and then— bang goes your meal ticket. Why not string them along a bit? Take their money while you can. When the day comes that they ask you to do something illegal, or you catch them doing it, then's the time to tell them to chase themselves.'

'I intend doing something like that,' said Jeremy, 'but

I'm relying on you not to leave any tracks that can be traced back to me.'

'You're a funny fellow, Jeremy. You've a streak of your father in you after all. He was a great stickler for legality. Now me—I never ask questions about money that flows in my direction. But I ask a hell of a lot if it shows a tendency to go the other way. I think that's why I've a first class digestion, sleep a good eight hours every night and like to hear the rustle of a silk petticoat once in a while. Now you, Jeremy boy, you're only just over half my age. Your hair's going grey at the sides, I see. You work harder than you have to, neglect a dashed good-looking wife and don't have any fun at all. You're even drinking that sherry as though it's something the cook bought at two bob a bottle to put in the soup, whereas it's going to cost you about two bob a sip.'

*   *   *   *   *

Roddie Macdonald shivered. He was, also, very tired. It had been a long day. Ignatius Turner had left his service suite in Park Lane at nine-fifteen a.m. to visit a West End barber's shop, where he had remained over an hour. After that he had met a tall man, evidently by appointment, on a seat in St James's Park. The tall stranger had been there first. For a few minutes they had ignored each other. Then Turner had asked to look at a newspaper the other carried and, as strangers will, they had got into conversation. It had been a disappointing half-hour for Roddie. He had hoped to be able to hear some of the conversation, but dared not approach too closely. When the two men parted Roddie had been torn between following the tall stranger, and thus losing the trail of Turner, or carrying out Jeremy's instructions. Roddie resolved that never again would he do his trailing alone. The tall stranger might have yielded much information.

Turner then took a taxi to the City, stopping at an office building in Cannon Street which Roddie already knew had several entrances and exits. It was not possible to ascertain to which set of offices he went, but as he appeared to know the way Roddie did not waste time making enquiries. Turner would probably pay another call there. When Turner was safely seated with Lady Penmanby at a table in the Ritz restaurant, Roddie had time to visit a near-by Lyons teashop, snatch a bun and a cup of tea, and wait more than half-an-hour outside the Ritz for Turner to emerge. Roddie did not care to risk entering the Ritz again as several of the staff had already eyed him suspiciously.

In the little arcade on the Piccadilly frontage of the Ritz Roddie was able to spend a pleasurable few minutes admiring an incipient pimple on the side of his nose. It bid fair to become a noble specimen of its kind, bright yellow and protuberant, surrounded at the base by angry, inflamed flesh. It nearly broke Roddie's heart that he was unable to find anything better than a shop window in which to view this latest eruption.

Turner occupied the afternoon in making short calls at private addresses in the West End. There was no time here to make enquiries, so Roddie carefully noted the addresses. One was in Knightsbridge, two in Marylebone, one in a handsome block of flats in St John's Wood, and the last overlooking Regent's Park. Then Turner had returned to his suite in Park Lane, emerging to keep a dinner appointment at the Savoy, where he joined a party of three men in the lobby. When at eleven o'clock Turner had gone back to Park Lane by taxi, most sleuths would have assumed that he had gone to bed. Not so Roddie, who argued that after such an apparently innocent day there might follow a night of wickedness. Roddie was not disappointed. Turner emerged from his suite within fifteen minutes, hailed a passing taxi and drove to a large but seedy house in Maida Vale.

There was much to occupy Roddie during the three hours which followed. A succession of private cars—Roddie noted all the numbers methodically—set down expensive-looking folk in evening dress. At one time, assuming Turner to have been the first arrival, there were not less than eighty people in the house.

'They seem to be giving a party,' remarked Roddie uneasily to a policeman who had three times flashed a bulls-eye lantern in his face.

'They 'aven't wasted much time, then,' said the policeman. 'The ruddy 'ouse was empty las' week when I was on this beat. I'll make a note of it. Wouldn't you be more comfortable at 'ome and in your bed?' he asked meaningly.

The policeman moved on. Roddie shivered and resumed his vigil, reflecting that not for anyone else on earth but Jeremy—kind, generous, magnificent Jeremy Dowbiggin—would he endure such cold, such agonising tiredness.

It seemed an eternity before Turner finally emerged. It was actually after three a.m. when Roddie caught a glimpse of him in the hall, putting on his hat and coat. For a few seconds he talked to a very beautiful woman—one of the most beautiful he had ever seen—and then other figures blocked the view. Turner walked the two hundred yards to Maida Vale, turned right in the direction of the Edgware Road and Marble Arch. Since at that time of the morning it was not possible to follow on foot without being observed, Roddie watched his quarry out of sight and presumed that he was returning to his Park Lane suite.

Roddie himself, being reluctant to take a taxi to Battersea, found a corner table in an all-night café at Marble Arch and, ordering a cup of coffee, fell into a sleep of deep exhaustion, from which a waiter shook him every few

[128]

minutes until the early buses began to run. He had an appointment at Victoria Station at eight o'clock with an unemployed reporter of his acquaintance who had agreed to take over the day's watching of Turner, after which Roddie himself intended to go over the previous day's wanderings with a view to finding out more about the addresses visited.

There were eleven different firms housed in the Cannon Street office building visited by Turner the previous day.

'Excuse me,' said Roddie at each, 'but did Mr. Turner leave his gloves here yesterday?'

'Never heard of Mr. Turner!' or some such variation of the theme, came from the first four offices visited.

'I don't think so,' said a girl at the fifth. 'But I'll ask.'

The name of the firm was 'Gardenia Investment Trust, Inc., New York, Paris, Montreal.'

'No, Mr. Turner didn't leave anything,' said the girl.

The first two of the private addresses visited the previous afternoon revealed themselves as flats, partially converted into consulting rooms, and occupied by psycho-analysts. Enquiry revealed that they had both just moved in.

For five days Ignatius Turner was trailed from morning to night by either Roddie or his helper, and the mass of information resulting filled a small notebook which Roddie had bought at a Woolworth counter for one penny.

Much of the information conveyed very little, but the points underlined in blue pencil for Jeremy's benefit revealed that Turner had visited in all seven psycho-analysts, one ordinary soothsayer, one astrologer, one palmist, three city offices which dealt with stocks and shares, a firm of private detectives, two gambling hells (one of them occasioned the all-night vigil in Maida Vale) and a café off Wardour Street frequented by waiters and other restaurant personnel, chiefly foreigners.

Roddie was a little hurt that Jeremy showed so little enthusiasm for the painstaking work of those five days, but he did not know that Jeremy had been given much food for thought.

Jeremy was thinking of what he had heard Lady Penmanby say the previous evening.

'I've just come from *the* most marvellous man. He psycho-analysed me. It was as though he could see into the innermost recesses of my soul.'

'Who is he?' someone asked.

'Levant, his name is,' replied Lady Penmanby. 'He has moved to Porterhouse Square—Number 443, I think. I have his phone number here somewhere. I never can find things when I want them.''

Jeremy pricked up his ears, metaphorically at least. Levant had been one of Turner's callers.

For days, or so it seemed to Jeremy, everyone he met was loud in praise of this man Levant.

Jeremy attended a series of tea parties, chiefly given in the houses of well-known people. At one of these—Lord Mandleton was the host—Jeremy listened eagerly to the conversation around him.

'I confess,' he heard one lady say, 'that I dislike the idea of going to a psycho-analyst. It sounds to me like undressing in public.'

'My belief,' observed another woman, 'is that this craze for psycho-analysis is part and parcel of some sinister plot of the Roman Church. They want to get us all back to the confessional.'

'I wonder, dear lady,' said Turner in his honeyed tones, 'whether the confessional was so bad an institution as some people believe. I don't know, of course, because I've never been to one. I know also that the confessional could be abused, with disastrous consequences. But the human soul has strange needs. In the minds of most of us dark thoughts lurk at times. Do you never feel the need to unburden your soul—not necessarily of sinful deeds and thoughts—but of the weight of care which oppresses? Would it not sometimes ease your way through life to be able to talk with absolute frankness to some sympathetic, understanding person, who might be able to shed a light upon your problems?'

'Where does one find such people?' chimed in another voice.

Lord Mandleton took the questioner aside, while Jeremy strained his ears to hear what passed. Lord Mandleton recited an account of his own visit to the famous Mr. Levant.

'Does he do it for money?' asked the lady.

'He will accept money, but he asks no fee. I understand that from most of those who go to see him he will accept nothing,' said Lord Mandleton. 'He is a most saintly man. His insight into human problems and troubles is almost godlike.'

Jeremy looked searchingly at Lord Mandleton, who in Edwardian days had borne the reputation of a rake. It was hard to imagine this grossly materialistic-seeming man interested in such matters, or in the neurotic people who thronged his drawing-room. Lady Mandleton, too, was not the type. She was the sort of horse-faced, heavy-footed Englishwoman whom foreigners delight to caricature. She was more at home in the stables than in the precious atmosphere created by the guests. Jeremy was skilled in the art of detecting boredom in others. As a salesman he had learned when to stop. It was obvious that Lady Mandleton's interest in the people around her was assumed. Only with a conscious effort could she bring her thoughts back to the chatter and jargon of the drawing-room.

The whole expression on her face changed when Jeremy remarked to her: 'This is too lovely a day to be in London, don't you think, Lady Mandleton?'

'What some of these people need,' was the surprising reply, 'is a ten mile tramp in the heather. Psycho-analysts! They make me sick. You don't go to them, Mr. Dow-biggin, do you?'

'Good Lord no!' exclaimed Jeremy with a gesture of horror.

'Then what on earth are you doing here?' asked Lady Mandleton.

'I was just about to ask you the same question,' retorted Jeremy, 'but I remembered in time that you were my hostess.'

Lady Mandleton gave Jeremy's arm what might be called an affectionate squeeze—she was over sixty—and resuming the bored look, circulated once more among her guests.

In some strange fashion most of the cranks of Mayfair seemed to attend the tea parties which Lady Penmanby managed to organise for Ignatius Turner's benefit, although the latter figured only as an ordinary guest. Turner, to Jeremy's eye, seemed to weave through these gatherings, paying his attentions to men and women who might be useful and appearing not to see the others.

But always the talk centred round psycho-analysis, palmistry, astrology and the other pseudo-sciences. Turner smiled serenely through it all, never voicing opinions on the main subjects of conversation, listening intently, always suave and courteous, but utterly non-committal. Slowly, imperceptibly almost, Turner gathered around himself a small group of satellites and it was obvious to Jeremy that when this little group had been formed to Turner's satisfaction the round of tea parties ended. Turner began instead to give discreet little dinner parties to these people, prominent among whom were Lady Pen-manby and Lord Mandleton. Jeremy instituted enquiries regarding these last two, learning without much surprise that whereas a few months previously both of them were being hounded by creditors, they had recently paid all their outstanding bills. The inference was that the considerable sums involved had come from Turner's apparently bottomless pocket.

All the time Jeremy looked in vain for the least sign that Turner was recouping himself for the large sums he was paying away, but Turner seemed content with what he was getting for his money. The thought occurred to Jeremy that perhaps Turner was getting a rake-off from the psycho-analysts and the other fakes who were levying toll upon an ever-widening public, but he dismissed the idea. Turner was playing for bigger stakes than that.

At Jeremy's instigation Roddie Macdonald went the rounds of all the psycho-analysts, palmists, astrologers and the rest whose names were being bandied about, but nothing interesting or significant emerged from the calls except that their waiting-rooms were crowded with the curious, the worried and the neurotic people who flock to consult the oracles.

'I don't understand it at all, Roddie,' said Jeremy. 'I'm worried. What does it all mean?'

'There's nothing new about it,' said Roddie. 'All through history it's been the same. When the world is in an upset condition people go with their perplexities to the soothsayers. The war turned the world upside down and it hasn't righted itself yet.'

'I grant you that, Roddie, but it's a long way from explaining what Turner hopes to get by all this. How much did you pay Levant when you went to see him?'

'Five shillings!' said Roddie. 'He must make about a quid an hour for an eight-hour day if everyone pays him five bob.'

'And he pays £700 a year rent for his flat. By the time

he's paid that, the staff and all the incidentals, how much rake-off would there be for Turner? Chicken feed—that's all. I'd bet my last shirt that Turner has to subsidise these fakes or they'd never cover their expenses. Why?'

Chapter Twelve

JANET SEYMOUR gathered up the pile of letters which Jeremy had just signed. She showed a disposition to linger. For a few moments Jeremy appeared to ignore the fact that she was still sitting beside him.

'Do you know, Jeremy,' she said when he looked up inquiringly, 'that I have to-day completed ten years working for you?'

'Is it really as long as that?' asked Jeremy. 'We're getting old, Janet. Ten years, so it is! I think it calls for some sort of a celebration.'

Jeremy looked at Janet appraisingly. 'Good Lord!' he said. 'I suppose you're about thirty now. Do you know, Janet, that I still think of you as the bright kid at the old offices when I first came there. Somehow you haven't grown up. Are you free this evening?'

Janet nodded assent and there was a sparkle in her eyes as she did so.

'I was going to go to a dull dinner party, but I'll get out of it somehow. Where do you live these days, Janet?'

'Since my people died I've been spending the winters at a girls' club in Kensington and the summers down near Maidenhead.'

'Then let's go to dine and dance somewhere up the river, and then I can drop you at home on the way back to town.'

'Lovely!' cried Janet. 'It's about eight years since I

[134]

thought so, but I really believe you're a nice man after all.'

'After all what?'

'After eight years.'

'Stay where you are, Janet,' said Jeremy, 'and I'll be back in fifteen minutes.'

Jeremy was back within the fifteen minutes, bringing with him a dainty diamond-and-platinum wrist-watch, which he kept in his pocket. He was feeling a little ashamed and conscious that over the years he had not been appreciative, or at any rate not demonstratively so, of Janet's hard work, efficiency and loyalty. She had given him all these in full measure—for ten years.

As they were leaving the office together Janet pointed to the suitcase which Jeremy always kept there ready packed, containing dinner jacket and etceteras. 'Bring this, too!' said Janet. 'You can change at my place and it'll give me the chance to wear something pretty. Funny! You've never seen me looking pretty.'

'I've never seen you looking anything else,' replied Jeremy stoutly and obtusely.

Janet ignored this. She would show him.

Janet did show him. The early autumn light was fading as she emerged from her bedroom in the little cottage near Boulter's Lock. Jeremy, already changed, was shaking a cocktail, wondering as he did so at the excellent taste evident everywhere in the cottage. It took him several seconds to recognise Janet in the soft light. For one thing her head and face were a different shape, or so it seemed. All the severity associated with the office had gone. Before him stood a tall, graceful young woman, with fair, naturally curly hair, done in some entirely new style—to him. She was wearing a frock of black and pale blue velvet.

The look in Jeremy's eyes was Janet's reward. He had made a mental note while waiting for her to remind her of some matter at the office which would require attention in the morning, but the office and the glamorous creature who came into the room were irreconcilable. Jeremy tried to think of something to say, but he felt tongue-tied, like a schoolboy. He fumbled in his pocket for the wrist-watch, fumbled when opening the box and fumbled even more while clasping it on Janet's wrist, thanking his stars the while that he had bought a really good one.

A little later Jeremy admitted to himself that he was enjoying the evening more than he had enjoyed one for months. The dinner had been good. They had had enough wine. The dance band was excellent and the room not over-crowded.

'Hullo!' he said as, on returning to their table, a woman's voice called to him by name. 'That's torn it!'

The woman who spoke was not only a friend of Sybilla's—Jeremy did not mind that, for he had no guilty feelings where she was concerned regarding this perfectly innocent evening—but an intimate friend of the woman whose dinner party he had cut that evening.

'May as well be hanged for a sheep as a lamb!' he murmured inwardly, and danced every dance with Janet for the next two hours. He was discovering things about this secretary of ten years standing: not only was she lovely, but she danced superbly. In fact, it was the first time he had danced with a woman whose dancing compared with Sybilla's.

The woman who had hailed Jeremy made it impossible for him to avoid introducing Janet, whom he introduced as Miss Seymour, without—of course—mentioning that she was his secretary. Janet returned the woman's hostile scrutiny with a well-bred insolence that Jeremy liked, and then they escaped.

They danced, these two, until the band packed up and Janet, looking at her new watch, announced that it was two o'clock. Torrential rain was falling outside, which seemed to emphasise the snug intimacy of the car.

'I won't let you go in this,' said Janet when they reached the cottage. 'I'll mix a drink and you must wait until it eases.'

But it didn't ease. If anything the rain became heavier. Summer gave its last dying kick that night, going out to the accompaniment of a spectacular thunderstorm. Perhaps, even if it had been a brilliant starlit night, Jeremy would have found a good enough reason for spending the night there.

He awoke with dawn's first light and, looking intently at Janet's face, as she slept peacefully beside him, wondering how ten years could have passed without him noticing—many things.

'I'm not going to the office to-day, Jeremy,' she announced over the breakfast table. 'I can't quite explain to you what I mean, but it would seem immoral, and I don't feel the least bit immoral. It will take me at least twenty-four hours to feel, look and behave like a piece of the office furniture again. You go on alone and I'll turn up to-morrow morning. I'll try to look very plain, very demure. I shall call you Mr. Dowbiggin, and so long as you forget this and continue to treat me like a piece of furniture, I shall probably continue for another ten years to be an efficient, unobtrusive secretary. But I simply couldn't face it to-day, Jeremy. . . .'

There was a wail, almost of anguish in Janet's voice as she said this last. It was born of a vague fear that she would never be able to return to the office. There were so many things about her that Jeremy hadn't known. On the day that, lurking behind the bookstall on the Continental Departure platform at Victoria, she had seen Jeremy and Sybilla go off to Paris, something had died inside Janet. She had believed—probably without justification—that she meant something to Jeremy. Then this other woman with the husky contralto voice had come along. The only thing which had persuaded Janet to remain in Jeremy's service had been her very real devotion to him and a sort of quiet certainty that one day Jeremy would need her. Over the years young men, some of them quite eligible, had pursued her, but Jeremy had been, so to speak, her standard of comparison, and none had stood that comparison.

It had not been in her mind the previous night that their little celebration should end this way. She had wanted to make herself as beautiful as she knew how—in the very limited time available—just to make Jeremy realise that she was not merely the object at which he hurled notes at lightning speed and relied on to keep his appointments straight, but a desirable woman.

Well! She had succeeded, more completely than she had anticipated. Jeremy had recognised her womanhood. What now? Janet wanted twenty-four hours to answer that question to her own satisfaction.

'I must warn you, Jeremy dear,' she said as he left for London, 'that I may never come back to the office. I'll try to, but it won't be easy.'

Jeremy knew better than to argue then, but he drove slowly back to London with the consciousness that the night had created its own problems.

The following morning there was a note from Janet— it was a Friday morning—to say that she would be back on the Monday. By Monday morning events had taken another turn.

For Jeremy there was a gloom over the weekend. The domestic atmosphere was tense. The flat was filled with the usual collection of strange people.

'I think you might take some notice of your guests,' remarked Sybilla acidly, finding Jeremy reading alone in the small library.

[138]

'They're not *my* guests,' he replied. 'I don't consider people invited without my knowledge as guests—if they have been invited at all.'

This occurred on Saturday evening. Sybilla and Jeremy avoided each other for the rest of the weekend. Jeremy, naturally enough, wondered whether Sybilla had already been told of the encounter up the river. Wives probably, like husbands, were the last to be told of these things.

When Jeremy reached the office on the Monday morning Janet had just arrived. She greeted him in the cool friendly way to which the years had accustomed him. He was in the office less than an hour, leaving to keep a luncheon appointment in Birmingham with the newly-appointed publicity man of the Birmingham-Simplex car.

Just as Janet was thinking of going out for lunch the door of her private office opened without a knock. Sybilla stood framed in the doorway. Janet had not seen Sybilla since the day years before on Victoria Station. Officially, therefore, she had never seen her.

'Miss Seymour?' asked Sybilla.

Janet inclined her head.

'There's a small job of typing I want done in rather a hurry, Miss Seymour. Just a matter of about three hundred invitations to this bothersome charity ball. When they're done would you mind posting them? By the way, is my husband in?'

'There are several husbands in the office. Which particular one are you looking for?'

'There's no need to be impertinent, Miss Seymour,' said Sybilla. 'You know perfectly well that I am Mrs. Dowbiggin.'

'Then I don't need to tell you, Mrs. Dowbiggin,' said Janet, 'that I was not engaged as your social secretary. Unfortunately, Mr. Dowbiggin is in Birmingham, or should be by now. I'm sorry, Mrs. Dowbiggin, but I have my own work to do. There is a very efficient typing agency in this building. Why not try them?'

It was no part of Sybilla's plan to lose her dignity and her temper. Enough had happened already for her purposes.

As Sybilla left the office Roddie Macdonald came in. He had only once in his life seen Sybilla and even then was not aware who she was. Roddie found Janet in tears.

'Why are you crying, Janet?' he asked gently. His devotion to Janet was only second to his devotion to Jeremy. She, also, had been kind to him in an unkind world. 'Did that woman upset you?'

Janet nodded.

'Why did you let her?' asked Roddie.

'She's Jeremy's wife,' sobbed Janet.

Roddie tried to conceal his amazement. He would not tell anyone except Jeremy himself what he knew: this was the woman he had seen for a few moments framed in the brightly-lit doorway of the gambling hell in Maida Vale, talking to Ignatius Turner.

'So that's it!' said Roddie to himself. 'That's why I've been following the man. I see! Jeremy didn't like to tell me about his wife and that's why he told me to follow the man. He's going to divorce her and wants evidence.'

In Roddie's twisted soul there was gladness. He liked the idea of spying upon a woman, especially a beautiful woman like this one. The fact that it was serving Jeremy made it much better.

Roddie trailed Sybilla as far as the Berkeley. When she and another woman were seated, Roddie went to the telephone and called in his reporter friend to aid him.

From that hour for over two weeks Sybilla's every footstep was dogged. Roddie watched Sybilla in and out of hotels, restaurants, taxis, the houses of friends and even on her shopping expeditions. It was mainly luck which

prevented Sybilla from realising that she was being followed. On one occasion she gazed full into Roddie's
eyes, wondering at the malignance she saw there, little
dreaming that it was for her.

*   *   *   *   *

When Jeremy returned from Birmingham, Sybilla was
out for dinner. On the following night he had a dinner
engagement, and the night after that he and Sybilla had a
joint engagement.

'Some evening when we have the flat to ourselves,'
Jeremy remarked, as the car took them through the gathering darkness to the Savoy, 'I should like to have a talk
with you, Sybilla.'

For the rest of the evening strangers and acquaintances
remarked on their happiness together. Neither revealed
by the smallest look or word the burning resentment which
was hidden by the mask of convention.

Sybilla knew her Napoleon. She did not wait for
Jeremy to launch the attack, but launched hers as soon as
they had closed the door of the flat. Her voice was
ominously calm, her manner coldly polite and through
both came the note of hurt pride which was uppermost.

'I'm not going to read you a lecture on moral grounds,
Jeremy,' she said, closing the drawing-room door and
taking one of the chairs near the fire, 'but I do wish you
would be just a little more considerate to me and less—
I suppose flamboyant is the word—when you go away for
the night with your secretary. I never did like that Mrs.
Cartwright anyway, but I did as you asked the other night
and made your excuses about being called away suddenly.
Naturally, she didn't like it. Women don't like having
their numbers messed up at the last moment. I wouldn't
have minded, therefore, nor been surprised if she had been
very rude to me when she phoned me on Sunday evening.

As it happens she was sweet and sympathetic, which was worse. She made me sick, telling me incidentally that not content with dancing with your Miss Seymour for four hours at some low haunt near Maidenhead—I've always thought it the most inappropriately named spot in England —you introduce her to a party of your friends. I can only believe that you did it as a deliberate affront to me, Jeremy. If there is any other explanation than the somewhat uncharitable one I have accepted, all I can say is that I wish you would let me have it. These things coupled with the fact that you did not return home to sleep are, you must agree, even to the most charitable mind, suspicious. Did you sleep with her, Jeremy?'

'Your suspicions don't entitle you to make scenes in my office, Sybilla,' said Jeremy, angrily and evading the question. 'We agreed long ago that it was far better that you didn't go to the office. Domestic and office affairs don't mix. . . .'

'That's really the burden of my complaint, Jeremy. You appear to have been mixing them. I had always supposed —stupidly so it seems—that the fair Miss Seymour's duties were strictly secretarial. To tell you the truth I've been sick of the sound of her name for years, but I accepted your word that she was—just your secretary, and I find it rather nauseating at this late date to learn that in all probability this sort of thing has been going on for years. Do you take her to hotels, Jeremy, or do you run some subsidiary establishment—that is the usual term, I believe, used to describe a love nest—which is it?'

Jeremy smarted under a sense of injustice. He was out-raged at the thought that Sybilla could believe him capable of years of deception such as suggested by all she implied. One woman had been harbouring resentment for years that he had behaved so utterly impersonally, and had made him feel a heartless cad. Now another woman—this one his wife—was blackguarding him for precisely contrary reasons. No matter what he did he was wrong, or so it seemed. An hour previously he had entertained an uncomfortable sensation of guilt. Now, since he had to bear the burden of indiscretions he had not committed, his anger enabled him to forget the night with Janet at her cottage.

'Let me tell you, Sybilla,' he said with narrowed eyes, 'if anyone came to me—man or woman—with filthy stories about you, I would confront you with whoever it was and have the story repeated to your face. Common decency demands that you give me and I give you the benefit of any doubt. . . .'

'I quite agree, Jeremy,' said Sybilla quietly, 'and that is precisely what I am doing. Of course, if you don't mind a scandal—I confess I don't want one—I'll phone Mrs. Cartwright and ask her for the names of her friends who saw you. She did tell me, but I've forgotten. If it will take that injured-innocence look off your face I'm quite prepared to use force if necessary and confront her with you. But I really don't see what good that's going to do unless you assure me that the whole story is a tissue of lies. . . .'

'I didn't say the whole story was a tissue of lies, but I do object to the construction you have put upon what you've heard.'

'Then give me some other construction to put on it, Jeremy. I'll try hard—really I will—to believe it. But please don't lie to me. I should hate that.'

'I haven't lied, Sybilla,' Jeremy stormed.

'I know you haven't,' was the calm reply. 'You haven't yet denied anything. I'm waiting for your denial of the whole story. When I get it—and you can't deny that I'm entitled to it—I shall know what to do.'

'While you're in this mood, Sybilla, it's no use trying to discuss anything with you. . . .'

[143]

'What mood? Really Jeremy, for a wife who suspects that she has been wronged, I think I'm behaving with admirable restraint. Of course, if you feel you'd like another day or so to think up a good story, Jeremy, or you'd like to consult this Seymour person before you commit yourself, I have no objections. But to-morrow morning I am moving out of the flat and I shall stay out of it until two things have happened. I want a satisfactory explanation of the whole story, and to hear that this Seymour person has been dismissed from your office. If you want to retain her services as concubine I have no objection, but I insist that you do so discreetly, unless you want a scandal.'

Jeremy sat on where he was, while Sybilla swept out and to her own room.

An hour later Jeremy hesitated outside Sybilla's door and then, with a shrug of the shoulders entered his own room. It occurred to him in a mood of self-dramatisation that he would probably never see Sybilla again. He intended leaving the flat early in the morning and he would learn by telephone during the day whether Sybilla had adhered to her threat. One thing was sure: he was not going to endure any more of Sybilla's cold sarcasm. Pride would not now let him tell her the truth, which was that for ten years his relations with Janet had been impersonal to the point of brutality. Since he would not tell the truth and a lie was going to serve no useful purpose, Jeremy realised that he had reached an impasse. Sybilla couldn't divorce him, whatever she might suspect.

His last waking thought was to wonder just how much he was going to miss her.

Chapter Thirteen

IGNATIUS TURNER had the air of one who was bursting to say something but did not quite know where to begin. He was Jeremy's guest. They were dining at Jeremy's flat as being the place where they would be least likely to be disturbed. Turner had suggested dining at the Piedmont, but Jeremy liked where possible to be the host.

'Mr. Dowbiggin,' said Turner, after they had chatted of trivial things for a while, 'you once said to me that, given the chance and the necessary money, you could create a great public figure from a nonentity. I'm going to give you the chance and the money.'

'Are you the man?' asked Jeremy bluntly.

'No, I am too modest to wish to be a public figure.'

'Tell me who it is,' said Jeremy, 'and I'll tell you whether I can do what you want.'

'I haven't made up my mind yet,' said Turner. 'Perhaps you can help me. I am undecided, you see, with the choice of three persons, one of whom is to head the Christian Movement in England.'

'If you're going to start that here,' said Jeremy, 'why not try the Archbishop of Canterbury?'

'I am being serious, Mr. Dowbiggin,' came the quiet rebuke. 'The three persons I have in mind I would like you to meet as soon as possible.'

'Do the people in question know that they are being considered for this high honour?' asked Jeremy.

'Most certainly not!' replied Turner. 'I have not broached the subject to anyone except you. I place great reliance on your judgment.'

'Well, don't place too much. I may be a good advertising man, but I'm not much of a Christian. Anyway, who are they?'

'Have you ever met Lionel Mossbank?'

'Do you mean the fellow who ran for Parliament as an independent and was beaten in a by-election? I've not met him, but I've heard a good deal of him. Supposed to be a wonder orator with no brains.'

'I wouldn't go so far as to say he had no brains, Mr. Dowbiggin, but I will agree that he is a little naïve at times. I will be frank with you and say that of the three persons I have in mind Lionel Mossbank is the most likely. The other two persons are both clergy and, therefore, have what might be termed the sectarian taint. . . .'

'Clergymen would be no good for your purpose,' said Jeremy. 'For every convert a clergyman secured he would drive off two more from rival denominations. An honest layman is much better. Is Mossbank honest?'

'I think it would be as well if you were to meet him, Mr. Dowbiggin,' said Turner. 'Would I be trespassing upon your hospitality if I asked you to telephone him and invite him round here now?'

'Delighted!'

Lionel Mossbank, who had evidently been expecting the summons, arrived within twenty minutes. He proved to be a young man, in the late twenties or early thirties. He was strikingly handsome, wore his clothes well, walked well and was possessed of a very pleasing speaking voice. There was about his face a quality which can only be described as spiritual. It was apparent to Jeremy within five minutes that Mossbank was conscious of all these things himself.

'I've been telling Mr. Dowbiggin,' said Turner, 'that you have joined our Movement. Mr. Dowbiggin would like to hear your ideas as to how we should broaden the scope of our work.'

'Just tell people about it, that's all,' said Mossbank dreamily. 'I'd like to lecture to people about it,' he said more brightly. 'I'm sure I could influence people. I nearly got into Parliament, you know. At one of my meetings there were three thousand people. You could have heard a pin drop.'

'How was it you couldn't get in?' asked Jeremy.

'It was the Labour candidate, I think,' said Mossbank vaguely. 'They told me afterwards that he bribed somebody, or somebody bribed him. I forget which. He was an unpleasant person.'

'I'm delighted to have met you, Mr. Mossbank,' said Jeremy, almost throwing the man out. 'Will you have lunch with me to-morrow—and Mr. Turner, of course? Anywhere in particular you'd like to go to?'

'I should love to go to Simpson's,' said Mossbank eagerly. 'I just adore the saddle of mutton there. When I was Lord Rustington's private secretary I used to lunch there every day.'

'Excellent!' said Jeremy, helping him on with his coat.

Mossbank did not seem conscious of the fact that he was being hustled out of the flat. He said good-night dreamily and left.

'Am I to understand that Lionel Mossbank isn't satisfactory to you?' asked Turner when the door had closed.

'He's perfect!' exclaimed Jeremy. 'Provided he really can speak well in public and hasn't at some time or another blotted his copybook too badly, I can turn him into a Messiah for you. I assume, of course, that you have ways of making him do as he's told . . .'

Turner glanced up quickly before replying.

'Yes, I think I may say that Lionel Mossbank will be, shall we say, amenable to discipline. He hasn't many original ideas, I am afraid. . . .'

'So much the better!' said Jeremy. 'I have clients with what they call original ideas, and I don't want any more. I'd like to hear him speak—somewhere where he doesn't know I am in the audience. I'll give him all the original ideas he can use. Now, as you may have noticed, Mr. Turner, I go in for plain speaking. What have you got on our Lionel?'

'I don't quite follow,' said Turner thoughtfully.

'You say the man's amenable to discipline. What kind of discipline? What reason have you for believing that when it comes to the point he will do as he's told to do?'

'I have been able to be of some small assistance to him in the—er—financial sense, Mr. Dowbiggin.'

'Money, eh? Then keep him short. Better still, let me be paymaster. The dog always sits up and begs best for the person who usually gives him the lump of sugar. Excuse me, I want to put in a telephone call. . . . That you, Roddie? Listen. Be a good fellow and slip down to Fleet Street for me. I want you to hunt through a newspaper morgue for me and let me have everything they've got about Lionel Mossbank. Remember him? He was the bloke that got beaten in a by-election somewhere. Dig down deep for the dirt—if any. Thanks Roddie!'

'You are a very practical man, Mr. Dowbiggin,' said Turner beaming. 'I admire the man of action. There are times when I feel myself to be very ineffective—a poor tool for such a noble work.'

'I'm practical enough for the two of us,' said Jeremy shortly. 'So long as you don't forget how to sign cheques —some of them will be big ones, too—I'll get to work on Lionel and before I'm done with him I'll have a million suckers eating out of his hand for you. Provided, as I said, he hasn't some skeleton in the cupboard, a pale, neutral creature like Mossbank is the perfect raw material. There'll be no fundamental change in the man, of course, but he will exist as an ideal in the minds of the multitude. It's what they will think he is, rather than what he really is, that will count. I've always wanted a job like this—

with virgin soil to work on. I have theories about this sort of thing. . . .'

'Don't you think, Mr. Dowbiggin, that before you do anything else you should study a little more the under-lying principles of the Christian Movement. It is the Movement, not the man, that I am seeking to publicise.'

'I know enough for my purpose, thanks. When I have done with Lionel he will be enshrined in a million hearts as a saintly, unselfish, sincere man who seeks only the betterment of mankind. People—the mass of people—will accept the man. The ideas he expounds are really secondary. Once he has been accepted by the mass his ideas—or what the mass will regard as his ideas—will be accepted automatically. People—ordinary human beings —come under the spell of a personality, not of an idea. There are too many ideas already, most of them bad. Some of the popular film stars have such a personal following that the mere fact of them using some face cream, eating oranges or drinking champagne out of teacups, makes millions of people imitate them. If Steve Donoghue—he is a well-known jockey—if Steve Donoghue at the height of his popularity had burst into print advocating birth control you'd have had to hunt for the next generation.

'Take our Prince of Wales as an example of what cleverly directed ballyhoo can do. He is a Hero and a Prince Charming to countless millions of people all over the world—people who have never seen him, are never likely to see him and who know absolutely nothing what-ever about his private life, his likes and dislikes or his true character. Mind you, I don't say that if they knew all these things they would like and admire him any the less. The fact remains, however, that they know nothing except what gushing newspaper reporters tell them. He is seen on the screen golfing, kicking off at a football match and riding losers in races. For all they know to the contrary he may loathe football, golf and racing. Argentine *vaqueros*, Canadian lumberjacks, Parisian mannequins, miners in Australia, fishermen in Iceland and perhaps even Volga boatmen cheer madly when his face flits across the screen. He is the embodiment of the most successful publicity campaign ever staged to make him live as an ideal in the affections of millions. Any idea advanced by the Prince of Wales to-day—however absurd and impractical it might be—would be accepted avidly and without thought by millions of people in almost every land on earth. Lord Kitchener during the war was just such another ideal—the popular concept of the upright, courageous soldier. When he called for men they besieged the recruiting offices. They were following the lead of a man. They didn't care two hoots in hell for Belgian neutrality. Many of them didn't even know what neutrality was. Kitchener wanted them, so they went, even though well-informed people knew very well that Kitchener's ideas of warfare were out of date. They would have followed him if he had armed them with bows and arrows. . . .'

'Your enthusiasm and your evident knowledge of your subject positively enthral me, Mr. Dowbiggin,' said Turner beaming. 'Let me tell you that I have no more earnest desire than to see you a member of the Christian Movement. Your force, your eloquence are what we need.'

'You can have my force and my eloquence, Mr. Turner,' said Jeremy coldly, 'but my job is to put the bait on the hook—not to swallow it, thanks. I knew an advertising man once who thought it was his duty to use all the things he advertised. We gave him a wonderful funeral, poor chap. This is business, Mr. Turner. You want a job done and you've come to me as an expert. I'll do the job and I'll do it better than any man in the Kingdom, but between you and me there must be the semblance at least of frankness. Think of me as a potter, if you like. You give me the shapeless mass of clay—Lionel Mossbank—and you tell me what you want it made into. You want a twentieth-century model, streamlined Messiah. Right! He's yours, but don't expect me to do anything except sit back and admire my own handiwork. . . .'

*   *   *   *   *

Lionel Mossbank was on the verge of tears. Nobody had ever spoken to him in the way this man Dowbiggin was speaking.

'From now onwards, Mossbank, you've got to do as your told to do,' Jeremy was saying. 'You're going to be a great public figure, which means that a lot of people will think you great. You and I will know differently, of course. This means that you are going to have no private life, or rather that you will have no intimates. The body-guard I'm going to provide for you will be instructed to keep everyone at bay. On the public platform, Mossbank, you're superb, but in five minutes conversation face-to-face a blind man could see that you are a brainless twerp. Do you know how emperors have always kept their thrones, Mossbank?'

'No, Mr. Dowbiggin,' was the tremulous reply.

'Then I'll tell you. Emperors have always surrounded themselves with an aura of mystery. Emperors have never been known to have colds in the head, water on the knee or constipation. They are above such frailties, or so their loyal subjects have always believed. So far as their subjects are concerned, emperors only have one illness and that is the last one. Actually, of course, emperors have probably been very ordinary creatures like you, Mossbank, and like you they have had excellent advisers who have stood between them and the common herd, so that the common herd never found out how very ordinary they were—the emperors, I mean. I'm your adviser now,

Mossbank, which means that while you are visible you must do at all times exactly what I tell you to do. In the privacy of your own rooms you may do what you please.

'The first thing you must do is to learn to hold your head a little higher. When you speak in public I am going to have a spotlight on you from above. To get the full effect you must hold your head so that your face is not thrown into dark shadow. With face turned upward to the light you will look more spiritual. Nobody would believe you capable of eating what you have just eaten. A three pound sole is enough for most people for a day, but two helpings of the saddle of mutton on top of it—Simpson's helpings too—is excessive. Most people would agree with me and, what is more important, nobody known to consume food on such a scale could possibly maintain a reputation for spirituality. Let me tell you what Lionel Mossbank has to eat. For breakfast he eats a little fruit and a glass of milk. For lunch he eats a salad with some cheese and another glass of milk and in the evenings a little vegetable broth and perhaps a small piece of fish. . . .'

Lionel Mossbank groaned. The look of horror on his face was more eloquent than words.

'Which reminds me,' Jeremy went on remorselessly, 'that you're a strict vegetarian. You believe that it is not consonant with the dignity of God's four-footed animals that they should be slaughtered for man's delight. You don't believe me? You'll read it in print before long. Talking about slaughter reminds me that you have an appointment with a surgeon this afternoon. I want to see if he can give your face a more interesting appearance. You're goodlooking already in a nambypamby sort of way, but you don't look like a man. These plastic surgeons are wonderful . . .'

'Do you mind passing me the cheese,' said Mossbank,

who had been eyeing a superb blue Cheshire for some while.

'I think,' said Jeremy, turning to Turner, 'that while we're about it we may as well have him wormed, don't you?'

'Mr. Dowbiggin does love his little joke, Lionel, doesn't he?' observed Turner uncomfortably. 'But you mustn't mind that. He is a genius, you know. I will lend you my set of his wonderful Walk-with-the-gods advertisements which were prepared for the Sigismund Pulitzer course. You should read them. They are an inspiration to any man. How is Dr. Juniper Berry, by the way?'

'I visited him last week in a nursing home. He will not stick to his own diets. He's very sick, poor chap. He ate an infected pork chop after drinking a few gins and tonics. He calls it botulism, but I think there's a certain amount of bottleism too. His new book has gone off with a bang. Twenty thousand copies subscribed, and reprinted within forty-eight hours of publication. I gave him the idea. The book provides a diet for rheumatic subjects. People with rheumatism, you see, are tired of going to doctors and getting no benefit. I believe there are over a million persons with rheumatism in the country. He's bound to sell a copy to ten per cent of them. It won't cure them, of course, but it will prevent them from doing the things that aggravate rheumatism and he'll follow it up with another book on how to prevent rheumatism.' . . .

There was something about Ignatius Turner which impelled Jeremy to be flippant. He knew that under the man's unctuous mask there was a cold cynicism which matched his own, but while Turner maintained his sanctimonious exterior it was impossible for them to associate upon a we're-just-a-couple-of-crooks basis. It would, therefore, be difficult for Turner to propose really dirty work in plain language.

Nevertheless, Jeremy tackled this new task with zest.

With his private affairs in such a muddled state he was glad to be busy. Some men took refuge in drink, golf, venery or fishing. Jeremy was accomplished in none of these things. Work was his only refuge.

It had been a pet theory of Jeremy's for many years that there was little or no relationship between the public and private lives of great men. A man's private life was something which existed as a fact, while his public life existed merely in the imagination of the public. It was a conception. For all the world knew to the contrary, Gandhi loathed goats, which did not alter the fact that in public Gandhi and his goat were inseparables, although very likely the goat was just 'an act' used to distract public attention from something else. It is a known fact that men and women who do not caricature well very rarely rise to any eminence in the public esteem, which is another way of saying that a person does not become a public figure until a great number of people has formed a mental picture of him, quite regardless of whether that picture is an accurate one or not.

Let a reporter with an overdeveloped sense of humour write a story about some purely fictitious person who, shall we say, boils his mother-in-law in oil. Three million people read the story at breakfast, another three million before lunch. By the evening not less than ten million people will be discussing the horror, having formed mind-pictures of the method of procedure. Although this man never existed at all, and therefore never boiled his mother-in-law in oil, he will continue to be a public character for years, because not one in ten will trouble to read the denial which is printed in the following issue of the newspaper, or having read it, will permit the denial to wipe the picture off the slate of the mind.

People—the great mass of them—love their little illusions. Who should know that better than Jeremy Dowbiggin?

Had he not been the instrument which had enabled millions of people to cure themselves of ailments from which they had never suffered? Had he not persuaded a vast army of whisky-drinkers that a magic label had imbued a very common spirit with remarkable properties?

Then what was the difficulty in taking this poor husk of a man—Lionel Mossbank—and building around him for the benefit of the masses an aura of sanctity? Greater miracles than this were performed many times yearly in Hollywood, where the arts of the publicity departments transformed photogenic morons into supermen, effeminate lounge lizards into red-blooded he-men, and man-eating nymphomaniacs into simpering virgins. There was nothing—nothing that the power of suggestion could not accomplish. People believed what they wanted to believe, especially about their heroes and their heroines, quite regardless of facts. Much human happiness was derived from phantasies. Human pleasures were largely vicarious, which explained why an industry timidly begun in Hollywood counted its revenues in hundreds of millions. It explained why parents read fairy stories to their children. For most of the people in the world life consisted of toil, food, sleep and illusions, and the most precious of them all were the illusions. Let them believe that their kings were kingly, their great men truly great and their professional holy men holy; that what was denied to them in this life would be granted to them a thousandfold in the next.

Jeremy had once visited Runcorn, where foul vapours seemed to have blasted all green things from the earth and where people lived and died in a man-made inferno. He remembered wondering how these people, who had erected many churches, could believe that any hereafter could be worse than what they were already enduring. They retained their hold on life, he decided, only because they believed and hoped that the hereafter would be that much better, and it was this illusion of a golden hereafter which made life worth living. Certain it was that those who had dwelled in Runcorn could have no fear of hell.

Lionel Mossbank's wonderful vocal chords, directed intelligently, would transform this poor thing into a leader whom the masses would revere. When the picture of the new Lionel Mossbank was firmly implanted into the minds of enough people, they would not only take him to their hearts, but accept him with acclaim as a new Moses who would lead them out of the Wilderness of reality into the Promised Land compounded of their own dreams and longings. As they accepted Lionel Mossbank, so too would they accept the ideas he propounded. . . .

The England of the 1930's was a befuddled land. So many idols had been shattered and there had been nothing to replace them. It was the propagandist's paradise. Most of the forty odd millions of people could read and write. Therefore, they thought themselves educated. Human knowledge was growing at a greater rate than the capacity of anyone to absorb it, so people imbibed their knowledge in tabloid form. It was mental indigestion on the grand scale.

There were huge surpluses of goods—almost everywhere, so slogans were coined to whip people into buying and consuming more of everything. 'Eat More Fruit!' screamed the greengrocer's window. 'Drink More Beer!' exhorted posters on van sides. 'Eat More Bread!' said huge press advertisements to people whose digestions were already upset by eating the devitalised pap sold to them. 'Drink More Milk!' was the ironical plea to mothers who could not afford it. That there wasn't a 'Play More Grand Pianos!' campaign is merely evidence that there was not a surplus of grand pianos.

It did not occur to people that the benefit from obeying

an advertised command accrued to those who inspired and paid for the advertisements rather than to the masses who read them. Nor did it occur to people that in the days when such things as vitamins were secrets in the womb of time, their ancestors managed to live exceedingly well without them.

People would read in their newspapers that such and such a comet was approaching the earth at so many million miles per hour, but that the chances of it striking the earth were so many quadrillions to one against, so the danger could be ruled out. But it did not stop people from throwing their money into football pools and exotic sweepstakes, where the odds against them were also astronomical.

Photogenic nincompoops from Hollywood were given receptions which rivalled that given to conquering Cæsar returned from the wars, while the truly great men of the age died as they had lived, unknown and unsung. For every tear shed on the anniversary of Edith Cavell's murder, a small river of tears was shed to commemorate the death of an Italian waiter, Rudolph Valentino, by nit-witted women who had never seen him in the flesh and to whom it had never occurred that their over-publicised hero probably reeked of garlic.

Maltreating innocent babies, hounding people to their deaths by blackmail, and the rape of young girls, all ranked in the eyes of the law—and still do—as lesser offences than counterfeiting, forgery and other offences against property, which is only understandable when it is remembered that the laws of the land were made by those who owned property of various kinds with the idea that nobody else should share it. But it did not prevent England being known as a Christian democracy. It was in the 1930's that Honest Stanley Baldwin was elevated to the House of Lords; but Ramsay Macdonald, who had—however unwittingly—done almost as much harm to British prestige, was allowed to die plain Mr. Macdonald.

It was in the 1930's that, in an Empire which has always boasted of religious freedom, the sectarian religious feelings of a minority were allowed to play a large part in removing the King-Emperor from his throne. Even the fact that the exchange has proved a very happy one cannot have prevented many millions from asking themselves why the Moderator of the Presbyterian Church, the heads of the other Christian denominations, the Chief Rabbi, the Aga Khan and the Grand Mufti of Jerusalem were not also invited to take their part in the proceedings? In the British Empire Christians of any kind are in a minority, while Anglicans are a microscopic minority.

But there was football, dirt-track racing, the dogs, the movies, the Sunday newspaper astrologers, and the perennial circus of Westminster to occupy the minds of the masses, so these questions were not asked very forcibly.

In the light of these things, therefore, it is not so hard to understand that Lionel Mossbank was swallowed by a world which had long since ceased to marvel at sword swallowers. In a very ugly world his frail figure, spiritual face and modest demeanour carved a place for him in the seats of the mighty. The cadences of his lovely voice were vastly more important to his audiences than the thoughts to which they gave words. It didn't matter much what he said; it was the way he said it which won for him an army of followers.

Who cares whether Clark Gable is an authority on bimetallism?

Chapter Fourteen

A GREAT MANY PEOPLE jumped to the not unreasonable conclusion that Lionel Mossbank, having failed to get into

Parliament by the usual methods, was trying to do so by climbing aboard the religious bandwaggon. It had been done before.

The series of lectures opened in London at the Empire Hall to some four thousand persons, or so near capacity that the few vacant seats were not noticeable.

Lionel Mossbank was introduced by the Rev. Charles Courthope-Lumley, formerly Vicar of St Bartelmy's, Knightsbridge, who had horrified his own wealthy and fashionable congregation beyond all forgiveness for having preached a sermon which had for its text: 'Sell all that thou hast and give to the poor.'

It is hardly necessary to add that the reverend gentleman was a very tactless person and did not last long in the parish.

As one of his churchwardens said afterwards: 'The masses have enough fantastic ideas already without having more put into their heads—from the pulpit of all places.'

'But you don't surely deny that those were Our Lord's words?' said Courthope-Lumley. 'Or that those words expressed his wishes?'

'My dear chap,' replied the churchwarden, 'it isn't for me to admit or deny such things, but since you raise the subject I am strongly of the opinion that a too literal interpretation of the Bible—Old or New Testament—can cause a great deal of trouble and misunderstanding. If it comes to that, we pay you a pretty handsome sum every year. Do you give that to the poor?'

'Most certainly I do,' was the astounding reply, 'all except a very small amount which I require for food and shelter.'

'Good God!' exclaimed the horror-struck church-warden. 'You're nothing more than an agitator. Don't you believe, as laid down in the Prayer Book, that it is enjoined on us to "do our duty in that state of life unto which it has pleased God to call us?" You're simply inviting people to become discontented with their lives . . .'

'Your very apt quotation has nothing to do with Holy Writ,' retorted Courthope-Lumley. 'It is taken, as you say, from the Book of Common Prayer, which might be described as the partnership agreement between Church and State, devised by the over-privileged to keep in subjection the under-privileged.'

The Rev. Charles Courthope-Lumley had forthwith ceased his efforts to preach the doctrines of Jesus Christ in Knightsbridge. Without any intentional cynicism a colleague had advised him that he would be a great deal happier in a poor district in the East End. Courthope-Lumley had taken this advice, but abandoned Holy Orders. His presence as Chairman of Lionel Mossbank's meeting, therefore, was responsible in large measure for the good attendance. Jeremy ensured his presence by a donation of £50 to the East End mission to which Courthope-Lumley was devoting his life and talents.

'I talk to you to-night,' began Lionel Mossbank, 'as a very simple, ordinary man, claiming no divine inspiration, who believes that the Sermon on the Mount is the only rock upon which civilisation can endure. That sermon was one of the shortest ever recorded. In it there are no long and ambiguous words. It contains the essence of Our Lord's mission on earth. If you try sincerely to live by that sermon you are entitled to call yourself a Christian —but upon no other terms.

'In a great library a few weeks ago I counted over three hundred volumes written, or so their authors said, to explain and amplify the teachings of Christ. Do these simple words need explaining? How dare any man presume to amplify them? In this great hall to-night is there one man or woman who will stand up—I promise he or she will not be made an object of ridicule—who will stand up and tell me—tell us all, of an inability to understand one single rule of human conduct as set forth in the Sermon on the Mount?'

Lionel Mossbank paused. A deep hush fell over the hall.

'Smart idea of mine that, don't you think, Janet?' whispered Jeremy. 'I told you nobody would speak.'

'Sh-h-h!'

'In front of each seat in the hall,' continued Mossbank when a full minute of silence had passed, 'is a slip of paper on which the Sermon on the Mount is printed in full. I urge each one of you to take that home to-night and read it. To-night I am not going to try to explain or amplify those simple words. They stand there unchanged and unchallenged as they have stood for nearly two thousand years. Nothing has happened in these nineteen centuries to alter one word. No justification has ever arisen for one iota of change. Many things have happened since those words were uttered. New prophets have arisen. Men have adopted new ways of life. Learning has advanced beyond the wildest dreams of those who heard that sermon delivered. But nothing—nothing I tell you—has happened to date those words. They were applicable when uttered to those who heard them. They are equally applicable to us now.

'Why, one is forced to ask, have we seen through the ages so many men who have sought to modify and pervert the simple words of which I speak? Surely the reason is not far to seek. Christianity, as we know the word, did not gather momentum until several centuries after the death of its founder. When the tyrants and oppressors of that age found that nothing would stop the tidal wave that was sweeping and cleansing the world, they harnessed it to their own base uses. Christian leaders entered into alliance with temporal rulers, not so much to bring

Christian precepts into government, but to use Christianity as a tool of oppression.

'There was nothing new in this. The unholy alliance of the priest and the politician has always been one of the greatest forces in the way of human spiritual progress. . . . If Our Lord were to return to earth to-day I wonder would He find one single Christian sect which teaches its followers to worship God in the way the Son of God himself told men to worship?

'The simple fishermen from the Sea of Galilee, who cast aside their nets to follow Him, were told in words a child of ten could understand to preach the Gospel in poverty and humility. "Go ye forth into the world. . . ." Every man and woman here to-night knows the substance of that injunction if not the entire quotation. Does anyone—can anyone doubt its meaning? Are there to be found in it two meanings? Will anyone stand forth in front of his fellows and tell them that that exhortation can be interpreted as licence for the more than royal magnificence which surrounds the bishops and archbishops of the Christian churches of this age? Not even the genius for hairsplitting shown through the ages by ecclesiastical lawyers can justify this monstrous transgression of the simple, direct exhortation. It is not my purpose to single out one Christian sect from another, but I say that all in varying degree have bowed down to Mammon. The strength of a Christian sect to-day is measured by financial standards and the richness of their material treasure shows up in stark relief the poverty of their spiritual force . . .'

Lionel Mossbank spoke for two hours. Despite the scathing terms he used in his indictment, not one protest came from those in the hall.

In the press leaving the hall Jeremy heard one man say: 'By Jove, that fellow's a spellbinder. He'll have a following of a million within the year.'

'I wonder,' said the speaker's companion thoughtfully. 'It depends on what sort of people are here to-night.'

'I don't follow you.'

'Well, what I wonder is whether he's going to attract in his following people who have a sincere belief in Christian teachings in their original purity, or whether he's merely going to attract those who dislike the churches. There's a tremendous difference, you must realise. . . .'

'Did you hear that?' Jeremy asked Janet. She nodded. 'That fellow has hit the nail on the head. There are thousands of people—like me for example—who don't care a curse about religion, but who like sniping at the churches. Even if the churches were to cleanse their stables, it wouldn't make any difference to me, or to the people I'm talking about. Mossbank is going to attract the anti's round him, but I can't see him ever doing anything constructive. What a speaker, Janet! Did you ever hear anything like him? It sounded as though he believed every word he uttered and yet you and I know that he hasn't an idea in that head of his—not even a bad one. I take my hat off to Turner for finding him.'

'It frightens me, Jeremy. You know I'm not religious, or anything like that, but if Mossbank is going to drive people away from the churches and give them nothing to take their place, he's merely destroying something—bad as it may be. It's somehow like taking away a pair of damaged crutches from a cripple because he might slip with them. But without them he's helpless.'

* * * * *

Jeremy, Turner, Mossbank and the Christian Movement, to say nothing of her own irregular status, worried Janet. She had at bottom a very conventional mind. In one sense she was happy, for she was devoted to Jeremy. They were now living together. Jeremy maintained the old flat

[163]

because the lease still had a few months to run, but he was rarely there. Janet would have been happier if Jeremy had sometimes spoken of Sybilla and his intentions where she was concerned. Whenever she herself raised the subject Jeremy snarled at her. One of these occasions occurred on this evening after Mossbank's first lecture.

'What are you going to do, Jeremy—about her?' Janet asked when they had eaten an omelet and drunk some coffee.

'What can I do?' said Jeremy with a shrug of the shoulders.

'What do you want to do?' asked Janet. 'What you want to do you will do. You always get your own way —in everything.'

'The first move's up to Sybilla. I've heard nothing from her since she left the flat. I don't even know whether she wants a divorce. I can't divorce her. I've nothing on her.'

'But would you if you had, Jeremy?'

'I don't know,' he replied slowly. 'I think I would.'

'Then why don't you have her watched? For all you know to the contrary, all sorts of things may have been going on for years.'

'You haven't the slightest right to say that, Janet,' said Jeremy in a cold hard voice. 'If you want to know whether I intend to get a divorce from Sybilla and marry you, the answer is that I don't know.'

Janet winced, but she had known Jeremy in these moods for too long to be really hurt by what he said. He was always like this when he was turning over any problem in his mind and finding difficulty in reaching a solution. Nobody could help him—that much Janet knew. With every year that had passed she had watched Jeremy stripping himself of illusions. More and more it was to his keen hard brain that he turned for the answer to all his problems. The evening when they had gone up the river together on the spur of the moment was the first impulsive action on his part she had seen for years. Perhaps, Janet argued, if Jeremy were to act more on impulse and less on calculation, he would be happier.

In the office, on Jeremy's insistence, their relationship was as nearly as possible what it had always been. Janet was well content with this for, as she saw only too clearly, to inject personal things into Jeremy's working life would force him to drive her out of the office. She could not stand the thought of some other woman taking her place there, even if Jeremy's evenings were hers.

There was something rather laughable, if it had not also been a little tragic, in the way Janet transformed herself in the mornings into a prim and rather staid secretary and reversed the procedure in the evenings.

Long ago Janet had once asked Jeremy why, with his good brain and personality, he was content with putting them to such shabby uses.

'You can make shoddy, worthless, cheap things and ideas appear to people as though they were real, fine and beautiful,' she said. 'Wouldn't it give you more satisfaction to devote yourself to things that weren't just shams?'

'Of course it would,' Jeremy had snapped, 'but people with fine, worth-while ideas and honestly made things don't need advertising men to help them. Did Marconi have to hire an advertising agent to make the world see the possibilities of his invention? Do Savile Row tailors spend money on buying advertising space? Have you ever seen an advertisement for Fortnum & Mason's food departments, for rare vintage ports, for the finest hand-made shoes, or superbly made chronometers? Of course not. And you never will. The people who have the best for sale—goods or ideas—don't need any help selling them. Good things really good things—can only be produced in limited quantities, just as there are only very limited numbers of people with the discrimination to recognise goodness when they see it. The rest of the goods are like the people who buy them—cheap imitations of the best.'

'But some people haven't the money to buy the best, Jeremy,' Janet had countered timidly.

'How much do you spend on a pair of shoes?' Jeremy asked.

'Up to about twenty-five shillings. . . .'

'Well, I pay five guineas a pair for mine, and I'm prepared to bet you a month's salary that you spend more on shoes each year than I do. I pay fifteen guineas a suit for my clothes, but you spend more on clothes than I do.'

'Meaning, I suppose,' Janet had replied, with a woman's gift for reading something personal into an impersonal remark, 'that I'm cheap and nasty.'

'Meaning,' retorted Jeremy, 'that you, like millions of others, haven't yet learned the lesson that the cheap things are the most expensive. If an overcoat won't keep you warm, no matter how cheaply you may have bought it, it is still expensive—at any price at all.'

Janet had never been able to find fault with Jeremy's logic, but deep inside her she knew with an unerring certainty that Jeremy would have been much happier always if he had not allowed cold logic to rule his life.

Janet was able, at least in part, to forget some of her heart-burnings in the work involved by the launching of Lionel Mossbank.

Ignatius Turner wrote most of the lectures in draft, submitted them to Jeremy, and both of them worked to put them into shape. The first few lectures were entirely religious in character, and then a series was prepared entitled: 'Christianity Seven Days a Week.' These lectures propounded the remarkable idea that Christianity was not just for Sundays. The silver tongue of Lionel Mossbank was heard declaiming throughout the land that Christianity was not merely a theoretically perfect set of ideas, but a basis for everyday life. The good Christian, Mossbank declared, must make of his office, workshop, foundry and field a temple in which industry, honesty of purpose and the betterment of mankind were deemed of more importance than the making of high profits or the receiving of high wages. To work upon any other basis was to prostitute God-given talents and was the utter negation of Christ's teachings.

Jeremy was not in the smallest degree religious, but it appalled him sometimes to hear fine and noble sentiments coming from the mouth of such a poor creature as Mossbank.

After the lectures Jeremy had seen on the faces of some of those who listened a seraphic, adoring look. The body-guard of four ex-policemen often had difficulty forcing a passage through the throng because of the hundreds who sought merely to touch Mossbank before he went from among them. Even Jeremy, who knew the truth, found it almost impossible to realise that Lionel Mossbank did not care a rap for the beautiful thoughts which he illumined with his beautiful voice, and was more concerned with what he was going to have for supper than with the spiritual welfare of the thousands who flocked to hear him.

Jeremy and Roddie Macdonald preceded Mossbank wherever he went, finding in every town and city influential people prepared to sit on the platform in support of Mossbank. The lectures were widely advertised everywhere, in the press, on the hoardings and outside the houses of those who lent their support. In the West of England and the Midlands there was a tendency on the part of Nonconformist clergy to be hostile. In one

Midland town Mossbank could not finish his lecture because of interruptions.

'It won't do to antagonise the churches—just yet,' counselled Jeremy. 'We must tone down the references to the failure of the churches. We want the support of the churches to begin with. When the clergy have once declared themselves for Mossbank it won't be so easy for them to withdraw.'

Ignatius Turner nodded agreement and Mossbank was given lectures which flattered the clergy as individuals, while still pointing to the weaknesses of the organised churches.

'After all,' Jeremy argued, 'if Mossbank is never allowed to depart from his one main contention—that the world needs the Sermon on the Mount unembroidered—it is going to be very hard for any parson to find fault with him.'

Lionel Mossbank's rise to fame was steady, without being sensational.

'Say your little piece on the platform,' Jeremy insisted, 'and after that keep out of sight—be inaccessible. You must appear remote and above human weaknesses. The more people you meet face to face, the less your influence. Remember that emperors retained their thrones because of the aura of mystery around them. An emperor with a pain in the belly or a cold in the head would have become an object of ridicule. We're not going to say that you don't eat, but we're going to imply that you don't by never allowing people to see you eating. They'll think of you as purely spiritual. . . .'

This conversation took place in a hotel suite in Birmingham after one of the lectures.

'Three thousand people went home to-night with a mind picture of you clearly delineated,' Jeremy continued. 'Under the spotlight you looked spiritual, aloof, ethereal.

[168]

Do you follow? Every word you uttered heightened that impression. You rebuked that heckler mildly, gently, sorrowfully. Can't you see now that that way is much more in keeping with the picture people have of you? It would have been much easier, I know, to have said something smart and cutting, but as it was the people were with you, merely because they were against a heckler who tried to embarrass such a saintly man as they think you are. Get me?'

Lionel Mossbank, his mouth full of steak and onions, mumbled assent.

'But,' said Jeremy remorselessly, 'what do you think those same people would have said if they could have watched you eat that grilled sole and then wolf an underdone steak big enough for two navvies? Does that bottle of burgundy look spiritual and saintly? In future we're going to arrange for a tray to be sent in to the room where you meditate before the lectures. There will be on it an apple, a glass of milk and two or three rusks. I'll eat the apple or one of your body-guard will if I'm not there. You can pocket the rusks, leaving half of one on the plate, and pour half the milk down the lavatory. Then the people who come into the room after the lecture is over and you have gone will say: "How modestly and frugally this saintly man lives!"

'Get this into your head for all time, that it isn't what you are that's going to make you famous, but what people think you are. All the time you are visible to the naked eye you've got to be in character. . . .'

'You speak as though I were not sincere,' said Mossbank gently.

'Good God!' exclaimed Jeremy when he saw Ignatius Turner a moment or two later. 'The bloody man has forgotten already that he gets his lectures written for him. He's just been talking to me about sincerity. . . .'

Ignatius Turner pursed his lips and shook his head sadly.

'Listen, Turner,' said Jeremy fiercely, 'don't waste time turning your synthetic sanctity on me. I'm doing a job of work as well as I know how to do one. You're paying me for it. My job is to make the public believe that that sanctimonious little squirt Mossbank is a saint. I'll make a million people believe he has a halo round his head before I'm through with him, but unless you want to drive me into a lunatic asylum don't try to sell me ideas like that.'

Jeremy could have bitten his tongue out after this outburst, but contact with Mossbank irritated him beyond endurance. The man was living the part for which he had been cast.

But it was evidently no part of Turner's plan to allow this outburst to endanger the relationship between him and Jeremy. Turner smiled his benign smile.

'I suppose, Mr. Dowbiggin,' he said in mild tones, 'when you were a small boy and your father took you to see a conjuror you always knew how the tricks were done, or if you didn't, you found out afterwards?'

'As a matter of fact you're right,' said Jeremy.

'Then hasn't it since occurred to you that the little boys and girls who allowed themselves to be deceived derived much more pleasure from the entertainment than you did?'

'Perhaps they did,' replied Jeremy, 'but if I have to derive pleasure from self-deception I don't want pleasure. I happen to think there's a lot of amusement to be obtained from life by merely watching other people being stupid and indulging in self-deception. . . .' And then Jeremy became a little boy again for a few seconds: 'You don't fool me a bit, you know, Turner!' he said with a grin. 'I don't pretend to know what your little game is, but I do know that you're not the innocent mug I once thought you were—for a very little while.'

'It is one of the doubtful privileges of the gods that they cannot be deceived, Dowbiggin,' said Turner, dropping the 'Mr.' for the first time since Jeremy and he had known each other. 'Be careful that you don't become a god. There's something I like very much about you, Dowbiggin. It is that you will not permit yourself the smallest atom of hypocrisy. You would be genuinely horrified if someone were to attribute to you a completely selfless motive for anything, wouldn't you? Like you, I believe, you see, that hypocrisy is a very ugly thing, but I do not think I could go on living unless I cherished a few of my little illusions. You will say that it is an illusion I have about you. I happen to believe that two things will cause you to remain my colleague, adviser and collaborator for a long while. One is your insatiable curiosity about me and my works, and the other is the extraordinary form which honesty takes in your make-up. It would allow you, for example, to sell me shares which you knew to be completely worthless, but it won't allow you to accept my money for doing a specific job and then not do that job, or botch it.'

'My honesty, as you call it, Turner, is merely conceit. I should hate to have a shoddy job of work labelled with my name. It so happens that I am enjoying this job, even if I don't quite know where it is leading me. I've always had a theory, you see, that deception on a colossal scale is easier than a number of little deceptions. I suppose really it would be more satisfying to create an entirely new religion—I've thought of doing that more than once —but you are doing the next best thing, in trying to re-build an old one out of its own ruins. Any architect would tell you that it's easier to build a new house than restore an old one.'

'We shall get along well together, Dowbiggin,' said Turner with a beatific smile. 'Our little chat has cleared the air. Now we both understand one another, which is a fine thing.'

'I wish I understood you as well as I pretend to, nevertheless,' said Jeremy to himself.

Chapter Fifteen

RAIN BEAT AGAINST the upper deck windows of the omnibus, which was parked on a slight eminence, commanding a view of thousands of streaming umbrellas, glistening in the half light of evening. The spotlights had just been turned on to the figure of Lionel Mossbank, who had mounted a raised platform in the centre of the assembled multitude. High above the platform, so that it did not interfere with the spotlights, was an awning which kept the platform dry. Lionel Mossbank spoke to a group of men standing beside the platform, and in a few seconds it became apparent to everyone in sight what he had said. The awning was rolled back.

'If they can stand in the rain to hear me, I can stand in the rain to speak to them.'

The murmur which went through the crowd—a murmur of appreciation—was almost as though they had heard the words.

'I told you that would fetch them,' said Jeremy to nobody in particular, as the spotlight picked out Mossbank's slight figure, his pale face shining in the rain and sodden clothes clinging to him. He waved aside the raincoat which was proferred to him.

Ignatius Turner nodded approvingly.

'The poor man will catch pneumonia,' said Janet.

'Pneumonia nothing!' snorted Jeremy. 'He's wearing a complete suit of oiled silk underneath that. When it looked like rain this morning I bought it for him. Look at them!

[172]

He hasn't spoken a word yet. My God! If that fellow only had brains there's no limit to what he could have done!'

Janet shivered a little, although it was a warm June evening.

'It seems terrible to me, Jeremy—rather frightening—to see the way they worship him. I wish you'd never had anything to do with it. Deep down inside me I know that it's wrong to fill people's heads with false ideas. . . .'

'But their heads aren't being filled with false ideas,' snapped Jeremy. 'Lionel Mossbank is teaching Christianity in the nearest to its pure original form that this or any recent generation has heard. What you mean is that you don't like hearing beautiful sentiments expressed by a man whom you know to be anything but a paragon himself. Truth is truth, you know, regardless of who utters it. The square root of sixty-four is eight, whether this conclusion is reached by a professor of mathematics or the chorus at the Hippodrome. Not even a twerp like Mossbank can kill the truth and beauty of the teachings he expounds. Let them think him a saint! What does it matter? The unkindest thing of all would be to let them know the truth about him. I think that would be a crime. . . .'

The massed voices, singing a lovely old hymn, died away and Mossbank's melodious voice became audible, amplified by a chain of loudspeakers suspended from trees and temporary posts. The river at foot of the meadows was jammed with hundreds of pleasure boats as far as the eye could reach. Loudspeakers on the banks carried his voice across the stream, while on the roadway, cars and lorries were halted and the police vainly tried to keep the traffic moving.

From the sea of umbrellas came no sound. All eyes were fixed patiently on the speaker, who paused occasionally to wipe from his eyes the water which streamed down his face.

Lionel Mossbank was speaking on 'The Failure of Democracy.' There was now no hall in the country which could begin to accommodate the thousands who flocked to hear him. Many of those present, prompted by a section of the press, believed that Mossbank was in this, his last lecture, going to declare himself a fascist.

Instead, Mossbank delivered the most violent attack upon fascism ever heard in England. The failure of democracy, he contended, was not because of any inherent weakness in democracy but because of the apathy of people who took freedom for granted. What was the use of sending elected representatives to Westminster and then allowing them to serve privileged interests? The same apathy which had allowed Christians to stand by while their churches became great business institutions was making democrats stand by idly while a handful of powerful men ruled the country from behind the scenes, pulling the strings of government to suit themselves.

There was nothing particularly new or startling in what Mossbank said. It was the way he said it which held his audience.

Jeremy sat dumbfounded. Perhaps of all the thousands of people, drawn from all walks of life, who listened to the magic of Lionel Mossbank, Jeremy, who had made the man, created him almost from nothing, was the most bewildered. To one so cocksure as Jeremy the state of bewilderment is an unenviable one. It was like a rising tide which was encircling and destroying the sand castle of his self-confidence.

*　　　*　　　*　　　*　　　*

The shadowing of Ignatius Turner was almost fruitless. It proved merely that the man was an incurable gambler. He was a frequent visitor at the private-house gambling parties which had sprung up all over London. The meeting between Turner and Sybilla had proved to be entirely accidental. They never saw each other again. Sybilla, too, Jeremy was learning, loved gambling. In the conversation Roddie Macdonald and Jeremy had, which revealed that Sybilla and Turner had met, Roddie had not disclosed the fact that he had arranged for a continual watch on Sybilla. Nor had Jeremy discussed with Roddie the breach between himself and Sybilla.

Uncle George had returned from New York with virtually nothing which shed light upon the true intentions of Turner. The legal firm which paid out money on behalf of Paul Lefroy and, therefore, presumably Ignatius Turner, defied all efforts at investigation. Mercutier, Flashman & Gulbrandsen were highly reputable lawyers who acted for a number of prominent corporations and persons, and were unlikely to be mixed up in anything shady. Turner's frequent calls upon brokers and financial houses were merely another aspect of his love for gambling. He speculated in stocks and shares, usually with success; bet on horses extensively, and was prepared to lose sleep playing roulette and chemin-de-fer. The only real crumb of information which Uncle George brought back with him was the recollection of when and where he had met Ignatius Turner.

'He used to be known on Broadway as "Iggy the Priest",' said Uncle George. 'He hasn't been seen in New York for years, but a lot of the boys still remember him. He was always a bit of a mystery. Nobody knows anything definite about him, but he is suspected of having been mixed up in a psycho-analysis-blackmail racket. I had a look at his record at police headquarters. Ignatius Turner is his real name. He's never been arrested, but on several occasions stool pigeons have tipped off the police. Enquiries never revealed anything against him. I met him aboard ship going to Havana for a gamble. He and

I and two or three others played poker going out—big poker too, but as far as I can remember there was no suspicion that he played anything but a straight game.'

This was enough to make it extremely unlikely that Turner was what he pretended to be, but it was a long way from anything tangible. His interest in psychoanalysis was confirmed by his calls on several of the gentry in London who practised that peculiar profession, but the men on whom he had called were without exception men of good repute against whom nothing was known or suspected.

'Take my advice and stop worrying, my boy,' said Uncle George. 'Here's how I've worked it all out. Turner knows that you suspect he's a crook, doesn't he?'

'I've as good as told him so,' replied Jeremy.

'Very well. He knows, therefore, that if he pulls anything very raw under your nose you'll tip off the police. He's suspected and knows he's suspected. He probably knows, too, that you've been fishing around making enquiries about him. You can't keep that sort of thing quiet. He probably recognised me. If he did he must have jumped to the conclusion that I'd tell you anything I knew. Unless he thinks that you are prepared to go in for unlimited crookedness with him—and I don't think he does think that—he must see as clearly as you and I can that he's got to keep his nose clean. I agree with you that the fellow's a crook, or has been one, but human nature is a funny thing: don't entirely dismiss the possibility that the man may have "got" religion, or that— and this is more probable—that the people behind him, whoever they are, have got it. Do you remember Charlie McGinnis? He used to be on Rum Row when we were there. Charlie shot two prohibition enforcement officers like dogs when he was boarded in a fog. Charlie was tough —really tough. But it didn't alter the fact that a few years

[176]

later he turned religious. He faded from sight. Someone told me he'd been seen in a little town in the Middle West where he was one of the pillars of the church. Turner's getting on in years and maybe he's getting funny ideas.'

'You're probably talking sense, Uncle George,' Jeremy had replied, 'but I'm worried. This thing has got big. It's going to be bigger. I just can't see where it's leading. . . .'

Then, during the months after Uncle George's return to England, Lionel Mossbank had gone from triumph to triumph, culminating in this huge mass gathering in the rain beside the Thames. It was obvious that, provided Lionel Mossbank did nothing stupid or out of character, his following would swell to gigantic proportions. There were already some forty odd stenographers employed to deal with his mail. They only replied to letters which called for reply. Letters, postcards and telegrams arrived by the thousands weekly. Some were congratulatory. Most were asking for help and guidance in spiritual matters, but a large number wrote to point out corruption, moral decadence in highly placed persons and the abuses which had crept into the public life of the country.

Although Mossbank had frequently declared that he did not want people to send him money—'It is your hearts I want—not your money'—hundreds did so. It was always punctiliously returned to those who sent addresses, while money which arrived anonymously was handed over to well-known and established charities. On Jeremy's insistence and Turner's eager agreement, a chartered accountant dealt with all these sums of money.

Jeremy looked across the omnibus to where Turner was sitting, his face bland and expressionless, looking thoughtfully out on to the sea of dripping umbrellas. Mossbank was nearing the end. He had spoken for nearly ninety minutes.

'Well, there's your Messiah for you, Turner,' said Jeremy, breaking a long silence in the omnibus. 'I once used to think there were only two things that would make an English crowd stand out in the rain, but I was wrong. If Mossbank told them now to shut their umbrellas and turn cartwheels and handsprings they'd do it.'

'You are right, Dowbiggin,' said Turner solemnly, 'but there are times when I wish you would not be flippant. How true it is that men will follow a man but never an idea. There is almost nothing that Lionel Mossbank could not do with that crowd at this minute, and yet you and I know, Dowbiggin, that the power which endowed him with his glorious gift of oratory forgot to endow him with brains. The potentialities for good or evil in that man are beyond calculation. The great brains of the world, the scientists, engineers and chemists, wield a power that is childish in comparison with his. In the last hour I have tried to detach myself from my knowledge of the man. I sat here listening, drinking in every word. Although I wrote most of them they came strangely to my ears, transformed and beautified beyond all recognition. What a sublime gift!'

Jeremy looked narrowly at Turner, realising that for once the man was not acting a part. He had fallen under the spell of his own words which came back to him through the vocal chords of another. Not even the metallic tones of the loudspeakers could kill the beauty of the tones. Turner had not been listening to words so much as music, which had enthralled him.

Lionel Mossbank had finished. The spotlights on the platform went out. Hanging lights beside the loudspeakers were turned on, to enable part of the crowd to get back to the cars parked half a mile away, while the majority went on foot in the direction of railway stations and bus routes. Lionel Mossbank disappeared into the crowd.

'And who could guess at this minute what Mossbank is thinking of as he fights his way here through the crush?' asked Jeremy. 'Is he thinking of the souls of those who have stood in the rain for ninety minutes listening to him? Is he wondering whether they'll catch chills or develop pneumonia? Is he thrilled to the marrow by the evening's triumph?'

'He might well be thrilled—and awed,' said Turner.

'He might be,' echoed Jeremy, 'but he isn't. Master Lionel Mossbank at this moment is wondering what we've brought in the picnic hamper.'

Jeremy looked at his watch.

'He'll be here in a moment, Turner. I'll bet you a level fifty quid that within thirty seconds of his arrival here he either opens the picnic basket himself or asks one of the bodyguard to do it for him.'

The bus vibrated as Mossbank and his escort mounted the lower platform and began to climb the stairs.

Jeremy would have lost his bet had it been taken, for Lionel Mossbank was already eating a ham sandwich which he had secreted in his overcoat pocket. His mouth was too full to reply to Turner's congratulations.

When the crowd had thinned out a little Mossbank and his escort went off towards London in one car, leaving Jeremy, Turner and Janet to return in another.

'That's that!' observed Jeremy. 'What next?'

'You've done a wonderful piece of work, Dow-biggin. . . .'

'I know I have,' snapped Jeremy. 'I hand it over to you. It's yours. But what I want to know is what you're going to do with it now you've got it. All he's accomplished so far is that crowds will turn out to listen to him. He's made a million people discontented and dissatisfied with all sorts of things, but he's given them nothing they can get their teeth in. You call it the Christian Movement.

[179]

A movement moves. That's why it's called a movement. But this doesn't move. The people who come to hear him go away thinking he's wonderful. They think a lot of their cherished old institutions are rotten. If this *is* a movement, for God's sake let it move. Give the customers something. Mossbank can't go on lecturing indefinitely. He's got his nucleus. Christian groups are established in every town and city in the country. They meet. They talk. They read the Sermon on the Mount. After this I suppose a few of them will begin badgering their Members of Parliament a bit. But they're not moving. They're surging around slowly in circles. Don't say I didn't warn you, Turner. I understand the masses and I tell you that the whole thing will fall to pieces as quickly as it has grown if you don't give the people something definite— a programme, or something.'

'How long will it take you to start a paper, Dowbiggin? A weekly, shall we say?'

'If it came to a showdown, I'd have one out by to-morrow night, but it ought to have some thought. It all depends on how much money you're prepared to lose. Are you going to give it away or sell it? Is it going to carry advertising? What are we going to call it?'

'I leave those matters to you, Dowbiggin, except that I would like to be consulted regarding the title. It should not be given away, but we do not wish to make a profit from selling it. The ideal would be to break even.'

'All right!' said Jeremy. 'Leave it all to me. Will you be ready to discuss plans by to-morrow night? I'll have everything lined up by then. Unless you want little Lionel to flop we shall have to hurry.'

'Janet,' added Jeremy a moment later. 'Get Roddie on the phone when we get back to town and tell him that the fairy godmother has made him the editor of a new weekly. Tell him, too, that it wants a staff.

No drunks! Humbugs who can write are what we want.'

*   *   *   *   *

In a quiet office just off Whitehall two keen-faced men were discussing the previous evening's mass meeting organised by the Christian Movement.

'You were there yourself, weren't you?' asked the elder of the two.

'Yes, sir! I was within twenty yards of the platform and heard every word clearly. I tell you, sir, you have to hear this fellow Mossbank to realise what a spellbinder he is. The local police say that there were between twelve and fifteen thousand people listening to him. To get them back to London special trains had to be run from Staines and Windsor. At two o'clock this morning there were still some hundreds stranded. I never saw a more orderly crowd in my life. They hung on every word he uttered. I had a stenographer there and the notes are being transcribed now, sir, but you may take my word for it that nothing was said to which we could possibly take exception.'

'Nevertheless, I expect to be kept informed about the man. I've had my orders from—well, never mind where, but they came from a source that compels me to go against my own better judgment. Very important people are interested in Lionel Mossbank. You still don't know who's behind him?'

'We believe it's an American named Turner, sir, but even of that we're not sure. . . .'

'But surely man, it's easy enough to trace the origin of the money that's being spent on advertising and all the incidental expenses?'

'Up to a point, perfectly easy, sir! The advertising is handled by a Mr. Jeremy Dowbiggin, head of the Hayward Fisher Agency. Short of going to him and asking him point-blank who pays the bills, I don't see what I can do, sir.'

'What do you know about Dowbiggin?'

'He's one of the best known advertising men in the country, sir. He's a rich man. Nothing whatever against him. Good war record. There was, about six years ago, a query from the New York police regarding his uncle, a George Dowbiggin, but nothing of any consequence...'

'What about the American, Turner?'

'The New York police say that there is nothing specific against him, but from the guarded way in which they phrased their reply to our cable I rather gather that the man has a shady past.'

'All right. So much for the few facts you have. What do you suspect, if anything?'

'I've talked to two men who were at school with Moss-bank, sir, and they both agree that he was a fool there, flunked every exam. and so forth. They both disliked him, but had nothing specific to say. Then I had a chat with the men who helped him when he fought the Smeddle-down by-election. They rather confirmed this view. They said he was amazingly conceited, spoke wonderfully well if someone else wrote his speeches for him, but hadn't an idea in his head. From this I deduce that someone is writing his lectures for him now. He lives in a suite at King Charles Mansions and there have been complaints from other flats that he rehearses his speeches half the night, apparently learning them by heart.'

'Have you ascertained whether he was a religious man prior to his association with the Christian Movement?'

'He definitely was not, sir, in the sense that he did not go to church, nor did he express religious views of any kind to those in close contact with him.'

'Would you then give it as your opinion that the man's a humbug?'

'When I read one of his lectures I was sure of it, sir, but I've heard four now and I'm not so sure.'

'Make your report out and let me have it to-day. I don't mind admitting to you that I'm having the life badgered out of me on this fellow's account. They are taking a great interest in him in exalted circles—very exalted circles. If the tip had come from almost anywhere else I should laugh at it, but—well, I can't, that's all. Keep me informed about anything connected with him. If you want more help ask for it.'

*   *   *   *   *

The newspapers at last regarded Lionel Mossbank as 'news'. A Liberal journal with a large Nonconformist circulation asked: 'Is this the long-looked-for revival of religion?'

A Labour paper devoted its entire leader page to the Thames-side meeting. 'We take issue with Mr. Mossbank on only one point,' it said. 'How can democracy be said to have failed when it is painfully obvious that it has never been tried? The major part of the wealth of our country is still controlled by a handful of its people. More than one-third of its land area is owned by a few families which produce nothing and owe their broad acres to the acquisitiveness of remote ancestors. Privilege still stalks triumphant through the kingdom, and the key to advancement in public services—entry to some—is family rather than ability, and the cries of the under-privileged still fall on deaf ears. But Mr. Mossbank is right, nevertheless, when he says that most of our social problems would vanish overnight if we, who call ourselves a Christian people, would try to govern our public and private lives by the simple words of the Sermon on the Mount.'

An august morning newspaper, which had hitherto not

recognised Mossbank's existence, at last recognised him:

. . . While we wholeheartedly deplore the social inequalities to which Mr. Mossbank so eloquently referred, we must not blind ourselves to the fact that in the last fifty years the social reforms instituted in this country have constituted the most comprehensive and far-reaching programme so far seen in the world's history. We must and shall go further, but reform, if it is to be effective, is of necessity a slow process. . . . We feel that Mr. Mossbank is right when he says that in the Sermon on the Mount the true principles of Democracy were expounded. . . .

Jeremy had a huge pile of press cuttings ready to show Turner.

'I expect you've seen most of these,' said Jeremy, 'but there's one here—the only one of the bunch as far as I can see—which hits the nail on the head. I'll read it to you:

'No greater tribute could have been paid to oratory than was paid by a crowd, estimated by our reporter on the spot at more than ten thousand, which stood in the pouring rain in a Thames-side meadow last evening to hear Mr. Lionel Mossbank speak on "The Failure of Democracy."

'Mr. Mossbank used a great many words and used them beautifully and effectively, but said very little. We have before us *verbatim* copies of this and Mr. Mossbank's other addresses, but one may hunt in vain through them for one specific constructive thought. He tells us that we call ourselves Christians, but ignore the teachings of Christ; that we call our country a democracy, while ignoring the very meaning of the word. Perhaps, as Mr. Mossbank tells us, we are bad Christians and worse democrats, but when those who heard him speak came away from the spell of his superb oratory, it must have occurred to many that he had not offered them one new thought. In our democracy we are used to the spectacle of the politician on the opposite side of the House from the Government of the day, building himself a reputation by sniping at those who form the Government. But we have noted how, when the pendulum of politics swings this same man into high office, he finds the task of formulating constructive policies a more difficult one than it had appeared from the other side of the House. We do not need Mr. Mossbank to tell us that our system is imperfect, but we would like to know in precise terms how he proposes to unfold the Utopia implicit behind his golden phrases.

'Great emphasis has been laid upon what this so-called Christian Movement is *not*, but before we pass judgment upon it we should like to know what it *is*, what it proposes to do and how it proposes to do it.'

Jeremy passed the cutting over to Turner, who remarked: 'The man who wrote that is no fool.'

'The man who wrote that,' said Jeremy, 'read but did not hear little Lionel.'

*　　*　　*　　*　　*

When Roddie Macdonald returned to London after the riverside meeting, he went to the St Charles's Square office to make a few notes and leave them for the stenographer who would arrive there early in the morning.

Finished for the evening, he came out into the fresh air to find that the rain had ceased. It was hot and airless. Roddie decided to take a stroll. In the crush emerging from the Haymarket Theatre Roddie caught a glimpse of the tall man with whom he had watched Ignatius Turner conversing in St James's Park a long time previously. He had often felt that if he could have overheard the conversation in question much light might have been shed upon many matters.

The tall man was with a striking-looking woman, whose face was familiar to Roddie, who was an ardent devotee of the weeklies which chronicle the doings of the socially prominent. The pair were ushered into an expensive private car and driven away. Roddie noted its number. It is a relatively simple matter for those who know how to ascertain the name of the owner of a car from its registration number. In less than thirty minutes Roddie had learned that the car was registered in the name of Señor Pablo Alfonso Medina, *Chargé d'Affaires* in London of the small South American republic of San Bernardino. Reference to the London telephone directory revealed that Señor Medina lived in Brook Street, W., and within five minutes of learning this a taxi had deposited Roddie two doors away from the address in question, outside which still stood the car which had brought its owner and his companion from the Haymarket Theatre.

Hardly had the taxi driven away when the tall man, presumably Señor Medina, emerged, accompanied by the woman who had left the Haymarket Theatre with him. As the pair entered the car Roddie sauntered away so as not to be conspicuous. It was then that Roddie remembered who the woman was—Lady Constance Charlesworth—daughter of the bankrupt Earl of Bromborough.

Lady Constance Charlesworth was one of those rare people who live to refute the cynics. Although possessed of very little money, which she had inherited from her mother, and despite the handicap of a bankrupt earl for a father, she occupied a position in Society which was the envy of many richer more beautiful and more talented women. Being over thirty years of age, she was neither of the younger nor the older set, but managed to maintain a position poised between the two and liked by both. Her popularity even surmounted the handicap of being intelligent, and when a little while previously she had announced her adherence to the Christian Movement, a number of other well-known women had followed suit.

Of these things Roddie was not aware. It remained only for him to confirm that the tall man and Señor Medina were one and the same person and to report his discovery to Jeremy.

It was a night of discoveries for Roddie, who loved to prowl in city streets after dark. Five minutes after leaving Brook Street Roddie found himself outside the building where Ignatius Turner still occupied a service suite in Park Lane.

A taxi drew up to the door. Out of it stepped a man and a woman. The man opened the front door with a latchkey, opening it to admit the woman. The woman was Sybilla Dowbiggin and the man was Paul Lefroy. The aspect of the matter which puzzled Roddie was that a cable had come only that same afternoon signed with Paul Lefroy's name.

Roddie went to a telephone-box at Hyde Park Corner and routed two unemployed reporter friends out of bed. When they arrived to relieve him it was after two a.m., by which time Roddie was tottering with fatigue, which made a taxi to Battersea a necessity. But even then Roddie returned to bed via Jeremy's flat. Securing no answer to his ringing, Roddie left a note in the mail box with a discreetly worded account of his evening's work.

There was a note for Roddie by the telephone in the hall of the house where he lived: 'Miss Seymour wants you to phone her, urgent.' But Roddie was too tired. He went to bed without knowing that he was the editor-elect of a weekly paper which, even as he put his tired head on the pillow, was in its birth pangs.

Chapter Sixteen

WHILE LIONEL MOSSBANK was compelled to spend some eight or more hours daily learning by heart the speeches provided for him, there was very little chance of his getting into mischief. But released from this drudgery, with time on his hands, he required discipline. Mossbank was, as Jeremy described him, 'punch-drunk with his own eloquence.' The spectacle of thousands of people listening to his words in reverential silence was too much for him. He began to look upon himself as a Messiah. He wanted to get out and among people, to hold court surrounded by followers and admirers. To have permitted this would have been to explode the fabulous reputation which had been built around him.

Crowder, the senior of the four ex-policemen employed as bodyguard, reported to Jeremy that Mossbank was becoming difficult to control. Twice he had eluded their vigilance, nor would he reveal where he had been and what he had been doing during his long absences.

Mossbank was growing to hate Jeremy, who was the only person who did not deal in flattery. He knew that Jeremy saw through him and his feeble pretences. He knew that Jeremy despised him utterly, regarding him as a very low creature. Mossbank was frightened of Turner, of that Jeremy was sure. The hold Turner had over him was something more than that of holding the purse strings. Turner, when speaking to Mossbank, whether in public or private, maintained an air of unctuous deference, but behind it all was a threat.

Mossbank had grown to look upon himself as a power, but between him and the realisation of his ambitions stood Turner and Jeremy. He forgot, if his vanity had ever fully permitted him to realise, that he was a manufactured product and that Jeremy was the manufacturer.

Mossbank's good-looking and somewhat featureless face had been given character at Jeremy's instigation, when a famous plastic surgeon, by two tiny incisions near the eyes, had changed and amazingly improved the whole facial expression. A theatrical hairdresser, employed by Jeremy, had evolved, after some weeks of patient work, a style of hairdressing which had given Mossbank's rather perky face an air of austerity. It was Jeremy who, knowing that Mossbank's magnetism was in his voice, had perfected for him the technique of abrupt endings to his addresses and the sudden, shy disappearances from the platform, so that audiences ready to applaud wildly, received the impression that this reserved, saintly man did not need their plaudits.

Jeremy, via Macdonald, had given out to the press stories calculated to heighten this reputation for humility and unworldliness, as well as crediting him with almost supernatural powers. Without Mossbank's knowledge, Jeremy one day arranged for his shoes to be treated with a preparation known to dog thieves in the Bethnal Green district. Prior to this Jeremy had slipped into the press a story which recorded how animals loved and followed Mossbank.

Three press photographers, tipped off by Macdonald, secured pictures of Lionel Mossbank followed through St James's Park by a horde of lecherous-looking dogs of all descriptions. Somehow the photographs gave an entirely different impression.

'Evidently, lechery isn't photogenic!' had been Jeremy's comment.

[189]

But millions of dog-lovers all over the world were thrilled by the spectacle of numbers of man's best friends cavorting across the greensward in hot pursuit of the saintly Lionel Mossbank, who guessed from the presence of the photographers that Jeremy had had a hand in the matter.

Lionel Mossbank looked with eyes of hatred at Jeremy, and as the public acclaim mounted to his head, the belief grew in him that Jeremy, far from creating him, was standing between him and some grand destiny which had been marked out for him. The climax in his hatred for Jeremy was reached when he overheard Jeremy talking to Macdonald about an address which was in course of preparation. 'Forget that, Roddie,' Jeremy had said. 'It isn't any good telling the little squirt to adapt himself to the mood of his audience. Get it into your head that he's nothing more than a bloody gramophone. Our job is to make the record and wind up the machine. Mossbank provides the needle. . . .'

One afternoon Mossbank, believing that his bodyguard was off duty, jumped into a taxi to go to the movies. Crowder just spotted him in time, hailed another taxi and followed, taking a seat two rows behind Mossbank in a big West End cinema.

Mossbank sat down beside a girl who was sitting alone. Crowder five minutes later saw the girl move along several seats. Mossbank followed. Once more the girl moved and once more Mossbank followed. A few moments later the girl screamed and every head was turned in their direction.

Crowder wasted no time. He picked Mossbank bodily from his seat and planted him on his feet in the row behind. 'Get out of the theatre quick and go home!' he whispered fiercely.

Mossbank needed no second invitation, escaping by an

emergency exit, but not before a girl attendant had flashed a light in his face. When he judged that Mossbank was clear of the theatre, Crowder followed. He did not want to be mixed up in the affair further, for if he were questioned and detained it would be discovered that there was a connection between him and Mossbank. Crowder had noted the flashlight which had illuminated Mossbank's well-known face.

Mossbank was back in his suite when Crowder arrived there.

'Come along,' said the latter, 'we're going to see the boss.'

'I don't know who it is you call the boss,' was the reply, 'but if anyone wants to see me he can come here.'

'Yes, and before you know it,' said Crowder, 'there'll be a couple of plain clothes men round here wanting to talk to you. Come on!'

Mossbank's brief assertion of himself collapsed. He walked down with Crowder to the taxi.

Jeremy and Turner were there, as Crowder had hoped, in the St Charles's Square office.

'He was mauling a girl in a cinema,' Crowder explained breathlessly, 'and an usherette flashed a light in his face before he got out. Chances are she recognised him.'

'But you've been with me the entire afternoon, haven't you Lionel?' said Turner. 'You've been working on the new paper.'

'Half a dozen people saw him arrive at the suite,' interposed Crowder. 'That won't wash.'

Turner took Crowder and Mossbank, the latter thoroughly scared, into a small room adjoining Jeremy's office. Ten minutes later Crowder and his charge left and Turner rejoined Jeremy.

'Handled properly,' said Turner smiling beatifically, 'this may turn out to be a most fortunate occurrence.'

[191]

'I don't get you,' said Jeremy. 'All I know is that if little Lionel is convicted of mauling a girl in a cinema the Christian Movement will die so damned quick that we shan't have time to get to the funeral.'

'But he won't be convicted,' said Turner confidently. 'He hasn't been to a cinema. I've arranged all that. Furthermore, his tendency to become troublesome will be curbed. He is a very frightened man. He will do precisely as he is told. Remember, Dowbiggin, Lionel Mossbank was here between two-thirty and three-thirty p.m. You and I were talking to him all the while, so he couldn't possibly have been to a cinema.'

Jeremy turned coldly to Turner, looking him up and down from top to toe.

'In England, Turner, there is a crime known as perjury, the maximum penalty for which is, I believe, seven years hard labour, or maybe it's penal servitude. I warned you once, and I meant what I said, that I'll have no hand in anything criminal. Get little Lionel out of the mess any way you like, but don't ask me to commit perjury for him. I don't want to be dragged into it and I give you fair warning that if I am I shall tell the truth.'

The mask fell off Turner for a moment. Fear and hatred gleamed from his eyes. The bland smoothness of his face was distorted. For a moment Jeremy thought Turner was going to hit him.

'You're a funny fellow, Dowbiggin,' said Turner evenly. 'You spend your life perpetrating deceptions, but when you are asked to perpetrate just one more, in order to save many months of hard work from being wasted, your conscience makes you baulk.'

'Call it conscience, or just intelligence, Turner. I happen to believe that intelligent people don't run foul of the law. I also happen to believe in the sanctity of an oath. Even if there were no danger of being caught, I still wouldn't commit perjury. You laugh. But I am a great believer in law and order. Perjury leads to chaos. Chaos would destroy my hopes of living comfortably in my old age. There are not many things left that I believe in, Turner, but one of them is that the vast majority of people—here in England—when they stand in the witness box and swear to tell the truth, the whole truth and nothing but the truth, so help them God, do just that to the best of their several abilities. That is why when we walk the streets at night we do not walk in fear of robbers. That is also one of the reasons why, when our daughters go out alone, we are not in perpetual fear that they may fall victims to religion-crazed sex maniacs. I'm afraid you've got several wrong ideas about me, Turner, and the sooner you sort them out the better for both of us.'

Jeremy turned on his heel and left Turner.

Roddie Macdonald, who had been trying all day to speak to Jeremy alone, followed him out of the office. Four days had passed since Roddie had seen Paul Lefroy and Sybilla enter the house in Park Lane together. He had tried to talk to Jeremy, but the latter had brushed him aside. Then Roddie had had to go to interview a firm of printers out of London and something had always prevented him from telling Jeremy what he knew.

'Go away, Roddie! I want to be alone for a bit . . .'

'You've got to listen to me, Jeremy,' pleaded Roddie. 'You've got to!'

'Sorry, Roddie! I didn't mean to be short with you, but I'm very worried.'

'I know that, Jeremy, and I'm afraid that what I'm going to tell you is going to worry you more.'

'Come back to my flat, Roddie,' said Jeremy, seeing that he was genuinely distressed.

When they were settled comfortably Roddie told Jeremy the story of seeing Sybilla and Paul Lefroy.

7*

'. . . and in the morning Cantrell, that's the man who's working with me, followed Lefroy to the American Express in the Haymarket, where he bought two tickets to the South of France. Cantrell thinks it was to Toulon. There was no time to consult you—I tried to talk to you twice—so I gave Cantrell money and told him to hang on to them. He went last night to Paris via Southampton-Havre and I'm expecting a wire from him this morning.'

'You've done very well, Roddie,' said Jeremy, trying to control the rage burning in him. 'Now, if you don't mind, I'd like to be alone to think things out. When you get back to the office send a wire to Lefroy in New York. Invent a reason that demands a reply and when the reply comes give it to me.'

'What about the new paper, Jeremy?' asked Roddie fearing that the glorious editorship would be dashed from his lips at this the eleventh hour.

'Go ahead as though nothing had happened, Roddie. I'll be at the office before the evening is out.'

When Jeremy was alone he rang for a cup of tea and, as he sipped it, browsed through the pages of a magazine lying beside him. It helped him to calm down. He had a murderous temper which, happily for him, he knew he must control.

As he sat alone in his flat Jeremy skipped a dozen generations of placid English forbears and went straight back to that Elizabethan progenitor, Jules d'Aubigné. His eyes went to pin-points, his jaw muscles knotted and his breathing grew almost stertorous with the emotions which shook him. Hot rage gave place to cold rage. Faculties numbed by the hot blood surging through him began to work again.

There was a tangle caused by some strange interlocking of lives which he did not understand. Sybilla and Lefroy were not so hard to understand. That might have no more significance than the obvious one. Turner's relationship to Lefroy and Sybilla was something quite different.

Jeremy did not mind the fact that Lefroy and Turner had used him in some big scheme which he did not even now understand. That was all part of the battle of wits that was the very essence of life itself. Jeremy had understood that from the very beginning. Indeed, he had rather enjoyed the situation. He was sorry now, in view of what Roddie had told him, that he had allowed himself to say so much to Turner that very afternoon. That had been a pity. He must heal the breach with Turner, for Turner probably was the key to the whole mysterious business. In any case, Jeremy felt little or no animus against Turner, who was just a clever crook. But Lefroy—that was another matter. Lefroy had done the one thing which a man of Jeremy's temperament could never forgive. The fact that he and Sybilla had allowed their marriage to go on the rocks had no bearing on the subject. Lefroy had stabbed him in the back, using Sybilla as his decoy. Lefroy and Sybilla were going to pay for that.

With a tremendous effort Jeremy went back to the office to resume the task of launching the new weekly.

'There was something I forgot to tell you,' said Roddie. 'Do you remember my telling you of the time when Turner had an appointment with a man in St James's Park? They met apparently as strangers on one of the seats. You do. Well, the other night I saw him coming out of the Haymarket Theatre. I followed him and I know who he is. He's a South American, Pablo Alfonso Medina, *Chargé d'Affaires* at the San Bernardino Legation. I don't know whether it has any significance, but I think it has, because the woman Medina was with was Lady Constance Charlesworth.'

'Good work, Roddie! Here's a present for you.'

Jeremy took off a valuable gold watch and chain and handed it to Roddie.

'You don't mean this for me?' asked Roddie, who considered that in a city with public clocks a watch was sheer extravagance.

Jeremy did not trouble to reply. He was glad to be rid of the watch. Sybilla had given it to him.

Turner came into the room.

'I'm afraid I got a bit heated this afternoon, Turner,' said Jeremy. 'Sorry if you got the rough edge of my tongue.'

'On the contrary, my dear fellow, it is I who should be offering apologies. I well deserved the rebuke you gave me. I confess that I was panic-stricken. I saw months of toil going for nothing and I allowed myself to propose to you a most immoral procedure. I have had a chat with Lionel. I rather think Crowder exaggerated the incident in the cinema. In any case, there have been no enquiries, as I am sure there would have been if anyone had recognised him. The chances are, therefore, that we shall hear no more of the matter. Lionel, by the way, assures me that he saw the young woman fumbling for a match in her handbag and offered her his lighter. I should be horrified if the construction put upon the incident by Crowder were the correct one. But I think you may take it that this was not so.'

'Well, let's forget the whole business, Turner,' said Jeremy heartily. 'We've both been working hard and our nerves are a bit frayed.'

*   *   *   *   *

The only thing Jeremy could remember about the Republic of San Bernardino was that it was in a perpetual state of tension with its near neighbour, the equally insignificant Republic of La Trinidad. Even this fact was remembered only because it had been the basis of an amusing if scurrilous story told by George Dowbiggin, who had once used one or other of these republics as a base of operations for one of his most nefarious schemes.

'San Bernardino, eh?' exclaimed George Dowbiggin. 'Do I know San Bernardino? Jeremy, my lad, one of the very few things that troubles me in my old age is a newspaper report I read the other day to the effect that San Bernardino and Great Britain were discussing terms with a view to arranging an extradition treaty. Do I know this fellow Medina? No, I don't, but maybe I knew his father. If he's the son of old General Luis Medina you can take it for granted that he's so crooked he can't lie straight in bed. When he got tired of a woman the old man would make her play poker so's he could win back jewellery he'd given her. Next day she'd see it worn by her successor. . . .'

'I'm in deadly earnest, Uncle George. Can you find out all there is to know about the Medina at the Legation here in London, whether or not he's the son of the man you think?'

George Dowbiggin looked up into his nephew's face.

'By God! Jeremy boy, I do believe you are in earnest. What's the fellow done to you?'

'I don't know, Uncle George, and the story's too long to tell just now. But I suspect him of a hell of a lot.'

'Well, don't forget that the man's a diplomat, Jeremy boy, even if he does represent a sawn-off apology for a republic. There's a look in your eye I don't like.'

'Somebody's made a fool out of me in more ways than one, Uncle George, and somebody's going to sweat blood for it. . . .'

'Woman trouble, eh?'

'What makes you say that?'

'Look at yourself in the mirror, my boy, and don't

[197]

ask silly questions. I never saw you all steamed up like this before, so it must be a woman. Sybilla?'

Jeremy nodded. 'But that's only part of it, Uncle George. I'm up to the neck in things I don't understand and I'm going to understand them before I'm much older.'

*　　　*　　　*　　　*　　　*

Jeremy was taking his Uncle George's advice—looking in the mirror. But his reasons for doing so were remote from those suggested to him. It was the year 1938. Jeremy was forty-four years of age. There had been a time, and not so very long ago, when women—most women, had made it very clear to him in their several ways that they found him attractive. It had been part of his equipment as a salesman.

Jeremy was wondering as he looked at himself whether during the past years of devotion to the twin gods of money and success he had lost the touch. It had been a long while since he had set out to charm any woman. Janet did not count. Not that he was not very fond of Janet, even going so far as to contemplate marrying her one of these days. Just now he was finding that her presence fussed him. Without any sort of a rupture he had gone back to the flat where he and Sybilla had lived together. He had tried to do it without hurting Janet, but having made up his mind to do a thing, Jeremy did it, without reckoning the cost in hurt feelings.

'Janet dear,' he had said, 'you've been very sweet and I know you want to be helpful. But I've got to straighten all these tangles myself. I'm built that way. I can't help it. They used to call me the "Lone Wolf" when I was bootlegging with Uncle George. In a few days, or weeks, everything will come right. I hope you understand. . . .'

Jeremy really did hope Janet understood. He was very much afraid that she wouldn't understand what he was about to do. Women were that way. Well, it was to be hoped that she wouldn't find out.

Jeremy dressed himself with great care. Women liked that. The little things were important where women were concerned, or so he had read somewhere. In actual fact Jeremy had never had to trouble about the little things, for the more careless he had appeared the more obvious were the conquests which could have been his. He hadn't cared. That was the point. This time he did care—in his own peculiar way, and he was worried lest this simple fact would spoil his technique. He had won Sybilla carelessly —if he had ever won her at all.

Salesmen are actors—superb actors the good ones, and Jeremy was a good one. This night he intended to put on the act of his life. There wasn't time to walk softly. There were things he had to know—quickly. Uncle George was ferreting behind the scenes to find out all he could about this man Medina. But it might take time. Medina might prove the key to many things. He had met Turner surreptitiously. There must have been good reason for this. He was a friend or acquaintance of Lady Constance Charlesworth, and she was the game Jeremy intended to stalk that evening. Turner, Lefroy or Medina had induced her to lend her name to the Christian Movement, in the certain knowledge that what Lady Constance Charlesworth did to-day a large number of well-known Mayfair nitwits would do to-morrow. Somehow, Jeremy was sure, the lady herself would prove to be the key to many things which puzzled him.

For the first time in his life Jeremy was scared—really scared. He was 'up to the neck' in something, and that something, he was fairly sure, was diabolical. He had to know what it was. He would stick at nothing to find out. His vanity was touched. Men were taking him for a fool.

So Jeremy studied himself carefully in the mirror. Two

quick drinks made him look less purposeful and more human. It was Jeremy the salesman who was dressing himself with such care. He was out to sell himself. Every atom of charm and personality he possessed would be turned on to achieve his object. It had been a long while since he had tried to charm anyone, but so far he had never known failure. On this night he simply dared not contemplate failure. . . .

It was careless of him not to have realised that one cannot take the daughter of an earl—even a bankrupt earl—to a charity ball and expect the fact to pass unnoticed. A press cameraman photographed Jeremy and Lady Constance Charlesworth as they entered the hall of the Dorchester together. While the latter was in the cloakroom Jeremy approached the cameraman, thrusting several pound notes into his hand.

'Who do you want killed?' said the young man, who modelled his life on the American reporter as portrayed by Hollywood.

'Nobody—yet, thanks,' said Jeremy with a smile, 'but I'd take it as a great favour if you would kill that picture you took of me and the lady I came in with.'

'It's dead!' said the young man, firing a flash bulb at a well-known actress who entered at that moment.

'You know—I'm going to call you Jeremy if you don't mind—you know, Jeremy,' Lady Constance Charlesworth was saying an hour later, 'I just can't see how you of all people are associated with the Christian Movement.'

'There's nothing wrong with my digestion, you know,' Jeremy replied, 'but I do the advertising for Columbine Stomach Powders.'

'You hard-boiled devil!' was the reply, and Jeremy was not slow to detect in the reply a certain admiration.

'But you believe in the Movement, don't you?'

'Within limits—yes. It's like a lot of other things, I

expect, as good or bad as the people who form the Movement. It could be very good, or it could be very bad.'

'Let's dance, Jeremy,' said she, thoughtfully.

Jeremy steered the conversation away from the Christian Movement, knowing that his companion would bring it back again. Despite his ulterior purposes, Jeremy was enjoying the evening. There were signs, too, that this daughter of an earl would, like the long procession of hundreds of other women about whom he had been quite indifferent, thaw in his presence. Barmaids, night club hostesses, flower-women, charwomen, waitresses, women in offices, married women presiding at their own dinner-tables, weather-beaten *vestiaires*, shop assistants and fallen angels—age and rank did not seem to matter. What a gay Lothario he could have been, Jeremy reflected. His own theory of it all was that there was some quite ordinary explanation: glands, radiations, or chromosomes. It was just a chemical formula.

'You dance beautifully, Constance,' said Jeremy a little later, stating the bare truth and noting that her body as she danced was softer, more yielding.

'The bow once said to the violin "How beautifully you play!" And the violin made a very obvious retort. There is only one man in London who dances as well as you do, Jeremy. I think I've danced with all of them.'

'And who is this happy man?'

'I don't think you know him—Pablo Medina. I'm going to make a confession. Actually I dislike and mistrust him, but he dances so superbly that I forget my dislike. . . .'

'I'm not so flattered as I was, Constance. I must meet this rival. Where shall I find him?'

'That oughtn't to be so difficult, for I met him through your Mr. Turner. . . .'

'What do you think of Turner?' asked Jeremy, not

wishing to sound eager to hear more of Medina.

'I don't know,' was the slow reply. 'I suppose I oughtn't to say it, but there have been times when I've wondered a little about him.'

Jeremy said nothing.

'You know him well, don't you, Jeremy?' she continued. 'Is he as saintly as he appears to be?'

'It isn't easy to answer that question,' replied Jeremy. 'You see, he doesn't appear at all saintly to me. I know he's very shrewd. But let's not talk about him.'

Jeremy found himself liking Constance. He wondered why she had never married. At this stage of their relations there was no profit in talking about Turner. She would not 'come clean' about what she knew and suspected.

'Things are rather dull here,' said Jeremy, 'let's go on to the "Gay Nineties". It's sure to be amusing.'

Jeremy looked blankly at several of the dance hostesses who came towards him, thinking that he was entertaining some out-of-town client, his usual reason for being at the 'Gay Nineties' and other resorts of the kind. The girls took the hint and ignored him. Constance intrigued them. She was smartly dressed and quite good-looking, but they knew that Jeremy could have the pick of really beautiful women. They themselves—and some of them were truly lovely—had angled often to catch his interest. He had been nice to all of them, given them money and treated them in essence as though they were wooden idols. From the distance they watched with interest while he turned the full force of his charm and personality upon Constance.

'I expect she's a client,' said one girl.

'Client nothing!' exclaimed another. 'This is the real thing. I'd love to know what it was he whispered to her just then. Look! She's blushing—all over her neck and shoulders. It makes her look rather nice, doesn't it?'

'I wish I could blush like that,' said a girl rather sadly.

'If you can't learn here you'll never learn. . . .'

'Gee whiz! Look at him now. Our Jeremy's come out of cold storage at last. . . .'

'I made a good resolution this year. I promised to be a good girl and only sleep with men for money, but if I could make him look at me like that . . .'

Constance, like any other attractive woman who has got out and about, was familiar with all the wiles and blandishments of the ordinary would-be seducer. They had always made her laugh. But this was something different. All her usual self-reliance seemed to melt. She became conscious first of Jeremy's great physical strength. To dance with him was effortless. An hour or two previously she had thought his face hard and stern, but now his face, lit with a serene smile, was beautiful. There was no other word for it. A sense of her own loneliness swept over Constance. Her life was really very lonely. Thousands of acquaintances, popularity—but no intimates. At two or three o'clock in the morning she was going back to her flat and he to wherever he lived. Constance suddenly found herself frightened at the thought. There would be a vacuum flask of hot milk beside her bed and a slip of paper giving details of phone calls. She must take hold of herself. When he looked at her like that she felt utterly reckless and—yes, abandoned was the word. This would have to stop. All she had to do was to ask him to have a taxi called. He was too finished a man to behave badly in the taxi. Once inside her own front door all these foolish thoughts would vanish. But were they so foolish . . . ? How absurd to set herself on a pinnacle above other women. They talked freely enough about their affairs. There had been times when a sort of envy had come over her at these confidences from other women. Instead of being ashamed, some of the cats had had the effrontery to look at her in a superior fashion. Perhaps they felt superior about it. O-o-o-h! His eyes! His lips, too. A few minutes ago I thought what a stern, strong mouth it was, despite the voluptuous lips. But now—they were soft and slack . . . his eyes were hard and brilliant light blue, calm and cold, but something has happened to them. They've turned dark blue, almost black, and at the back of them there seems to be the flicker of dull, red flame. . . .

'No, Jeremy, I can't dance any more,' the words came thickly as though her tongue was sticking to the roof of her mouth. 'Take me out of here—anywhere, anywhere at all, Jeremy. . . .'

'What a devil he is!' said a tall, voluptuous blonde, one of the dance hostesses. 'If he's like that in a public place, what must he be like in private?

'You'd better have a nice glass of cold water, Gloria,' said a voice. 'You'll feel better then!'

Chapter Seventeen

THE GARDEN OF *Rose Marie* was long and narrow. At the top was *Rose Marie*, very modern inside and ageless outside. The salmon-pink paint which had been applied to its outside walls covered what might have been—but was not—very old masonry. From the ground floor it was just not possible to see over the mimosa trees which formed a break against the *mistral*. From the top floor, which consisted of one room with windows and a *terrasse* all round, it was possible to see over the mimosas in front of the little private cove and yacht basin belonging to *Rose Marie*.

To the left, which was roughly East, it was possible on a clear night to see the flash of the lighthouse on Cap d'Antibes. To the right, which was South and West, were visible almost always the Ile du Levant, which according to local legend was populated entirely by rats and a nudist colony, the Ile de Port-Cros, and on clear days the Ile de Porquerolles where, as they tell you with pride, grape-fruit grow in the open.

On this hot, brazen afternoon in the early part of August 1938, the garden of *Rose Marie* was (as the previous occupant, a romantic lady novelist, had described it) 'an oasis of coolth'. One detachment of bees was working down the long jasmin hedge, others were exploring geraniums of over forty different shades of red, while a small party —very privileged—hummed and droned soothingly among the tall, stately tuberoses, which filled the garden with their sad sweetness. An unknown hand had painted the inside walls of the garden sky blue and against them had trained purple and scarlet bougainvillea. For the rest there were blue gums, a wise and ancient olive, several orange trees and a vast clump of brilliant metallic blue agapanthus.

A flight of shallow mosaic steps led down the centre of the garden to a mosaic *terrasse*, hewn from virgin rock, all that was left to remind posterity that a Roman military governor, hot from the conquest of troublesome Ligurians, had once built himself a villa on this spot. Down by the water's edge was a massive bronze ringbolt let into the rock where his galley was tied. Constance was sure that in the cool of the evening the sighs of the tired galley slaves could still be heard. But then, Constance was a little overcome with it all. Dishwashing, for example, was something she had always taken for granted. Now she was washing dishes. There had always been someone to mop the water off the bathroom floor, but now she had to do it. Jeremy was cook. He stoked the boiler which provided hot water, cleaned the vegetables, gutted the fish and disembowelled the scrawny chickens which came from the village. The rest of the domestic tasks fell to Constance.

Constance was happier than she could remember being for years. She recalled once having been sorry for the Sabine woman slung over the shoulder of the Roman soldier, but having been through much the same experience herself, felt that her sympathy had been wasted.

They had been at *Rose Marie* a week now. Someday, she supposed, they would go back into the world and face its problems, but her secret hope was that the day would be long postponed. She was, of course, madly in love with Jeremy. But for some of his strange, thoughtful silences and a far-away look in his eyes at times, she almost believed that Jeremy was as much in love with her. There had been times in years gone by when Constance had regretted having waited so long for the dream lover who never came. But now, gorged on love, burned brown with hot sun, careless with easy living, Constance hugged to herself the knowledge that, come what may, the lonely nights which might stretch on and away into the future would never seem quite so lonely and empty. To-morrow might bring an end to this sweet folly, but there was always to-day. Even so, she would have liked to know what was simmering in Jeremy's handsome head.

Constance looked at the three aged cypresses which guarded the lower approach to the garden. She remembered reading somewhere, without quite understanding what it meant, that Roman voluptuaries planted cypresses in their gardens—the Sentinels of the Dead they called them—because no pleasure was so exquisite that it could not be enhanced by the breath of a little sadness. Here at *Rose Marie* she had given way to the call of the senses as never before in her life, and now she, too, in the lazy drowsy aftermath of love, was able to conjure new delights by just gazing at the cypresses and drinking in the sad, earthy bitter-sweetness of the tuberoses.

'Let's go for a swim,' said Jeremy, breaking a long silence, during which he had been turning over in his mind just how he was going to approach the subject uppermost there. Even to him this week had been dreamlike. It had not given him the bliss it had given Constance, but it had made him realise that for the first time in his life he had idled away a whole week.

It frightened him to realise that he was probably going to hurt Constance—bitterly. He was a thousand miles from being in love with her, but he had found in her real goodness and kindness, which made him even more certain that her association with Turner was not of her choosing.

Jeremy resented the need for wasting the precious days. He was impatient to get to the bottom of the mysteries which faced him, but he realised that common humanity demanded that he never allow Constance to know that it had been the information she possessed, rather than herself, which had been responsible for his onslaught upon her. They went nowhere, these two, because they were too well known. There were a thousand or more English people idling on the Mediterranean coast who would have recognised them instantly. From the bedroom lookout which commanded a view of a by-road, they had already recognised two carloads of holidaymakers among their mutual acquaintances. When it became necessary to buy things in the village one of them went alone. Jeremy noted, not without surprise, that he did not find this enforced idleness wearisome. Had it not been for his impatience to probe all the things which puzzled him, he would have enjoyed it thoroughly. Constance was gentle, intelligent, sweet-tempered, a restful and delightful companion.

It was on a hot, scented evening that Jeremy broke the spell. They were swimming, mother naked, through the tepid water to the raft moored a few hundred yards offshore, their bodies leaving a white trail of phosphorescence. The trilling of the nightingales in the high boughs of the blue gums came clearly across the water. When the moon rose they swam out towards the silver pathway.

'Constance, my dear,' said Jeremy, 'I feel I have a right now to ask you a question I couldn't ask you back in London.'

As Constance looked up, a wraith of cloud crossed the moon, casting gloom between them as though a witch had flown across.

'What is it you want to ask me, Jeremy?'

'Is Ignatius Turner blackmailing you, Constance?'

'Blackmailing is demanding money by threats, isn't it?'

'Yes!'

'Then he isn't blackmailing me, but he has threatened to make public something I must keep private, and I suppose that's much the same thing.'

'I knew something was worrying you, dearest. You needn't worry any more. I'll take care of Turner. It was because of his threats, wasn't it, that you were dragged into the Christian Movement?'

'Yes!' replied Constance, choking with the flood of emotion which surged up in her.

'One more question, dearest: did that information—I don't want to know what it was—reach Turner through a psycho-analyst, or someone of that kind?'

Constance nodded.

Jeremy fought to keep the triumph out of his voice. He must, somehow or other, prevent Constance from guessing that this was what he had wanted all along.

'I'm glad you told me—glad I summoned up the courage to ask you, dearest. You're not worried by it any more, are you? Don't be. I know how to deal with Turner . . . and now, let's forget that beasts like him exist. . . .'

*   *   *   *   *

By telephone from the village *poste* Jeremy learned that Paul Lefroy and Sybilla were still at the hotel in St Tropez to which they had been followed by Roddie Macdonald's assistant, Cantrell, who was himself staying there. He instructed Cantrell to cease following them and to return to London.

It was with a tremendous effort that Jeremy reached this decision. The pleasure of beating Lefroy's smooth face to a pulp must be deferred, for there were bigger fish to fry, and it was no part of Jeremy's plan to reveal that he knew anything more than he was supposed to know. He was in a fever to return to London, but the tragi-comedy of *Rose Marie* would have to be played out for a few more days.

*   *   *   *   *

'How did *you* come to be mixed up with Ignatius Turner?' Constance asked Jeremy. 'Is he blackmailing you?'

'Not yet,' replied Jeremy grimly. 'I like money, you see, dearest,' he explained. 'Turner approached me through a man named Paul Lefroy. Know him?'

Constance shook her head.

'You haven't missed much. But as I was saying, Turner through this man Lefroy, offered me money on such a scale that I just couldn't refuse it. This Christian Movement was in the background then and Lionel Mossbank had nothing to do with it. Turner was represented to me as a harmless religious crank with more money than sense. I arranged all kinds of publicity stunts for him. I still can't see their purpose, but there must have been one, for Turner doesn't do anything without a good reason. I'm sure of that. In defence of my own intelligence I may as well say that I suspected Turner from the very beginning . . .'

'Then why did you go in with him, dear?'

'You're not an ambitious man like me, dearest, or you'd understand. I'm vain and greedy. I was vain enough to believe that events would prove me a good deal smarter than Ignatius Turner, and it seemed a pity to let all his good money go somewhere else. Events may yet prove me smarter than he is, but in the meanwhile, I find that I've been for many months the associate of a criminal, actively participating in criminal schemes. No jury in the world would believe me if I said that I knew of nothing criminal going on. One of these days soon the cat's going to jump out of the bag and Turner's going to say to me in effect: "You're in this, Dowbiggin my boy, right up to the neck. On the day a hand is put on my shoulder there'll be one on yours. So be a good boy and do what you're told to do." And unless I'm pretty smart that's just what I shall have to do. When I met you I knew you were too sweet and decent to have anything to do with a shyster like Turner unless things weren't quite as they appeared, and it wasn't until I began to figure out ways of getting you out of his clutches that I began to see day-light. . . .'

Tears streamed down Constance's face.

'Oh! Jeremy, my dear, I've had some awful moments lately. I began to think that you—that it was because you wanted—well, that all this was just make-believe on your part, just to trap Turner. I thought I would die with shame. You see, Jeremy dear, I'm not a very vain woman. I don't gaze into a mirror and tell myself how lovely I am, because I know I'm not. Then you came along and swept me off my feet and—well, I've never been so happy in my whole life . . .'

Constance threw her arms round his neck and kissed him.

' . . . I know I'm being foolish, dearest, but I just can't help it. You see how horrible it would have been if you'd just been—using me.'

Jeremy Dowbiggin was, no doubt, a self-centred, tough-fibred man, endowed with rather less than his share of humility and gentleness. But to say that he was touched by this is grossly to understate what he felt. It shattered him. Not only was he touched inwardly, but he felt himself to be cheap and nasty. All his self-sufficiency collapsed.

He could say nothing, for there seemed nothing to say. He just sat beside Constance, holding her hand with such a grip that he was brought to his senses by the sound of cracking in the bones of her hand.

But Jeremy had to have more information from Constance and it was only by a great effort that he brought himself to questioning her again. It helped his curious conscience to believe that he was doing it for her sake as much as for any other reason.

'Tell me, dearest,' he went on remorselessly, 'what do you think about the other well-known people who have lent their names to the Christian Movement? Are they, too, in Turner's clutches, do you think? I ask this because I knew, before you told me, that Turner was suspected in the United States years ago of organising a blackmail racket.'

'I can't say for sure, Jeremy, but I know old Lady Penmanby is scared of him, although she trots him around everywhere, and I can't see what some of the others can possibly have in common with him. This man Lionel Mossbank, too. I don't say as a fact that he's scared, but I've had a conversation with him and I'm quite sure he isn't capable of writing his own speeches. Then there's Lord Mandleton. Do you know him? He isn't the type either, and I can't think of any motive except fear, or perhaps greed, which would induce him to lend his name to Turner. And there are others, too. Some are senior officers in the three services. There's quite an important officer from Scotland Yard and a host of civil servants,

[211]

two or three Members of Parliament, two trade union leaders, the general manager of one of the big stores, and so on. I don't understand it, Jeremy. You see, it isn't as if Turner had asked me to do anything wrong. He hasn't —truly he hasn't. The only wrong thing, if you can call it that, that I've done is to pretend to think Lionel Mossbank and the wretched Movement are marvellous, and to rope in all sorts of people I know. I'm trying to be fair-minded, don't you see? I can truthfully say that not once, either in private, or at the meetings, have I heard one word uttered, or one suggestion made that isn't absolutely and entirely above suspicion. And Lionel Mossbank, on the platform at least, speaks like a saint. . . .'

'Turner and I have to put every word into his mouth,' interjected Jeremy sheepishly.

'I'm not surprised,' said Constance. 'But what does it all mean? They're not collecting money—I'm sure of that, and you'd expect people like that to be interested in money. What does it mean, Jeremy? Or is it all perfectly innocent, and there's something wrong with us that makes us read something sinister into it all?'

'It isn't perfectly innocent, dearest,' replied Jeremy soberly. 'There's something diabolically clever about it all. I don't know what it is, but I do know that I'm going to find out. I must go back to London soon and you'd better stay here for a bit, at least until I know more than I know now.'

They had their last swim together that night. The fisherfolk from the village were spearing *loup* by torch-light, giving the little bay a fairy-like appearance. Constance shuddered when she remembered that on the morrow, and perhaps for weeks, she would be living alone in the sad sweetness of *Rose Marie*. Now that the season was coming to an end along the coast she could find a *femme de ménage* to do the rough work and as company for her, but she dreaded the emptiness of it. Only Jeremy's urgent persuasions—almost commands—were responsible for her decision to stay.

*　　*　　*　　*　　*

As Jeremy drove back across France to Calais, the talk in the villages and towns was all of the crisis which had arisen in Europe. Would Hitler march against the Czechs, or would the Czechs cede the Sudetenland to Germany, and avert a European blood-bath?

Is England ready? they asked him. Fear, doubt, anxiety, bewilderment were everywhere. The harvests were nearly ready. Numb, uncomprehending peasants, who had never heard of the Sudetenland, looked up uneasily from their toil and wondered, as their fathers had wondered before them, whether their little lives were to be sucked into the maelstrom of events beyond their ken. It had always been thus. The rich and powerful and greedy spun their webs, and when the mad dreams ended in disaster, as they always did, it was the little people who shed their blood and went hungry until the gods were glutted with the sacrifices offered to them. Then once again the cycle of ploughing, sowing and reaping would begin, with nothing accomplished except that wives and mothers were left with empty aching hearts, while sons came back and toiled where their fathers had toiled before. The only reality left was the good land.

The vintage of 1938 was still on the vines.

*　　*　　*　　*　　*

Jeremy arrived in London in the evening, to meet Roddie Macdonald who arrived in the St Charles's Square office with a huge bundle of proofs which had just passed the scrutiny of Ignatius Turner. A printer's messenger was waiting. The first issue of *Deliverance*—

the 'Mouthpiece of the Christian Movement'—was due for publication three days hence.

Jeremy thought he detected relief in Turner's manner when the latter arrived in the office a few minutes later.

'We've been very worried about you, Dowbiggin,' he said mildly. 'There's been a great deal of work to be done.'

Evidently Turner was not ready to quarrel with him, Jeremy deduced.

The printing order for the first issue of *Deliverance* was 100,000 copies. It was to be sold exclusively by volunteer workers of the Christian Movement and was 'published weekly at not more than threepence per copy.'

In a signed article, accompanied by a carefully touched-up portrait, Lionel Mossbank, 'Founder and Editor,' explained that those who so wished could have a copy for nothing at any time, but that for those who preferred to buy their copies the maximum price accepted would be threepence per copy. 'We do not wish to lose too large a sum on the publication,' he explained, 'but in no circumstances whatsoever do we intend to allow a profit to be made, for it is not seemly that any person or group of people should commercialise the teachings of Him who desired above all things that His Teachings should reach the hearts and homes of the lowliest of His people.'

The name of the publication, of course, and a great deal of its subject matter was religious in flavour, but there were many articles upon the topical events of the day. Jeremy read every word, hoping that by so doing the underlying purposes of Turner's activities would reveal themselves.

The principal article was by Lionel Mossbank, entitled: 'Christian Duty and Patriotism.' In a rather windy 2,000 words the article pointed out the conflict which war, or the threat of war, created in Christian hearts. Was a Christian's duty to his country, or to his God? There were those who might argue that the forces of evil must be destroyed in accordance with God's word, while others with equal sincerity might say that God's love of peace came before all. It was all rather inconclusive, but the nearest to a conclusion reached in the article was that it was the bounden duty of Christians in all countries to strive for peace.

The Rev. Courthope-Lumley contributed a strongly worded article in which he deplored the tendency of the world to bow down between wars to Mammon and then, when the threat of war loomed over the horizon again, rush to the churches to pray to God to help maintain peace. If men would only eschew Mammon in times of peace and plenty there would be no wars, nor threats of war, for war was the crystallisation of human greed.

An anonymous American contributor warned Europe, without naming any country in particular, that 'this time American blood will not be shed in Europe's internal quarrels.'

A retired general—who had to resign from his clubs because of the article—said that the British army would never reach the pitch of efficiency of the Continental armies while it was ruled by 'an outworn snobbery inherited from feudal England.'

'The Pleasure Mad World' was contributed by a gloomy Nonconformist cleric, who pointed out that there were not in the whole British Isles six clergy of any denomination who had a tenth of the personal following which jockeys, professional cricketers and footballers, actors, actresses and cinema stars claimed as their right. Was this the fault of the people or the clergy? Had religion and the personalities associated with religion less appeal to the hearts and minds of the people? Perhaps it was that religion had not kept pace with the world. The article wound up with the implication, not very thinly veiled, that a people which had forsaken its God would in turn be forsaken by its God. Were we standing upon the brink of the British Empire's dissolution?

The last article worthy of mention suggested that France had been weakened in every way by the Stavisky machinations, which could not have failed to weaken the *entente cordiale*. The writer—a retired diplomat—hinted broadly that Stavisky's accomplices had not been confined to France, but were to be found in the City of London itself.

'What do you make of this stuff, Roddie?' asked Jeremy when he had finished reading it.

'It's muck, most of it, but there's a public that will eat it up . . .'

Jeremy nodded agreement. 'Did little Lionel write his own article?'

'Not he,' replied Roddie. 'He's been lying all day in his suite smoking hundreds of cigarettes and eating huge meals. I don't think Turner will allow him outside the door. There've been hundreds of phone calls for him, but the girl has been instructed to tell everyone that in the rush of work getting out the new weekly he is unable to speak to anyone. I took him over a proof of his own article. Thought he might like to see it. But he didn't want to read it. All he wanted to see was how the half-tone of himself had come out. . . .'

'Roddie!' said Jeremy seriously. 'There's something behind all this that I've got to understand. You know and I know that Turner isn't doing all this because he loves suffering humanity. But what *can* he expect to get out of tripe like this? All this bears the mark of an impractical, idealistic ass. Does that strike you as a good description of Turner? No, of course it doesn't. Now I'll tell you something, Roddie. Turner—and it doesn't matter how I know it—is a blackmailer, or something like it.'

[216]

'That explains something, Jeremy,' said Roddie. 'I've had the impression more than once that the contributors —those who've called here, anyway—were scared of Turner, and I couldn't see why. When the stuff they brought in wasn't exactly what he wanted he just ordered them to re-write it. And they all did. You may say in effect that almost every word in this issue was written by Turner. Certainly it was all inspired by him.'

'Then let's look at it all in another way, Roddie. Imagine yourself to be one of the nitwits who go to hear little Lionel. You get a copy of this issue. What is going to be the effect of it upon your mind? Since Turner obviously can't expect to make money from it, perhaps he is trying to create an effect on the minds of others and has some way of turning that into money. Do you see what I'm driving at?'

Roddie was slow to reply.

'I've thought along those lines myself, Jeremy, but to answer your question, I can only say that every line in the paper is destructive rather than constructive. I tried to imagine myself a historian a hundred years hence, picking up a copy of the paper and using it to convey to the people of that age how we thought and behaved. And if some-thing happens between now and a hundred years hence which does bust up this country and the Empire, I think that if I were that historian, reading this first issue of *Deliverance*, I should paint a picture of a people uncertain of itself, fearful of events which had passed beyond its control, and wondering what had happened to the touch of greatness and inspiration which enabled the Empire to be created. Furthermore, I think that historian, on reading this stuff, would argue that 1938 was the turning-point in British fortunes . . .'

'I think you've expressed the thought well, Roddie. I feel just that way, too. But it doesn't get us any nearer to figuring out how Turner is going to make any money out of the situation, does it?'

'Don't think I've gone crazy, Jeremy,' said Roddie timidly, 'but I have a hunch that in some way Turner, Mossbank, the Christian Movement and this rag are bound up with the European situation. You say you can't see how Turner can make any money out of it all. Perhaps he *has* made it already . . .'

'I don't get you, Roddie.'

'Suppose he's being paid by some wealthy pacifists. Would the effect of all these articles and some of the rubbish that Mossbank spouted be to convince large numbers of people that we should be foolish and un-Christian to risk a European war by helping the Czechs? There are plenty of wealthy pacifists, on both sides of the Atlantic. Isn't it just possible that cranks like that have financed Turner?'

'Thanks, Roddie!' exclaimed Jeremy, jumping to his feet. 'I believe you're on the right track—at last. I'd like to sleep on this before I do any more. . . .'

Then Jeremy remembered that he had been in the office for more than two hours and had not even been in to Janet's room to see if she were there.

She was sitting there, dressed for the street, wearing the unmistakeable air of one who has been ready for a long while.

'I'm terribly sorry, Janet,' he began and stopped short. He had been away for nearly two weeks. He had gone without telling her. He had not written or wired while he was away. Indeed, she had scarcely crossed his mind.

'Go on, Jeremy! I'm interested. Tell me all about your holiday. It must have been enjoyable. You look very well.'

'I haven't been on a holiday, Janet. It may look like that to you . . .'

'It does look like that to me, Jeremy. You have a wonderful coat of tan. Was she nice?'

[218]

'Janet dear, one of these days I'll tell you all about it, but just now I'm worried and harassed and I have more on my mind than you know about.'

'I don't doubt it, Jeremy. Perhaps she was married. Indignant husbands are troublesome sometimes. But you don't have to worry on my account. I'm only your secretary and—just occasionally and when it pleases you—your mistress. I have no chains on you, Jeremy. You're as free as the air. I waited for you to-night on the off chance that there might be some real reason why you let me go on worrying about you without a word. But there isn't a reason, and you know it far better than I do. You have guilt written all over you. I give you a week to find another secretary, but if to-morrow, or any other day during the next week, you remind me that I'm your mistress, I shall probably be sick and will certainly walk out of the office there and then. I don't want your lying explanations and I won't listen to them. You're a dirty swine, Jeremy Dowbiggin!'

Chapter Eighteen

JEREMY HAD KNOWN many crises and difficulties in his life, but they had all been of the kind that called for direct action. Jeremy understood direct action. Now, however, he found himself in a situation where direct action appeared not only useless, but fraught with considerable risks. Jeremy, now in the middle forties, had matured. With maturity had come an understanding of how desperately easy it is for one human being to hurt others. He was still ambitious, but the keen edge of his ambition had been blunted by a desire to be less hurtful to others.

What he wanted to do above all things was to take a

riding crop to Paul Lefroy. But since Paul Lefroy and Ignatius Turner in the matter of the Christian Movement were the key to the whole business, Jeremy realised that an open breach with one was tantamount to an open breach with the other. His own strength, if strength it can be called, lay in appearing to have had his suspicions lulled, if not allayed entirely. There was Constance to be thought of also. He owed it to her somehow to extricate her from Turner's clutches. Even towards Sybilla he felt less animus. The chances were, he believed, that she, too, was in some devious way in Turner's clutches. There was the fact also that he had been unfaithful to her, although he still felt a certain sense of righteousness in that she had been prepared to condemn him without any real certainty on the point. But most worrying of all to Jeremy was the prospective loss of Janet Seymour. Not only was she the perfect secretary, and probably of all human beings the one who showed the greatest understanding of and sympathy with him and his problems, but he was very fond of her. He had more than once contemplated marrying her. Now, after all these years of close association, the prospect of losing her was unthinkable.

In an illogical way Jeremy reasoned that, with the world's affairs blowing towards a crisis, it behoved people to settle their private affairs, or the little—relatively little—personal problems would soon become lost in the greater storm which threatened soon to break upon the world.

The first thing to be done was, he was sure, to make his peace with Janet. Somehow or other this had to be done. While Jeremy was reaching this decision he heard Janet leave her office and go along the corridor to the washroom, preparatory to leaving for the day. He was in her office when she returned.

'Will you come out somewhere and have a talk with me, Janet?' he asked.

Janet took off her hat and sat down at her desk. 'Let's talk here,' she said in a cool voice. 'I'm listening.'

Jeremy the salesman knew that an untidy office at the end of a day was not the ideal setting for the sort of talk he had in mind. He would have liked to use the garden of *Rose Marie* for an hour or two. There he would have had for allies the soft Mediterranean night, the sensuous perfumes and the religious calm of a walled garden.

'Janet,' he began in a hurt voice, 'you called me a liar last night. Have you ever known me to lie—barring the ordinary white lies of courtesy?'

'No, Jeremy, I haven't—not until last night. I have never deceived myself that you have a very noble or beautiful character, but one of the things I have always liked about you has been that you are less of a liar than anyone I know. I'm talking about personal matters, of course, and not some of the advertising you have inspired. . . .'

The ghost of a smile lit Janet's face as she said this. Jeremy took it for a good omen.

'Thank you, Janet!' he said. 'That makes it easier for me to say what I'm going to say. Try to believe that I'm not lying now, will you? I'll lay my cards on the table and tell you that I'm desperately frightened that you will carry out your threat and leave me. I need you, Janet, as I've never needed anyone in my life. I'm not going to pretend that I don't need you here in the office. I do. But I need you personally. I'm in a mess and I don't yet know how big a one, or how seriously involved I am.'

Janet sat with expressionless face.

'I won't try to defend my callously going off and leaving you without a word,' he continued. 'There is no excuse for it. My reason was that I was worried and that I'm a selfish swine who put my own worries above yours. That's all. Now I'm going to strain your—affection for me. I'm

[221]

going to ask you to believe that I did not go away on pleasure, although I went to the Riviera. I'll also admit that I went with a woman, but you must believe me that she means less than nothing to me. She had information I wanted—information which may save me from God knows what. I got that information, Janet, and when I tell you the whole story, which I promise to do in a few weeks, I believe that, much as you will hate what I tell you, you will believe I did the only thing I could do. I'm not saying all this lightly, Janet, but I want you to accept this half-baked explanation for a while. Will you, my dear?'

'I don't believe one woman in ten million would accept it, Jeremy, but I will. I'm banking, you see, on the fact that over the years you haven't been a liar. You've been most other things, Jeremy, but not that.'

The little sigh which escaped Janet, as Jeremy folded her in his arms, was compounded of weariness and relief in equal parts. She, too, had found difficulty envisaging a future without Jeremy, even though—and she had been prepared to face that—it meant merely the impersonal contacts of the office. She had endured so much humiliation at Jeremy's hands that a little more did not seem to matter much.

Jeremy himself would have been happier at this reconciliation if he had been able to get out of his mind the picture of a woman sitting in a walled garden overlooking the Mediterranean, watching hopefully for the arrival of the postman.

*   *   *   *   *

Then, suddenly, a world which had always thought of Munich in terms of its beers and the sentimental, music-loving burghers who drank them, coined a new phrase with Munich as its key-word. It remains yet to be seen whether 'to do a munich' will take its place in the English language as a symbol of weakness and fear, or as a synonym for longheadedness. Let that be as it may, the gravity of the week in which Mr. Chamberlain flew to Munich may best be judged by the fact that the early football season was given much less space in the newspapers, while buyers of the 4th edition of *The Star* were seen, for the first time in the memory of most of the newsboys, to turn to the front page before turning to page four to absorb the wisdom of Captain Coe.

The week was also memorable for the fact that in it was published the second issue of *Deliverance*. The original printing order for the first edition had been 100,000, which the printers—although they forbore to say so—thought wildly optimistic. When they had printed a further 150,000 copies they thought otherwise, and when they were given an order to print 300,000 of the second issue they took a chance and printed an extra 100,000 for luck.

Lionel Mossbank's article created a sensation. In vivid phrases he painted a picture of 'the greatest and proudest Empire the world has ever seen, on its knees before a little Austrian paperhanger who, six months previously, meant no more than a music hall joke.' The article—which incidentally Mossbank did not see until it was on the streets—hinted broadly that England and France did not trust each other: 'We are told so often and so loudly that Anglo-French relations were never in the history of the two countries upon such a firm basis of understanding and goodwill, that the thinking man is forced to reflect that Truth does not require constant reiteration.'

The article went on to prove that the unpreparedness, the divided counsels and the mistrust in the two countries —Britain and France—were the direct outcome of having forsaken God for Mammon.

The arguments were inconclusive. At any other time

the article would have been a subject of ridicule. But before it was even written, ten millions of people were already asking themselves what *was* wrong with Britain. If the Astronomer Royal had come out with a statement that it was sunspots, such was the bewilderment of British people at that time, the explanation would have satisfied many. Any explanation was better than none, and to the thousands who clamoured to buy *Deliverance*, it served, for man has always been ready—when at the end of his resources —to fall back upon the hocus-pocus of the witch doctor for succour. Thousands who had heard Lionel Mossbank speak, and even more thousands who had not, were hypnotised into forgetting that God is always on the side of the strongest battalions. They forgot, too, when the war clouds seemed to have lifted, the tired old man of seventy who, flying for the first time in his life, had gone to Munich to abase himself, because of the knowledge he bore in his heart that if he did not do so history would be written differently. At a cost to himself—nobody will ever know how great—Neville Chamberlain, who had inherited a legacy of chaos and inertia from his predecessor, bought for his country a year of grace in which to grow strong.

It has been said that nations, like individuals, always run true to form. This applies not only to their own actions but in their interpretation of other people's actions. The Germans, to whom the story of David and Goliath has always appeared absurd, misinterpreted Britain. History will record that the British, to whom the infinitely more subtle story of Samson and Delilah has always seemed faintly ridiculous, misinterpreted Germany.

*   *   *   *   *

It was a new experience for Jeremy Dowbiggin to feel small. It had not occurred, when he came to think of it, since the last time he had stood waiting outside the headmaster's study in his schooldays, wondering whether six or eight with the cane would be his portion. It is a part of the technique of those who dwell in Scotland Yard to make callers feel uncomfortable, to sap their *morale*. The man who boasts loudly the night before that 'the police can go to hell, for they'll get nothing out of me,' sometimes sings a different song when replying to questions posed by courteous, keen- and hard-faced men who have spent their lives probing into guilty consciences. First it is the quiet and coldly impersonal atmosphere which chills, and then the air, worn by these men, of knowing much more than they admit is disconcerting even to clean consciences.

Jeremy had over an hour to wait before he could see the man he wanted to see and then, just as he was being invited to take a chair and smoke a cigarette, a uniformed man entered the room and laid upon the desk a bulky file. Jeremy would not have been human if he had not jumped to the conclusion that the file in some way concerned him.

'Now, Mr. Dowbiggin, what can I do for you?' said a shaggy-browed official, who looked as though he had shed his last illusion about his fellow men some twenty years previously, and whose courtesy seemed to mask the iron hand which lay beneath.

'I want to secure your help and advice in a very grave matter,' said Jeremy. 'I've come to the conclusion I ought to have paid this call a year ago. I have a long story to tell you, so I hope you will have patience to hear it to the end.'

'You don't appear the type to come here with fairy stories, Mr. Dowbiggin, so take all the time you want. Do you mind someone taking notes?'

'I don't actively object, of course, Mr. Inspector, but I'd much rather not. Don't construe that as meaning I won't sign any statement I make. Say the word and

I'll dictate the whole thing to my secretary and sign it. . . .'

'Just as you like, Mr. Dowbiggin,' said Mr. Inspector with a smile, pressing the button under his desk to indicate that the shorthand note of the conversation was to be taken from behind a screen in the next room. 'Let's go into the other room. It's warmer there.'

His next remark rattled Jeremy more than a little. 'I don't mind telling you, Mr. Dowbiggin, that we've been wondering when you'd pay us a visit.'

It would have annoyed Jeremy very much if he had known that Mr. Inspector not only had never heard the name of Dowbiggin before, but did not know whether Jeremy had come to complain of being blackmailed, report a stolen car or to lay information against a share-pusher.

Jeremy began his story from the day when he first met Paul Lefroy, confining himself to facts rather than suspicions.

' . . . and that brings me to the end of the facts,' said Jeremy some forty minutes later.

'As facts, you know, Mr. Dowbiggin,' said Mr. Inspector, 'they're not very damning. This man Turner is probably a humbug, as you say, but that isn't a crime here, or there wouldn't be so many people at liberty. Furthermore, there's no law here which can make a man divulge where he obtained the money he spends. If Turner had been raising funds here we'd be entitled to ask him questions, but you say most positively that he has not. You imply that you have suspicions. I should like to hear them.'

'I was suspicious of Turner from the hour I met him. He didn't run true to form, if you understand me. I'll admit that I allowed myself to be blinded. I thought, you see, that I might as well have his good money as the next man. But I knew then that whatever his real purpose might be, it was nothing like his declared purpose, but in my own defence I must add that I did not think there

[226]

was anything sinister behind it all. Now I'm certain of it. . . .'

'What makes you so certain, Mr. Dowbiggin?'

'I'm afraid I have to bring a lady's name into this. I count upon your discretion. The lady admits that her association with Turner was forced upon her by Turner, who has some knowledge which she desires not to be known.'

'Do you know what this something is, Mr. Dowbiggin?'

'I have no idea. I did not ask. It didn't seem relevant. The fact that pressure had been brought to bear on her seemed enough. She also declares that five or six other people—perhaps more—are in the same boat, as unwilling associates of Turner, who have been compelled under threats to lend their names.'

'Where is the lady now?'

'In the South of France.'

'Then I think the sooner she returns here the better. Have you the other names?'

'First,' said Jeremy, 'there's Lady Penmanby. I happen to have independent evidence that she was very hard up. Lord Mandleton is another. I did not make a note of the names of the three Members of Parliament, or the civil servants, but I can get these for you. Corbin-Witherspoon, the general manager of Munglefords, is another. I'm certain in my own mind that General Ditchling wouldn't have anything to do with a fellow like Turner unless the element of compulsion were there somewhere. He's the brother of the Duke of Hampshire. He has bags of money, a fine military reputation and friends in the highest circles in the land. If he'd suddenly turned religious, which I don't believe, he could have started a religion of his own and been sure of a following. Why would he associate with an oily scoundrel like Turner?'

'You do yourself, Mr. Dowbiggin!'

'But I've made lots of money out of it, which makes a difference, you know. . . .'

'Perhaps General Ditchling and the others have, too. You're not the only man in the world who loves money, Mr. Dowbiggin.'

'Perhaps not, but I'm probably the only man in the country who could have put Turner's scheme across. He knew it and paid me accordingly.'

'What do you know of this Turner's antecedents?'

'I found out through roundabout channels that the New York police have suspected him for years of being mixed up in a psycho-analysis-blackmail racket, but they were never able to prove anything against him. He was too smart.'

'As far as we are concerned, Mr. Dowbiggin, that is tantamount to saying that the man has a clean, unblemished record. I hope you will forgive me drawing your attention to another thing, Mr. Dowbiggin. It is that you do not seem to have become seriously concerned in your own mind about the—your word was sinister, I think—the sinister aspects of this matter until it came to your knowledge that Paul Lefroy was on—shall we say—intimate terms with your wife. I cannot help observing that it gives me the impression that you care a great deal more about this personal affront—and I sympathise with you deeply—than you do about the—er sinister aspects.'

'Mr. Inspector,' said Jeremy, 'do you suppose for one minute that I didn't know that crack was coming? But I tell you frankly that my opinion of Scotland Yard's intelligence will fall considerably if you allow that fact to influence you. You haven't asked me yet, but you will, so I'll admit freely that the incident which concerns my wife made me very angry. I'm not the sort of man who likes—to use an Americanism—being played for a sucker. My wife's infidelity is only material in so far as it is responsible for me being here *to-day*. I should have come here anyway, sooner or later, but I should probably have had more patience to see the thing through on my own if my personal feelings had not been affronted in the manner I have told you. Give me credit for a bit of imagination, man, even if you haven't any yourself. I know perfectly well that you're not going to believe anything I tell you until you have independent corroboration. I know also—I knew it before I came here—that I either had to come here prepared to tell you everything, or not come here at all. You birds would ferret out anything I didn't tell you. I came here and I've told you everything. I haven't spared myself, or tried to produce high motives for what I've done. You know it all: facts, motives and suspicions. I thought Scotland Yard had got beyond the *cherchez la femme* school of investigation, but apparently I'm wrong.'

Jeremy rose impatiently from his chair and walked towards the door.

'There's no hurry, Mr. Dowbiggin, you're just beginning to be interesting. Sorry if I offended you, but it's all a part of my job. Sit down and have a smoke. Cool off for a minute or two . . .'

'Sorry if I blew up, Mr. Inspector,' said Jeremy a minute or so later.

'We like people who blow up, Mr. Dowbiggin. We really like them. It's when people sit in the chair you're sitting in and allow us to say insulting things without resenting them—it's then we grow just a little suspicious. You see, if we didn't occasionally play little tricks we should have to waste so much time. I wouldn't go so far as to say that a man who was lying or hiding something material would always be discovered—at once, but it's usually painfully easy to learn whether a man's telling the truth. Now that we're back on a more friendly basis, Mr.

Dowbiggin, let me say that I believe your story entirely. I agree—in principle, as they say in Whitehall—with your suspicions. But—and it's a very big but—it isn't a job for Scotland Yard. We can't touch it, for a lot of reasons which will shortly be apparent to you. . . .'

'Who will touch it?' asked Jeremy.

'Could you tell me some place where you can be found this evening without trouble? I shall be sending along someone to talk to you—someone from a department which deals with matters outside the scope of Scotland Yard. We have to go upon proven facts, unfortunately. You see we haven't got a soundproof cellar where we can belabour suspects with a length of hosepipe to make them talk. There are times when I wish we had. Criminal investigation would be so much simpler. We are strictly orthodox, but Colonel Smith—that's the man who'll be looking you up this evening—isn't quite so hidebound in his methods as we are. Now where and at what time?'

'I shall be alone at my flat from seven p.m. onwards. Would Colonel Smith care to dine with me, do you think?'

'I'm sure he'd be delighted. Shall we say eight o'clock? And the address?'

*　　*　　*　　*　　*

Jeremy reached home at tea time. It seemed to him, when the maid brought him tea in the huge lounge-cum-drawing-room where Sybilla used to give her cocktail parties, that it was the first time he had ever derived any enjoyment from the room. It was warm and, although the term is usually applied to small rooms, cosy. Rain beat against the windows, heightening the comfort within. It was a pity, he reflected, looking around the room, that he and Sybilla had not hit things off well.

Nobody, or perhaps everybody, knew that they had parted, for Jeremy had made no sort of announcement of the fact to anybody except Roddie and Janet.

The telephone rang. The instrument was within reach, but Jeremy nearly allowed it to go unanswered.

'I thought you'd like to know,' said Roddie's voice, 'that Paul Lefroy is in town.'

'Where's he staying?'

'At Turner's place. I followed him from the office.'

'Get a couple of men on to him and see what happens. Thanks for phoning me, Roddie.'

That, Jeremy mused, probably meant that Sybilla was back in town.

The telephone rang five minutes later. This time a woman was on the line, a friend of Sybilla's, whose name escaped him.

'This is Priscilla talking, Jeremy. How are you?'

'Fine, thanks. And you?'

'We're all well, thanks Jeremy. . . .'

'I wonder who *we* is,' mused Jeremy.

'By the way,' continued Priscilla, 'I'd like to speak to Sybilla. Is she there?'

'No, she's not here. Sorry.'

'What time do you expect her, Jeremy?'

All these people might as well know immediately what they would be bound to know soon, Jeremy concluded. One of these gabbling women would soon tell the others and then it would be the best thing to close the flat and put paid to the whole business.

'Not only is Sybilla not here, Priscilla my angel, but she isn't likely to be here—ever.'

'But I saw her at the Berkeley to-day. She was with some people, so I know she's back, Jeremy. Stop pulling my leg.'

'I'm not pulling your leg,' said Jeremy. 'I don't know where Sybilla is. I haven't known for some weeks and—funnily enough—I don't much care.'

'Oh! Jeremy, I am sorry!' came a delighted voice.

'You're not a bit. You're just itching to tell everyone, so I won't keep you on the line any longer. Good-bye!'

As he hung up, Jeremy wished he had expressed himself differently, but he shrugged his shoulders and poured out another cup of tea.

Then the front door bell of the flat rang.

'I'm out,' he said to the maid who hurried through the room to answer the bell, 'no matter who it is.'

A moment later in walked Sybilla.

'I have a key, Jeremy,' she said lightly, 'but I thought it more tactful to ring. Nice of me?'

'Charming!'

'You don't seem pleased to see me, Jeremy!'

'I'm not. What do you want?'

'Among other things, I want a few of my belongings, Jeremy. I suppose you have no objection to my removing them. Also all Claire's things are here. I should like to pack them up and send for them in the morning. In the meanwhile, if you're not too busy, I should like a cup of tea and a little talk with you, Jeremy.'

'Help yourself to the tea,' said Jeremy curtly, walking to the door, 'and to any of the things here you want. I'm expecting someone to dinner with me at eight o'clock and I should be obliged if you will make it convenient to be finished here before that. So far as the talk is concerned, Sybilla, I've nothing to say and there's nothing I particularly wish to hear. If you've come back here to try and stage a reconciliation, don't waste time. We're through, all washed up, *finito*. Better write down the name of your lawyers before you go. You know mine.'

'As you please, Jeremy,' said Sybilla with the knowing air which she knew irritated him. 'I didn't come to stage a reconciliation, of course, but I did come to tell you something which might save you a great deal of trouble

—and unpleasantness. However, I won't press the matter. . . .'

Jeremy walked out of the room. His nerves were frayed and he did not trust himself to remain in the same room with Sybilla without revealing what he knew. He felt sure that Sybilla had come there for the express purpose of finding out what he knew—if anything—about her recent doings.

The phone rang again. There was an extension to the library where he had taken his tea.

'Hullo, Jeremy old man!' came Paul Lefroy's voice heartily. 'They told me at the office you were at home. How's everything?'

'Fine thanks, Paul, and with you?'

'Just got in this afternoon. Busy to-night?'

'Afraid I am, Paul. See you in the morning.'

'How's Sybilla?' Lefroy asked.

'She was looking very well a few moments ago. . . .'

'Fine! I want you both to dine with me one evening soon. Give me a ring. I'm in the next suite to Iggy Turner. How is he?'

'He's okay. See you in the morning, Paul. Thanks for ringing. Good-bye!'

Jeremy put down the telephone receiver and turned towards the portrait of his remote ancestor, Jules d'Aubigné, which he had discovered in an Exeter sale catalogue.

'Jules, old man,' said Jeremy softly, 'you don't look as though you allowed people to take liberties with you. I don't either. You'd have known how to handle this Lefroy. I think I'll have to take a leaf out of your book.'

Sybilla came into the library. She looked at Jeremy and then at the portrait of his ancestor. She had come to ask Jeremy to arrange to send some trunks for her, but the look she caught in his eyes frightened her. She felt

[233]

instinctively that if she remained, Jeremy would do violence to her. In all the years she had known him she had never seen such a look, and Jeremy's jokes about this remote ancestor who had made his victims walk the plank took on a new meaning. They were no longer jokes. Until she came into the room there had been an idea in her head that it would not be difficult to twist Jeremy round her little finger, but when she looked at Jeremy she knew those days were over—if they had ever existed. She became deadly scared lest Jeremy should ever find out about her and Paul Lefroy. How much *did* he know? Sybilla shivered and, leaving unsaid what she had come to say, left the room. A moment later Jeremy heard the door of the flat slam.

*   *   *   *   *

If one were to go to a London theatrical agent and say: 'I want a character actor to play the part of a chota-peg-hellfire-curry-pukka-sahib-ex-Indian-Army-colonel, the agent would thumb through his card index and produce something so like Colonel Smith that their mothers would not know them apart. Jeremy's heart dropped into his boots when Colonel Smith entered the room. Here, he took it for granted, was one of the well-connected, fairly amiable, incompetent boobs who may be found in sadly large numbers in peace or war, holding down £800 to £1,500-a-year jobs in Whitehall. This, he moaned inwardly, was the man prepared to do things in a somewhat unorthodox manner, according to Mr. Inspector at Scotland Yard.

'Have a drink, Colonel Smith,' said Jeremy barely politely when the introductions were over.

Colonel Smith looked at his watch, the implication being that only at certain times did he indulge in a drink, whereas Jeremy was quite sure that the only time the man didn't drink was in his sleep.

'I do like a peg about this time,' boomed the Colonel genially. 'Old habits die hard, you know.'

'I'll bet they do,' mused Jeremy, pushing the whisky bottle and siphon towards him.

He reminded Jeremy, by reason of his experienced grasp of the bottle and the way he splashed rather than poured out the whisky, of a fellow passenger across the Atlantic who always used to tell the bar steward to 'Just cover the ice, my lad. Cover the ice.'

When they went into the dining-room Jeremy hunted around for the cayenne pepper and put it ostentatiously beside Colonel Smith. It was not until dinner was finished and they were comfortably sitting beside the fire in the lounge with coffee, cigars and a bottle of liqueur brandy —and Jeremy was longing with a great longing to throw Colonel Smith down the lift-shaft—that a transformation took place. Colonel Smith's *pince-nez* dangling on a wide black ribbon, disappeared. The set, rather inane smile left his face and with it the puffy, grog-blossomed cheeks seemed to collapse; the watery boozer's eyes suddenly became keen and hard.

'Not likely to be interrupted now, are we?' said Colonel Smith in a brisk voice. 'Fine! Then we'll cut the comedy.'

The transformation was too obvious to require explanation.

'Sorry!' said Jeremy with a wry grin.

'That's all right, Mr. Dowbiggin,' was the reply. 'You see, I find it more effective than a false beard. Now let's get down to things. You needn't trouble to go over all the details, as Mr. Inspector gave me a copy of the transcript of your conversation with him. . . .'

'That's the one he wasn't going to have taken down in shorthand, I suppose?'

[235]

'That's the one!' said Colonel Smith genially, and then continuing as though the matter were not worth further discussion: 'I read through it all very carefully before I came along, and I believe you've stumbled on to something big, Mr. Dowbiggin, something a good deal bigger than you might suppose. Tell me now, in the plainest language, what you believe this Christian Movement is. You've been close to it all. You must have seen and heard things that can't have been mentioned in your conversation with Mr. Inspector. You're an intelligent man and you must have formed a mind picture of it all.'

'Do you remember, towards the end of the war, '17 or '18, I think it was,' asked Jeremy, 'a criminal trial at the Old Bailey, during which there was a great deal of talk about a German "Black Book," alleged to have contained the names of 46,000, or perhaps 47,000, persons in this country vulnerable to blackmail? You will probably remember that it was suggested that the German espionage service put the screws on people in that book —those in key positions anyway—to make them play Germany's game. A lot of people laughed at the allegations, but I've always felt that the disclosures touched upon the fringe of something real. We should have heard much more, I believe, if some of the names in that book hadn't been quite so exalted.

'Briefly, then, there is the picture I have formed. I believe this fellow Ignatius Turner is scheming on behalf of someone who wants something "on" people who can be useful in a certain eventuality. The amount of money which he has spent—which I have not mentioned, because I can only guess—is so great that he simply must have behind him an organisation to which money means nothing, which in turn is likely to mean a government— governments being the only organisations which don't care how much they throw about. I have deduced, there-

[236]

fore, without the smallest shred of evidence, that Turner's backers are in fact the German Government. If they are not, then we must believe Turner's story, that he is backed by a group of death-bed-repenting American millionaires.'

'How much money do you know Turner has spent here?'

'I *know* he's spent over half a million sterling,' said Jeremy. 'I've handled more than that for him myself and I've made a clear £35,000 for myself. My guess is that he has spent more than double this sum. The way things are it looks as though the paper *Deliverance* is going to lose between £10,000 and £15,000 monthly, and it doesn't seem to faze Turner a bit.'

'You don't suspect that he is deriving revenue from blackmail right now?'

'I'm sure he's not. The people he has in his clutches haven't got any money. I think the boot is more likely to be on the other foot. I think on the one hand he is threatening certain people with exposure if they don't lend their names to the Christian Movement, and on the other he's helping them financially. It's a new role for a black-mailer—a mixture of blackmail and bribery—and a very effective one, too, I would imagine.'

'Has Turner anything "on" you, Mr. Dowbiggin?'

'Of course he has,' replied Jeremy. 'He has proof positive that I have expended large sums of money for him. He probably knows to a five-pound note how much I've made personally and he argues that it is to my interest to shield him from suspicion.'

'But he has no other hold over you?'

'None whatever, but I think that's plenty, if my suspicions are correct.'

'Do you think it at all possible,' asked Colonel Smith, 'that he has the least idea you have been to Scotland Yard?'

'I'm absolutely certain he has no idea whatever, unless there is someone at Scotland Yard who has tipped him off. I made my appointment to go there from a public telephone box. I drove to Richmond Park, parked the car for fifteen minutes in a lonely spot, drove at over seventy miles an hour down the Kingston By-pass to Esher, Walton and Shepperton, using lonely by-roads, and then drove back to town via Sunbury and Hampton, parked the car in Kensington and took a taxi off a rank to Whitehall Court, arriving there after dark.'

'Have you told anyone you went there?'

'Not a living soul.'

'Excellent! Here's a telephone number that will always reach me. What was your mother's maiden name?'

'Bedford.'

'If you use this number, remember you are Mr. Bedford. Carry on as you are doing. Don't pretend to be too stupid, because you're obviously not. Be a little suspicious and a little scared. Keep your eyes and ears open—and, by the way, will you arrange for the lady who is now in the South of France to have a chat with me as soon as possible. Get her back here and see that she remains out of sight. Thanks for the dinner and all that. We shall be seeing a good deal of each other, I think.'

Colonel Smith resumed his inane character and left.

It was nearly midnight when Janet opened the door of her flat to Jeremy.

'I don't think I can stand many more mysteries, Jeremy,' she said when he was vague about what he had been doing all the evening. 'I want to lead the sort of life where things are what they appear to be and where everybody isn't trying to be clever and wicked.'

Jeremy, who did not have the safety-valve of tears, wondered how he was going to endure life with Sybilla, Janet and Constance all in London together. He too craved a little simplicity.

[238]

Chapter Nineteen

It must have occurred to intelligent foreign observers many times during the last couple of centuries that if the British people were as stupid, as careless and as inefficient as they sometimes appeared to be, the survival of the British Empire through its many vicissitudes must be due either to the special protection which Allah is said to extend to the afflicted, or to the fact that behind the façade of hopeless mediocrities in whom power of recent decades has apparently been vested, there must have existed— behind the scenes—a few persons with brains. It must also have been apparent to those same intelligent foreign observers that from the moment when the ink was dry on the Treaty of Versailles up to roughly the year 1937, the vast majority of those persons with brains were either fishing in Scotland or writing their memoirs, leaving certain animated tailors' dummies to conduct the business of the nation unaided.

Certain it is that during the two decades in question the only Englishman visible to the naked eye who said or did anything forthright in the realm of foreign affairs was the late lamented Philip—Lord Snowden.

What a catalogue of incapacity is represented by those two decades: Reparations! The American debt question! Anglo-French misunderstandings! The rise of Adolf Hitler! Abyssinia! The Spanish war and non-intervention futilities!

In view of all these and other things it is not surprising that beside the Potomac, the Seine, the Spree and the Tiber, along the caravan routes of the Sahara, in the bazaars of India and across the plains of China to the islands of Japan—tens of millions of people, of all colours and creeds and in not less than a hundred languages, simultaneously reached the same conclusion: that the British Empire was slipping.

The vultures, scenting carrion, sharpened their beaks and claws. The jackals timidly watched from cover.

Unless the Scotch, the Welsh and the Irish had consistently under-rated the English, the chances are that there would have been no United Kingdom. It is equally sure that if the British had always been as stupid as they looked, there would have been no British Empire, or alternatively, that it would not have held together long enough to make a worth-while impression on the sands of time.

The British system of representative government has always kept the limelight on the elected nonentities who, instead of protecting British honour and prestige—the chief purpose of their election—have been too busy vote-snatching. It is superfluous to begin to name these gentry for they have named themselves, and if those who have flitted across the screen since 1918 require a monument they have only to mount the roof of St Paul's and look around them at the scenes of desolation of which they are the architects.

They are brought into these pages solely for the purpose, albeit in a roundabout way, of introducing Colonel Smith who, needless to say, was not a colonel and was guiltless of the name of Smith. At the time he steps into this narrative he identifies himself as one of a small and unconsidered band of Britons who, without public plaudits, have been trying for two decades to undo the harm done by the bladders of wind dressed up to look like statesmen.

Colonel Smith was one of those strange people—thank God for them!—who loving their country, cheerfully allow others to claim the credit for their successes and with equal cheerfulness bear the onus of their failures. The Colonel Smiths, who are not hampered by red tape, precedent and the need for kissing august posteriors, are those who get things done, as opposed to those who, living in the limelight, are paid to get things done but never seem to find the time and the energy.

On leaving Jeremy's flat Colonel Smith learned over the trans-Atlantic telephone a number of interesting facts and near-facts. Chief among these was that the Federal Bureau of Investigation in Washington suspected the legal firm of Mercutier, Flashman & Gulbrandsen of being one of the channels through which the National Socialist Party of Germany transmitted funds to representatives all over the world. This eminently respectable firm had written a letter to a Danish-American businessman in Mexico City, advising him that his great-aunt, Emma Carstensen, had died naming him as her heir. Would he make it convenient to call with proof of identity upon Mercutier, Flashman and Gulbrandsen. Now this letter, for causes and reasons which do not matter here, was never delivered to the addressee. When, therefore, a drunken compatriot taxed him in a Mexico City bar with being the grand-nephew of Emma Carstensen, he indignantly denied having any relatives whatsoever of the name of Carstensen. From that hour great interest was taken in the correspondence of this legal firm and in the queer people from all over the Americas who came there ostensibly to claim fortunes.

Next Colonel Smith ascertained that (a) Paul Lefroy's mother's maiden name was Gerda Dorpmuller and that she was related distantly to the Krupps of Essen, and further that when the European war broke out in 1914 and American sentiment seemed to be with the Allies, she and her son Paul had gone to Germany, where the latter was educated; (b) that the Christian Movement in the United States (which studiously avoided the smallest suggestion of anti-Semitism) was being directed by an ex-

Lutheran pastor of known anti-Semitic sentiments and a friend of Jew-baiter Streicher, with whom he maintained a large correspondence and with whom two years previously he had stayed in Germany; (c) that Ignatius Turner, who had once been suspect of blackmail but probably unjustly, was the son of a certain Patrick Turner, late of County Cork, who had been executed in Cork for the murder of two policemen in the early part of 1918; and finally (d) that although Jeremy Dowbiggin appeared to be involved in all these matters, the long odds were that the story he had told was the simple truth.

But Colonel Smith was one of those rare people who leave as little as possible to the vagaries of chance. Between the time he retired to bed at five a.m. and ate his bacon and eggs at twelve noon, a number of things for which he was responsible had occurred. The valet of the service suites where Turner and Lefroy lived was taken ill suddenly and was replaced by an equally efficient man. Telephone instruments of ordinary appearance but quite extraordinary performance were installed in Jeremy's flat, his office in St Charles's Square, his office at the Hayward Fisher Agency, Janet Seymour's flat, Sybilla Dowbiggin's service flat in Curzon Street, and in the Park Lane service flats occupied by Paul Lefroy and Ignatius Turner.

Among the things heard by Colonel Smith's wakeful assistants were: that Jeremy to all intents and purposes lived with Janet Seymour; why (as told by the lady herself to Jeremy) Constance Charlesworth was frightened of Ignatius Turner (making it unnecessary for Colonel Smith to question her); that Janet Seymour was very suspicious of the existence of another woman in Jeremy's life; that the relations between Lefroy and Turner were becoming strained and that neither of them believed that Jeremy Dowbiggin had the smallest inkling of their purposes; that Sybilla Dowbiggin was a very naughty girl; and that if

[242]

the B.M.A. could have heard a conversation between Jeremy Dowbiggin and Dr. Juniper Berry (quite irrelevant to Colonel Smith's investigations) anent a new baby food account of the Hayward Fisher Agency, Dr. Juniper Berry would quickly have reverted to plain 'Mr'. Perhaps the most interesting thing to Colonel Smith, and one which comforted him greatly, was that Jeremy Dowbiggin revealed himself as an almost literally truthful man. Jeremy's accounts of various matters, passed on to Colonel Smith, tallied so exactly with what Colonel Smith had already heard, that the latter marvelled that so truthful a man could have got himself so involved.

Lastly, and because of obscurely phrased remarks heard over the telephone, Colonel Smith committed a grave breach of international etiquette by arranging for the installation, within the privileged walls of the San Bernardino Legation, of certain apparatus which would have horrified its occupants.

So for weeks of—to Jeremy—apparent inaction, the order was listen, listen, listen! The listeners filed, tabulated, checked, rechecked and listened again. New names were brought within the orbit of the enquiries and almost forgotten names brought back again.

Three women, on Colonel Smith's instructions, went the rounds of the soothsayers and psycho-analysts, telling them large but probable lies, lies invented for them specially by Colonel Smith. A few hours later those lies were being told to Ignatius Turner over the telephone, thence relayed by him to Señor Pablo Alfonso Medina, through whom the lies spread abroad, going as far afield as Dublin, Brussels, Paris, The Hague and Madrid.

Lies have one great advantage to their author provided he cuts them out of whole cloth: he can recognise them on sight as his own, and if he told them to only one

[243]

person—that is to say one lie per person—he can establish beyond a doubt how the lies travelled.

All this while Lionel Mossbank and *Deliverance* were going from triumph to triumph—the latter in particular. Circulation rose to over a million copies weekly, while thousands of readers clamoured for Mossbank to resume his public addresses. From Radio Aix-la-Chapelle Mossbank spoke for an hour—the B.B.C. had refused to grant him facilities. 'Peace in our Time' was the subject of his address, and in connection with this a curious thing happened.

In the original script submitted to and passed by the directors of the broadcasting station, Mossbank was to have described the Nazi Party in Germany as 'a gang of brutalised assassins'. At the last minute the script came back to Jeremy with the demand that this reference be moderated. Jeremy, therefore, substituted: ' . . . the handful of fanatics who have hypnotised the German people'. This was the phrasing used over the microphone. Mossbank went on to point out that the common people of all nations—the address was broadcast in eight European languages including German—had it within their power to halt all warmongers. 'Without the workers armies cannot march, nor factories turn out the deadly engines of war . . . if one fiftieth part of what we spend upon war were spent upon improving the living conditions of the masses, the world would turn a deaf ear to its warmongers.' Mossbank then went on to point out that one country which disarmed, while its neighbours did not, would be at their mercy.

There was a violent diplomatic protest made by the German Ambassador in Brussels within a few hours of the address being made, while simultaneously the *Volk- ischer Beobachter* fulminated against the 'loud-mouthed British evangelist, probably in the pay of the British

Government, who dares to refer to the leaders of the new Germany as brutalised assassins. . . .'

Jeremy began to see the light.

'I want to speak to Colonel Smith, please. This is Mr. Bedford speaking. . . . That you Colonel Smith? I've got something and I must see you right away. Very well, I'll wait here.'

Colonel Smith, catching the note of urgency in Jeremy's voice, joined him at the St Charles's Square offices within twenty minutes.

'Someone in this office,' said Jeremy slowly, 'must be in direct or very rapid communication with Berlin. The *Volkischer Beobachter* and the German Ambassador in Brussels complain angrily about remarks which Mossbank did *not* make in his address from Radio Aix-la-Chapelle. I changed the script at the last moment in my own hand-writing. Nobody but me in this office knew of the change.'

'There were no advance copies handed out to the press?' asked Colonel Smith.

'Waste of time!' said Jeremy. 'Newspapers won't give publicity to radio stations which are competing with their own advertisement departments. Not one advance copy was sent out to anyone.'

'Then what is your explanation?'

'Listen, Colonel Smith. I am a propagandist by profession, and I know what I'm talking about. When a man such as Mossbank gives a pacifist address at a time like this he lays himself open to the suspicion that he is in German pay, doesn't he?'

Colonel Smith grunted.

'The surest way he could set about preventing that suspicion from falling on him, then, is to blackguard the Nazis, isn't it? People say: 'here is a violently anti-Nazi speaker—a patriot, but one who loves peace.' When immediately afterwards the Nazi propaganda machine begins to abuse him he becomes even less an object of suspicion here in England. But the German Ambassador in Brussels and the *Volkischer Beobachter*, which obviously both received their information from the same source, acting probably on instructions from Goebbels, quote the sentence which I deleted from the address six hours or so before it was given. You have to believe that I, Janet Seymour, Roddie Macdonald, Paul Lefroy or Ignatius Turner—one of us or all five—passed a copy of the original unaltered script over to someone, who in turn put it into the hands of the German Propaganda Ministry in Berlin within an hour or two of it being typed. Find who that was and a lot of things will explain themselves.'

Colonel Smith again grunted comprehendingly. He was one of those irritating people who would not pass judgment upon a theory or idea at the time it was given to him. Colonel Smith left Jeremy in a state of wondering whether he thought him a lunatic or a liar.

*   *   *   *   *

Lionel Mossbank was now more than ever a prisoner in his flat. He was also a very unhappy man. He loved talking. While his radio address had not been so satisfying as looking down from a platform on to a sea of upturned faces, there was another satisfaction in knowing that he had had an incalculable number of listeners. The bodyguard was weary of talk. They had dropped even the pretence of politeness. Sometimes Ignatius Turner, and less often Jeremy, came to see him. But on these occasions it was Mossbank who had to do the listening, and he did not want to listen—to anybody. He wanted to hear the glorious cadences of his own voice, which even a hundred cheap cigarettes a day could not ruin, and to see a multitude hypnotised by its beauty.

To save his reason—or perhaps just to keep him quiet

—Turner installed in the flat a dummy microphone such as is used in broadcasting stations. It was a cruel farce, which vastly amused the guards, until they tired of his daily rehearsals of the speeches which, he believed, the B.B.C. were broadcasting every night. The microphone was connected—appropriately enough—to the garbage chute which led to the basement. At nine-thirty Crowder would go into another room and switch on the warning light, and when Mossbank was 'on the air' he would return to the other members of the bodyguard and resume the game of nap. As soon as Mossbank had finished his address—one night he went on for two hours—one of the bodyguard turned a switch which operated a gramophone record of handclapping and the roars from a huge crowd. With a spotlight turned on him and this sweet music ringing in his ears, Mossbank would bow twice and step away from the microphone, throwing himself exhausted into an easy chair, beside which on a table his supper awaited him. Mossbank was demanding his steaks less and less cooked until they were barely warmed through.

'How did I go over to-night, boys?' he would ask with his mouth full.

'Fine!' the bodyguard would reply in chorus, without looking up from the game of nap.

'I wonder how many people listened to me,' he would say.

'Millions!' came the chorus.

Drugged with nicotine, food and his own eloquence, Lionel Mossbank would totter off to bed.

Chapter Twenty

IT WAS NOT difficult for Jeremy these days to understand the state of mind of a man who in sheer desperation killed a clinging woman. Constance clung. Even the fact that she had every right to do so did not make it any the easier for Jeremy to endure, nor did the realisation of the ungallant rôle he himself had played. Besides, he had a duty also to Janet.

'You brought me back to London, Jeremy,' said Constance bitterly, 'and now you treat me like an acquaintance. I can't go on like this.'

Jeremy was relieved when Colonel Smith agreed that it would be as well if Constance returned to *Rose Marie*. The Colonel had already heard from her lips—even if it had been by means of a concealed microphone—what she had refused to tell him to his face: just what hold Ignatius Turner had on her.

'Jeremy, beloved,' said Constance in the taxi to Victoria Station, 'I would go back to *Rose Marie* happily if only I could shake off the vile suspicion that you have just been —using me.'

'I'm only thinking of your safety and happiness, dearest,' he told her. 'I will join you at *Rose Marie* just as soon as I can. I shall be thinking of you all the time. . . .'

The last part of the promise was not hard to keep, but he buoyed himself with the hope that Constance would forget him and that it would never be necessary to let her know that her clinging affection drove him almost to violence.

'Why will women be so possessive?' he asked himself in the taxi on his way from Victoria to meet Janet, knowing full well that his unexplained absence would cause recriminations and suspicion. He contemplated telling Janet that he would not have his movements questioned, but the answer to that would have been to lose Janet. Whether he was in love with her or not, Jeremy did not stop to think. All he knew was that he wanted her near him. Since George Dowbiggin had returned to live in the United States Janet was the only person Jeremy knew whom he had known for a long while. Janet was a link with happier, saner days.

Work, Jeremy's usual solace, failed him. Even reading was barred to him. He loathed fiction and suspected all factual books. He had for too long himself dealt in shoddy arguments, fallacious ideas and twisted facts to have any faith left in the printed word. Material success was not tasting quite as sweetly as he had expected. On top of these things was the strain of exercising restraint in the presence of Paul Lefroy. He dreamed one night with delirious joy of trampling on Lefroy's smooth suave face with heavy boots.

Colonel Smith, who could have provided Jeremy with another co-respondent, did not do so. Colonel Smith did not allow side issues to tempt him from his central purpose. Sybilla, therefore, believing that her relationship with Lefroy was unsuspected by Jeremy, was being troublesome. As far as he could do so Merryweather was stalling off Sybilla's lawyers, who were demanding that Jeremy regularise her position and declare his intentions.

It was irksome, too, to be told nothing of what was happening, by Colonel Smith who sucked in all the information he could, but never imparted any.

There was a message from Colonel Smith which Janet delivered as soon as she saw Jeremy.

'There's a Colonel Smith who wants to see you this evening,' said Janet with the air of expecting the arrangements for the evening to be broken. 'Who is he? Is his name really Colonel Smith, or did you get someone to phone me so that you could take some woman out?'

One of Colonel Smith's vigilant assistants heard the

discussion from afar and, since it did not matter a great deal whether he saw Jeremy the same evening or the next day, Colonel Smith came through on the telephone and suggested postponing the meeting.

*   *   *   *   *

'I'm free to admit, Dowbiggin,' said Colonel Smith when they were alone, 'that I'm up against a brick wall. What's more, I have learned a great deal more about Turner and Lefroy. In fact I've learned everything about them except the one thing I've got to learn—what they're trying to achieve. I've come to the point where I must take you into my confidence. . . .'

'You flatter me!' said Jeremy.

'This is bigger than personalities, Dowbiggin,' snapped Colonel Smith. 'Don't be petty. I'm looking to you to supply the missing link. First of all, I've come to the conclusion that instead of Turner giving orders to Lefroy, the boot's on the other foot. I know it, in fact.'

'There have been times when I suspected that myself,' said Jeremy, 'but as it didn't seem very important one way or the other, I didn't trouble to test the theory.'

'It didn't seem important to you, Dowbiggin, because you didn't know that Lefroy was educated in Germany and, whatever his private sentiments may be to-day, he is in the pay of the Nazis. You suspected that, I know, and so did I. But even now that I have proof it doesn't make sense, because neither Lefroy nor Turner seems to have done one single thing which would either hurt England or help the Hun. . . .'

'War hasn't broken out yet,' said Jeremy. 'Is it beyond the bounds of reason that they are the nucleus, so to speak, of an espionage system which will come into operation later?'

'It isn't beyond the bounds of reason, Dowbiggin, but

[250]

I don't think that is their purpose, although I grant you that they are in a position to gather a certain amount of information. I may go so far as to say that most of the Nazi agents are known to us. No, take my word for it just now that neither Lefroy nor Turner is a spy. Furthermore, the people—the British people they have under their thumbs—are not the sort of people who would turn traitor, which must follow logically. These people, whom we both know, don't mind lending their names to a crank religious organisation, because they believe it to be relatively harmless. But treason is another matter. Not one of them who has been bullied into supporting the Christian Movement would turn traitor under Turner's bullying. I'm sure of that. But what are Lefroy and Turner trying to achieve? Without that knowledge I admit I'm stumped. It all looks nonsensical, but it isn't. I grant you the Hun is pretty stupid, but he isn't laying out all this money through Turner and Lefroy for nothing. He is getting something in return, or hopes to get something in return. What?'

'I have a hunch—not evidence—that Medina will prove to be the key to all this,' said Jeremy. 'I have a hunch, furthermore, that as Lefroy is senior to Turner, so Medina is senior to both of them.'

'And I have a hunch, Dowbiggin, that your hunch is a good one. Furthermore, I believe we shall know that for certain to-night. Medina is meeting Turner and Lefroy to-night at the Park Lane suite. Would you care to hear what they say?'

'I would,' replied Jeremy. 'I suppose you have a microphone installed there?'

Colonel Smith nodded.

'And at my place?'

'Of course!' replied Colonel Smith without batting an eyelid.

'Well then,' said Jeremy, ignoring all the implications, 'how would it be if this afternoon I picked a quarrel with Lefroy and Turner and told them I was going to walk out on them? Wouldn't that be sure to come up for discussion at their meeting with Medina this evening? And if so, wouldn't that be likely to shed a little light in dark places?'

*   *   *   *   *

'I'd like a word with you, Paul,' said Jeremy. 'Got time for a spot of lunch with me?'

'Sure old man! Let's go somewhere quiet.'

'What's on your mind, Jeremy?' asked Lefroy when they were settled.

'Just this: I'm sick to death of working in the dark. I'm not the type, Paul. I like to know what I'm doing and why, and I don't know either. The whole thing is beginning to smell fishy to me.'

'What have you got to kick at?' asked Lefroy, dropping a little of his suavity. 'You've made the easiest money I ever saw in my life. Mind you, I don't deny that you've done a swell job, but what makes you think there's anything fishy about it?'

'I tell you flat, Paul, I don't believe this tale about the repentant millionaires. . . .'

'What other explanation have you got to offer?'

'None. That's what's bothering me. I don't mind carving up the bodies of millionaires who've probably done plenty of carving themselves, but I am as sure as I sit here that there's more to it all than that.'

'And supposing I tell you that there isn't any more? What then?'

'I should be too polite to say so, probably, but I should know that you were a bloody liar, Paul, and didn't intend to let me in on it, whatever it is. Get this straight Paul: I'm either right *in* this business or I'm right *out*. No half measures! I'm saying this to you because I know you better than Iggy Turner, but tell him what I've said and that I give him one week to make up his mind. Unless there's something criminal behind it all—and to be fair I can't see where it is—Turner need have no fear of my discretion.'

'Suppose, for the sake of argument, Jeremy, that there is something criminal. There isn't, of course, but just suppose.' Lefroy enunciated his words very slowly. 'Don't you think you're being a wee bit foolish in your attitude? If there were anything criminal, as you put it, do you think for one minute you could convince a judge and jury that Turner was guilty and you were innocent? Don't make me laugh, Jeremy!'

'Lefroy!' snarled Jeremy, who was thinking of another episode, 'I don't allow anyone—anyone, do you understand?—to threaten me. Take that superior smile off your face or, by Christ, I'll knock it off. . . .'

The temptation was too great for Jeremy to resist. His fist shot out and a second or two later Paul Lefroy was spitting two front teeth into the plate in front of him. With all the strength of his powerful right hand Jeremy seized Lefroy's nose between his index finger and the next, leading him to the door of the restaurant. A well placed boot sent Lefroy stumbling into the gutter.

A policeman who witnessed the entire incident had no choice but to intervene.

'Do you wish to make a charge?' he asked Lefroy.

'Go ahead, Lefroy,' mocked Jeremy. 'Make a charge. I should be delighted to pay a fine for the pleasure of telling a court full of reporters—and I'd see they were there—just what you said to me in there. Threaten me! Go ahead, constable! Do your duty! You saw me assault him. Charge me yourself if he won't.'

'I'll have to charge you both with making a disturbance,'

said the constable. 'You'd better come along with me, both of you.'

At Vine Street Lefroy declined to make a charge and both were released upon identification.

As Lefroy, who was released first, left Vine Street police station, all Jeremy's mock anger dropped from him in a flash.

'I enjoyed that two minutes more than I can tell you,' he said to the scandalised sergeant on duty, 'so will you give me the pleasure of letting me put something in the Police Orphanage box? No, it isn't bribery. I shall be delighted if you charge me. It's just that I have enjoyed myself so much that I feel I would like to celebrate it.'

The sergeant scratched his head as Jeremy folded several pound notes and dropped them into the box.

Janet Seymour, bringing Mr. Merryweather with her, arrived to identify Jeremy and arrange for his release.

'What would you do, Mr. Merryweather,' asked Jeremy in reply to the latter's expostulations, 'if a man were to threaten you? I ask you as a lawyer.'

'As a lawyer, Mr. Dowbiggin,' was the astounding reply, 'I should undoubtedly punch him on the nose.'

'That's what I did, only the punch landed two inches lower. It was a beautiful jab with the left. The napkin saved me from cut knuckles. Be a good girl, Janet, and take this napkin back to the restaurant and pay the bill for me.'

'I've just heard the dreadful news,' said Turner, who was at the office when Jeremy returned. 'Paul telephoned me five minutes ago. What can have possessed you to do such a dreadful thing? Poor Paul! He tells me he is in great pain.'

'Good!' said Jeremy. 'You go and have a chat with dear Paul, Iggy my friend. . . .'

'Don't call me Iggy!' snapped Turner.

[254]

'All right, Iggy! But as I was saying, go and have a chat with dear Paul and ask him what I told him, and unless you want some of the same medicine that he had, don't you threaten me. I'm tired of it all, do you hear? I'm sick of the sound of your sanctimonious voice. I'm sick of everything to do with the pair of you. I think you're a couple of crooks and I wish I could prove it. . . .'

Turner grabbed his hat and left.

*   *   *   *   *

Colonel Smith and Jeremy were sitting in a small room in Whitehall. In front of them was an ordinary loud-speaker. For an hour or more they had listened to a quarrel between Ignatius Turner and Paul Lefroy, which had been going on in their Park Lane suite. Punctuating their quarrel had come over the wire the sound of a bottle clinking against a tumbler, the splash of soda water from a syphon and the thin squeak as a cork was replaced in a bottle.

'You've had enough to drink already, Iggy!' came Lefroy's voice over the wire. 'You'll want your wits about you when Medina comes.'

'Don't worry about my wits, thanks,' Turner replied. 'I've got more brains drunk than he'll ever have sober.'

'Maybe, but if you won't take friendly advice perhaps you'll obey an order. Don't drink any more, Iggy!'

'You can't give me the run around, Paul, nor ten like you, and nor can that long Dago . . .'

'Shut up! Here he is. Put that bottle out of sight and pull yourself together.'

'I told you Lefroy was the boss,' whispered Jeremy.

'You needn't whisper,' said Colonel Smith. 'This is a one-way line.'

'Heil Hitler!' said a strange voice—strange to Jeremy. 'That's Medina,' said Colonel Smith.

'Heil Hitler!' echoed Lefroy.

'Well?' came Medina's suave voice.

'——Hitler!' came Turner's, all trace of unction gone from it. 'You birds can Heil all you like and who you like.'

'He's drunk!' said Medina angrily. 'Lost his nerve?'

'Something happened to-day,' said Lefroy. 'I had a row with Dowbiggin. He said he was going to walk out on us. I let him know that it wasn't that easy and he said I was threatening him. We finished up at Vine Street police station.'

'He pushed your front teeth in, Paul. Tell Medina about that. I didn't see any marks on Dowbiggin afterwards. I like Dowbiggin, even if he is a money-grabbing son-of-a-bitch of an Englishman. Smart fellow he is, too. I wonder what he'd do to you, Paul, if he ever found out about you and his wife. I hope I'm there to see it.'

'Why did you let this fool drink himself silly?' came Medina's snarling voice. 'There are important things to be discussed. It's no use trying to talk to him when he's like this.'

'Go ahead with your discussion, Medina. Leave me out of it. I'm all washed up, anyway. I think Dowbiggin isn't a bad judge. What's the use of more discussion? The job's been done, hasn't it?'

'The job is just beginning,' said Medina icily.

'Yours is, maybe!' said Turner, 'but mine's done. Count me out. I'm going back home where it's healthier.'

'You'll find yourself in a nice wooden box if you're not careful,' said Lefroy. 'Go to bed and sleep it off. Maybe you'll have other ideas in the morning. . .'

Turner evidently took this advice, for his voice did not come over the wire any more.

'He's in his own room,' said a watcher at another instrument a moment or two later.

'Keep listening!' said Colonel Smith.

For the next twenty minutes or so Medina and Lefroy spoke in such low tones that only the hum of their voices and an occasional phrase snatched out of its context came over the wire. It was evident that Lefroy was pleading for him.

'. . . I daresay he has done a good job, but he has gone too far . . . *in vino veritas*—loyalty and obedience . . . you are becoming sentimental, Paul . . . what is one man's life beside the issues that are at stake . . . you will have to carry on without him . . . somehow make your peace with Dowbiggin . . . you'll have to invent a story that will satisfy him. . . .'

'. . . that won't be so easy,' came Lefroy's voice, 'it would be a mistake to write him down a fool. . . . I'll manage it somehow, but I'm looking forward to the day when he isn't any longer useful. . . .'

'. . . there are no personal feelings where the Fuehrer's work is concerned. . . .'

'What do you make of that?' asked Jeremy when the line went quiet, except for the constant shuffling of papers.

'Not much—yet,' said Colonel Smith. 'Has Turner gone to sleep yet?' he asked an assistant.

'Not yet,' was the reply. 'He snores like a hog usually.'

There was a silence for some minutes. 'He's just turned off the light,' said Colonel Smith's assistant. The silence was broken shortly afterwards by Lefroy's voice:

'Are you awake, Iggy?'

'Go to hell!'

'I want to talk to you, Iggy,' came Lefroy's voice, this time more ingratiating.

'Well, what do you want?'

'I'm trying to save your life, Iggy, do you understand? If Medina reports what happened to-night they'll rub you out. In the morning you'd better see Medina and talk small. I'm telling you, Iggy.'

[257]

'Listen to me, Paul,' said Turner. 'I don't scare easily. I got mixed up with you and your crowd for my own reasons, but it wasn't because I liked it. There's only one race of people I hate and despise more than the Germans —that's the English. I haven't forgotten an evening more than twenty years ago, waiting in the rain outside Cork gaol with a handcart that was lent to me by a shopkeeper. The door opened. A black-hearted English warder said: "Are you Turner?" "Yes," I told him, "I'm Turner." "Then this is yours," he replied. "Grab the end." He and I lifted a rough deal box on to the handcart.

'What do you think was in that box, Paul?'

'How the hell should I know?' came the irritable reply.

'I'll tell you, Paul. In the box was my own father. His neck was twisted and broken. His poor face was black and his eyeballs was bursting out of his head. They had hanged him that morning and then, like a box of rubbish, they pushed him out of the back door of the gaol to his son. He shot an English policeman on Irish soil, so they hanged him. They called it murder to kill a foreign invader.

' "Be careful we don't stretch your neck, too," said the warder before he slammed the door, "you rebel Irish bastard."

'I shot him myself three days later, Paul, and caught the night boat for England. I hope he's still rotting in the pit of hell. . . . I took my old father back home on the handcart and that night I swore by all the Holy Saints that I'd make the English pay for the murder of Patrick Turner. They haven't paid yet, Paul, but they're going to. It won't be long now. I only wish that God had put into my hands some other instrument than your Nazi friends. But if I couldn't find a clean instrument strong enough I decided that a dirty one would do, Paul. So I joined up with you, and Medina and all the rest of the murdering scum that strut about Heil Hitlering. When you've destroyed England I hope someone comes along and destroys you and I hope I'll find God's pardon for associating with you. . . .'

'I'll talk to you in the morning when you're sober, Iggy!'

'Drunk or sober, Paul, you can't scare me. They'll rub me out, you say. Let them. I've done my life's work. I've planted the maggot of corruption in the hearts of the accursed English, to make it easy for you and the rest of Hitler's brave boys to finish the job, but don't think I did it for love of that Jew-murdering, cowardly son-of-a-bitch Hitler. My work's done, Paul. The maggot I've left here among the English is boring away, night and day. My little ventriloquist's doll, Lionel Mossbank, and Dow-biggin between them have rotted whatever brains they ever had. They don't trust their church, their army, their statesmen or their ally France. They look over their shoulders fearfully, wondering what's next. Their generals are incompetent, they believe. Their air force doesn't exist. They believe their statesmen have sold them down the river. The astrologers, the dirty rotten psycho-analyst fakirs, and all the rest of the leeches who are fattening on them, fill their heads with fears, rumours. Society women, men in high places, labour leaders, men and women in every walk of society, are spreading rumours, scattering the seeds of vile suspicion. Soon they won't have faith in anything, Paul—least of all in themselves. . . .

'So my work's done, Paul. Medina can rub me out now if he wants to. I've nothing more to live for. I've been tired of it all for a long while now. There was a time when I thought I'd go back to Ireland, buy a farm and settle down, but I'm too tired. It's been a long road, Paul. . . .'

There was a short pause during which Lefroy had evidently left the room. Then over the instrument connected with Lefroy's telephone came Lefroy's voice: 'That

[259]

you, Medina. Listen! Iggy's gone crackers. He'll have to be attended to to-morrow. Good-night!'

'That,' said Colonel Smith, 'was the death warrant of Ignatius Turner.'

'You think they'll kill him?'

'I know they will,' said Colonel Smith solemnly. 'Turner won't live another twelve hours. You may bank on that. They've no use for a man with ideas of his own.'

'But surely, man,' said Jeremy, 'you're going to do something about it? Tell the police, or interfere in some way?'

'And warn them all that we're on to them? No, Dowbiggin, I'm not a policeman. I'm after bigger game than a mere murderer—bigger than Turner and Lefroy and Medina. I don't fully understand what we've heard this evening, but I do know that for the first time in history the Hun is trying to be subtle. He's fighting with new and hidden weapons. It's like the story of the Trojan Horse all over again—the same story with modern trimmings. No, I'm afraid Turner will have to take his medicine. In a way I'm sorry for him. I understand how men like that feel. I have Irish blood in me . . . sh-h-h!'

The hidden microphone in Ignatius Turner's room once again picked up the voice of the condemned man: 'O! Heavenly Father, look down with compassion upon this Thy . . .'

'For God's sake switch off that machine, Smith!' exclaimed Jeremy. 'You can't eavesdrop on a man's last prayers. That's carrying toughness too far.'

'From you, Dowbiggin,' said Colonel Smith quietly, 'that's rich! But I'll switch it off nevertheless.'

'There was something about Iggy Turner that I liked,' said Jeremy, unconscious of using the past tense. 'He was a sanctimonious little swine in a way, but I admired his tenacity. They couldn't scare him!'

'In my work,' said Colonel Smith, 'I mostly come across

the men who are greedy for money and who'd sell their own mothers to get it. They are easy to track down because they always do the obvious thing. But it's the honest fanatics—men like your friend Iggy Turner—that I can't help respecting. This way is better than the way his father went. . . .'

* * * * *

When the Coroner's jury had brought in the verdict that Ignatius Turner had met his death by misadventure, the Coroner took the opportunity of expatiating on the dangers of having electric appliances within reach of a bath. At four o'clock in the morning, Paul Lefroy testified, he had heard the sound of a bath running. This did not surprise him as the deceased, who suffered from insomnia, often took a bath at strange hours. Witness heard nothing, but remembered that the time was about four o'clock. No! The deceased had been a deeply religious man and it was unlikely in the extreme that he had taken his own life. . . .

* * * * *

Constance Charlesworth was sitting on the mosaic landing stage at *Rose Marie*, reading for the hundredth time a letter.

Dear Constance:

I am sure it will make you very happy to know that you have nothing more to fear from I.T. Perhaps you will have seen the papers before you receive this. Anyway, that is the end of a sad chapter. I should not hurry about returning to London just yet until things have blown over. I am busy—as usual, but less worried. I will try to come down for Christmas. In great haste.

Affectionately, Jeremy.

The letter had arrived three weeks previously and it was now Christmas Eve—Christmas Eve 1938.

'No letter from monsieur?' the *femme de ménage* had asked that morning.

'No, Agnès, nothing. I expect there will be a telegram. He is busy and . . .'

'*Les affaires! Les affaires! Toujours les affaires, madame.* But it is to be hoped that monsieur will bring with him an appetite, for the turkey is *formidable*. The *pouding anglaise* is not yet made, madame.'

'I know, Agnès,' said Constance rather wearily, 'but it is an old English custom that those who eat the pudding must help to stir it. To-night, when monsieur arrives we will open a bottle of wine and we will all stir the pudding.'

One hour after the last possible train had arrived at Toulon that night Constance went to bed. There would be a letter in the morning, or better still, Jeremy would have arrived on the night train.

The postman trudged along the dusty highroad above *Rose Marie*. There was a letter and a parcel for the strange English lady who had no friends but who was always waiting beside the letter-box. When these were delivered he could return to the bosom of his family.

'*Bonne Noel! madame!*' he called gaily. 'There is a letter and a parcel this morning.'

Constance took them down to the old Roman landing to open them. The letter contained a Christmas card from her sister. The parcel was addressed in Jeremy's handwriting. In the parcel was a mink cloak. Constance searched through the parcel for a letter. There was none, only a card.

Agnès came down with a cup of coffee a few minutes later to see the mink cloak thrown in a heap on the ground. Agnès picked it up and stroked it lovingly. '*Ah! madame, qu'il est beau!*'

But madame evidently did not think so, for she was weeping. The matter of the *pouding anglaise* would have to be discussed later. They were strange people, these English. One would never understand them. A fur cloak such as that must have cost at least 2,000 francs. Surely not a matter for tears.

Constance wiped away her tears and, leaving the mink cloak where it lay, went up to the little villa, where she spent the rest of the day writing letters.

It was dark before she had finished.

'Take the turkey and the *pouding anglaise* to the village, Agnès,' said Constance. 'Cook them for some poor family. No, I am not hungry. Perhaps later I shall make myself an omelet. . . .'

There was no moon, but a bright star cut a silver swathe across the water. When Constance had first known the peaceful walled garden and the Roman governor's landing-place it had been high summer, lush with hot voluptuous perfume. Now it was cold, but no colder than the clutch which Constance felt all round her heart. Now, as she stood facing out to sea, it was hard to remember those velvety summer nights and the hot whispers she and Jeremy had exchanged. Her bare foot touched the soft silkiness of the fur cloak, which still lay where she had thrown it. It was this contact which decided Constance: out there, at the end of the pathway of light, was peace and oblivion, where men did not make false vows and then forget them.

*   *   *   *   *

Agnès found the neatly folded pile of clothes beside the fur cloak. 'To swim on a morning like this! These English!' Agnès shuddered. 'And to throw down, as though it was an old rag, a superb fur cloak like that! No wonder it is said that the English are rich!'

[263]

Agnès picked up the fur cloak to take it into the house, and as she did so espied a little white envelope, from which was peeping out a card. What a barbarous language English was, she mused as she tried to read the inscription:

T-O J-A-N-E-T W-I-T-H M-Y L-O-V-E J-E-R-E-M-Y

'If I had a fine fur cloak like that one,' muttered Agnès, 'I wouldn't be such a fool as to go swimming on a morning like this!'

*   *   *   *   *

It was Christmas Eve in London—the Christmas Eve when Peace reigned—the Peace which had been bought at Munich at a price which has not yet been reckoned.

Lionel Mossbank was orating in a mental ward. The Christian Movement, which had been built around him, had dissolved into thin air. There were still a few followers who insisted that Lionel Mossbank insane was preferable to the commercial sanity of certain more orthodox religious leaders, but they were very few. It requires much moral courage—of which most people are deficient—to announce oneself as the follower of a lunatic.

Paul Lefroy—co-respondent in Dowbiggin, J., *vs.* Dowbiggin, S. and Lefroy, P., on the undefended list—had returned to New York. His evidence at the inquest had been clear and concise. He had several times warned Turner about the danger of touching the electric fire in the bathroom with wet hands. Lefroy was glad to be out of England—glad too that he had been astute enough to avoid all suspicion falling on him.

Señor Pablo Alfonso Medina was pleased with life also. There had been nothing to connect him with either the life or death of Ignatius Turner. The fool was well out of the way. Small wonder the English had always found the Irish troublesome! It would have been very embarrassing to a diplomat to have been mixed up in the business.

Janet and Jeremy were giving a party. As the divorce case had yet to be heard they decided that it would not be quite proper if the party were given at Janet's flat. Jeremy had given up his own. It was not, of course, an engagement party, but the next best thing.

Janet invited an old friend and a couple of cousins, to give the thing a family flavour. Jeremy had asked Roddie to come along, three or four seniors from the Hayward Fisher Agency, and the advertising man of the Birmingham-Simplex car people, who was becoming rather difficult. As a last minute thought Jeremy had invited Colonel Smith. It was really a gesture, but Colonel Smith had accepted. He was a bachelor, without ties, and Christmas was usually a pretty dull affair for him. Besides, he found Jeremy an interesting character study.

Jeremy had booked a private dining-room at the Regency. There was a Christmas tree with something for everybody. At the last moment Jeremy had remembered to grab a box of clients' cigars at the office for Colonel Smith, who as the oldest man present, had been cajoled into donning the red gown and white beard of Santa Claus.

There was lots of drink, plenty to eat on a buffet, and even more laughter.

Colonel Smith was holding up a sumptuous cardboard box.

'This looks like something very special for——'

He blinked uncomprehendingly for a moment and then fumbled for his glasses.

'Let me see,' he went on. 'Must be getting old. This is for Miss Janet Seymour.'

Janet stepped forward to receive the parcel. All eyes were on her as she unwrapped it, so nobody noticed Colonel Smith slip a card into an inside pocket, or note that with the next and succeeding presents he had no difficulty identifying the names.

In imitation of the walk of a mannequin Janet swayed round the room wearing a lovely blue fox cape.

'You are a darling, Jeremy! Does it suit me?'

'Perfectly, darling!' said Jeremy swallowing hard.

While the women had disappeared to powder their noses, Colonel Smith prepared to depart.

'Thanks so much, Dowbiggin. I've enjoyed myself immensely. Make my excuses for me. By the way,' he added as an afterthought, 'perhaps it would be as well if this were destroyed. Don't want to hurt anyone's feelings and all that. . . .'

Jeremy took from Colonel Smith's outstretched hand a card on which was inscribed: 'To Constance, with love. Jeremy.'

Colonel Smith had gone before Jeremy had time to thank him.

'Damned careless of that girl in the shop!' Jeremy muttered. 'A mistake like that might have ghastly consequences!'

THE END